# *Brooklyn*
## *Love Story*

Janet Sierzant

Brooklyn Love Story
Copyright © Revision 2025 by Janet Sierzant
ISBN: 978-1-970153-57-6
Distribution: Ingram Book Company

*Maison*
La Maison Publishing, Inc.
Vero Beach, Florida
The Hibiscus City
lamaisonpublishing@gmail.com

# Cristoforo Colombo
## 1945

*O Sole Mio* streamed through the radio. Giuseppe Corrao enjoyed the live feeds, but they ended when Mussolini aligned with Nazi Germany and led Italy into WWII. Now, he had to settle for whatever the radio broadcast played. Like so many men in their Brooklyn neighborhood, he was born in Sicily.

Giuseppe left Sciacca at seventeen to come to America, where he married Anna. They had four daughters.

Jeanette was ten, the youngest, with dark eyes and a Buster Brown haircut highlighting her heart-shaped face. Her adventurous spirit had gotten her into trouble on more than one occasion.

They lived in an apartment on the third floor of 18th Avenue and 80th Street. Jeanette's grandparents lived in the apartment above them in the same building, and her aunts and uncles lived in the adjoining building. The doors were never locked. Jeanette ran up and down the stairs of the tenements to each of her cousins' apartments.

She could hear Sonny down on the street, yelling for her. He was her favorite cousin. Sonny was one year older than her. They had a special connection and were inseparable. Sometimes, on the weekends, he spent the night. They would lay the blankets in the living room and stay up late, whispering and giggling.

Jeanette stuck her head out the window. "I'll be down in a few minutes, I'm eating dinner."

Her older sister, Mariella, filled a glass of wine for her father while her mother took the pot off the white enamel stove and drained the pasta.

When everyone was seated, Luciana folded her hands and closed her eyes. "We thank you, Father, for this food we are about to receive."

"Amen," they all responded.

Luciana was two years older than Jeanette. She studied the Bible stories and knew about every saint.

"How was your first day working at the bakery, Mariella?" Giuseppe asked.

"The Morettis are so nice. Mr. Moretti said I could start behind the front counter, and he would let me help in the kitchen once I learn about the business."

"I don't understand why you want to work in that awful place," her sister Phyllis said. "With the oven blasting all day, it's as hot as the sweatshops on Fifteenth Avenue."

"I'm sure her future husband will appreciate her experience," Mama said. "You should start thinking about your future, Phyllis. Maybe you can get a job with your father at the fish market."

"Oh, Mama, I don't want to be some stupid housewife."

"What's wrong with being a housewife?" Mariella asked. "Mama's been doing it for years."

"Not me," said Phyllis. "I'm going to play baseball."

"Don't be ridiculous," Mariella said. "They don't let girls play baseball. They're not strong enough."

Phyllis slanted her eyes. "I'm going to show them that a girl can play too." Strong-willed, she loved baseball as a toddler and ran around the room crazily as if she were covering bases on a field of grass. A hopeless tomboy, she refused to give in to her femininity.

"I'm going to marry Sonny," Jeanette said.

Anna looked at Giuseppe with an alarmed expression, then turned to their daughter.

"You're only ten years old, too young to think about marriage. Besides, you can't marry Sonny."

"Why not?"

"Because he's your cousin!"

"I don't care. I love Sonny, and he loves me."

"Jeanette, where are you?" Sonny yelled, growing impatient.

She shoved the last bit of fish into her mouth, threw down her fork, and jumped up to leave.

"Make sure you take a jacket," Mama said. "And tell Aunt Giovanna I'll be down soon."

"Don't be late for the talent show," she said. "I'm performing, you know." Jeanette loved to sing and entertain her family.

A singer himself, Giuseppe loved Carlo Buti. He had always wanted to be a real singer, but he didn't know how to pursue a career, and his talents were limited to weddings and family gatherings. Papa had a tenor voice that could hold any tune. When he noticed his daughter mouthing the words, he lifted her onto a table and gave her the microphone. At first, she was nervous and shy, but her voice soared. From then on, he encouraged her to get on the stage with him whenever he sang.

Although he could speak English, he preferred to use his native language.

"Canta una Italiana," la mia piccola ragazza."

"I wish you wouldn't speak to her in Italian, Giuseppe. She is an American girl."

Anna constantly chastised him for filling the girls' heads with what he called the Sicilian way. Born in America, she knew only her Italian culture through her parents. Americanized, she insisted that the girls speak only English at home.

"It's important for a person to know where they came from," Giuseppe said. "How can you know your path in life if you don't know where you started?"

"You know how people discriminate."

"I understand, Anna, but I want my girls to be proud of their heritage."

After Anna cleaned the dinner dishes, she took her stool and knitting bag downstairs to join the family and neighbors. They sat in front of the building every night to enjoy the evening breeze. She was adept with knitting needles and loved making small gifts for the family from leftover yarn she collected at the textile mills down the street.

Summer nights in Brooklyn were magical, and only the adults minded the heat. They sat on milk crates and lawn chairs, fanning themselves.

The children played tag outside the building, under their parents' watchful eyes. A circle of older women huddled together as the children played hide-and-seek. Cousin Regina counted while the other kids ran to hide. Screams rang out as she tried to stop them from touching the wall so they wouldn't be *it*.

Grandma shook a bony finger when they got too wild. "Ti farai male!" she warned.

They played under the dim streetlights while the adults reminisced about stories from the old country. Each strived to give their children opportunities they would never have achieved in Sicily. They lamented how their children got away with much more than they did. They complained about how America had spoiled them. It was easier to blame American society for their children's brazen disrespect than for their permissive parenting skills.

"Kids had it so much harder in Sicily," Giovanna said. "They had to quit school so they could help their parents on the farm or take care of siblings."

"Well, I'm proud that my daughters will never know their ancestors' poverty," Anna said. She had heard stories of her parents' hardships in the old country and was grateful they made it possible for her to have a good life in America.

Their voices rose as they discussed morals and American values, and hushed as they gossiped.

"Did you see Tess?" Sadie said. "She got another black eye. Says she ran into the door."

"You don't believe that, do you?" Giovanna said.

"She should take a frying pan to his head," Anna said. "That poor woman has her hands full with three small children and a philandering husband."

Oblivious to the women's conversations, the men sat together playing cards, drinking cheap Chianti, and puffing on guinea stinkers they called cigars. They talked about Sicily and the horrors of another world war.

# Sicilian Steel

Giuseppe earned money working at the fish market in Elizabeth, New Jersey, with Caterina and her husband, Aldo. They had sponsored him to come to America and gave him a job. Every night, he came home with fresh fish wrapped in newspaper, the scent clinging to his clothes like the sea.

Around the dinner table, Giuseppe often told stories about his homeland.

Jeanette never got tired of hearing them — tales of Sicily, the sea, the village of Sciacca, and his mischievous youth.

"Can you tell us about Sciacca?" she asked one evening.

"I want to hear more about the mafia," Phyllis said, leaning forward. "Were Nonna's cousins connected?"

"No, Phyllis," Giuseppe said with a chuckle, "but the mafia was around. Most of them lived in Palermo, but they sometimes came through Sciacca. Our harbor brought all kinds of people."

He leaned back in his chair and rubbed his hands together. "When I was a teenager, my cousin Vincenzo and I used to hang around the marina, working odd jobs to make some money. We smelled like fish by the end of the day, but we didn't care. One afternoon, a truck pulled up. Two guys asked us to help load boxes of fish. Said they'd pay us when we were done.

"Well, we worked our tails off in that sun. When the truck was full, Vincenzo asked for our pay. The guy just laughed and said, 'Beat it, kid.'

"My father always taught me — never back down when something's owed to you. So I stepped forward and said, 'We want our money.'"

Jeanette's eyes widened. "What happened?"

"He punched me in the face and jumped in the truck."

Gasps came from around the table.

"What did you do?" Jeanette asked again.

"We went to Vincenzo's father, Calogero. When we told him what happened, he didn't ask questions. He just said, 'I'll take care of it.'

"The next day, they came back with their truck. Uncle Calogero was waiting. He didn't say a word — just walked up to the guy and punched him. Hard. He didn't stop until his hand gave out. Blood everywhere.

"'Don't you ever touch my family again,' he told him. 'Now get out of here — and don't come back.'

"But the guy wasn't just anyone. Turned out, he and his partner were sons of a mafia king from Palermo."

Phyllis sat up straighter. "What happened next?"

"We were worried there'd be a feud. The next day, we all showed up at the marina — brothers, cousins, even uncles — just in case. A truck and a sleek black car pulled up. Out stepped an older man, sharp suit, cigar in hand. He scanned the crowd and spotted my father.

"'Paolo!' he shouted.

"'Carlo?' my father said, surprised. 'I haven't seen you since grade school!'

"Carlo nodded. 'I'm sorry it came to this. I heard your brother hit my son.'

"'He did,' my father said. 'But it was my boy, Giuseppe, who was cheated. That's why.'

"Carlo looked at me. 'Tell me what happened.'

"I told him—how we worked hard, how they refused to pay us, how I got this bruise."

Jeanette touched her cheek in sympathy, imagining the pain.

Giuseppe continued, "Carlo turned to his son and slapped him across the face. Then again, harder.

"'Don't you know anything about family honor?' he shouted. 'You always pay your debts.'

"Then he turned back to my father and said, 'I'm sorry we had to meet again under such circumstances.'"

Giuseppe smiled at his daughters. "So, to answer your question, Phyllis—yes. Everyone in Sciacca was connected in one way or another."

# Snake Eyes

Every morning, Jeanette's first thought was of Sonny. The two of them were inseparable, which didn't sit well with his mother. Aunt Evelyn was always suspicious, demanding to know where they were going, and most days, she made them take his younger sister along.

Rosetta was only seven, so their adventures were limited. Sonny called her Snake Eyes because she watched his every move, always on the lookout for something she could report back and get him in trouble.

"Let's play tag," he told her one afternoon. "You're it. Close your eyes and count to ten—we'll hide."

"I'm always it," Rosetta pouted.

"If you want to play, you have to be it," Sonny said flatly.

Rosetta sighed and turned toward the brick building, covering her eyes and counting. By the time she got to five, Sonny and Jeanette were already gone.

Realizing she'd been ditched, Rosetta burst into tears and ran home to tattle.

Down in the cellar, Sonny and Jeanette were digging through the dumbwaiter shelves, hunting for scraps they could sell to the junkman—old wires, bottles, bits of metal. It was their secret treasure-hunting game. But before long, Aunt Evelyn's voice echoed down the stairs, calling Sonny home.

Sometimes Jeanette's mother babysat Sonny and Rosetta when Aunt Evelyn had to work. On Thursdays, the mobile rides came through their neighborhood, and Jeanette couldn't wait. Her favorite was the Half-Moon—a steel swing with long bench seats that soared higher with each pass. A single bar locked over your lap, but it barely felt secure once the swing picked up speed. The bravest kids sat at the top. Most closed their eyes, but not Jeanette. She lived for that moment when the swing paused at its peak, and the whole world dropped away beneath her.

That afternoon, she and Sonny scrambled to find enough money for a ride. Then Sonny had an idea.

"Let's send Rosetta to the store with the bottles we found this morning. We'll get a penny each."

He stuffed six milk bottles into a paper bag and handed them to Rosetta. "Hurry," he said.

But Rosetta never came back. They missed the ride.

Later, they found out she had fallen on the sidewalk. One of the bottles shattered in her hand, and she had to be taken to the hospital for stitches.

Jeanette felt terrible for Rosetta, but even worse for Sonny. Aunt Evelyn was furious. Jeanette feared it would be another reason for her to keep Sonny away.

That evening, she leaned on the windowsill, her head resting in the crook of her arms as she watched her cousins playing in the street below. She searched the crowd for Sonny, but he wasn't there. She wondered if he'd been punished, too.

*****

Phyllis tucked her long ponytail under a baseball cap and grabbed the mitt Uncle Alberto had given her for Christmas.

"I'm heading to the empty lot down the street," she called out.

"Be back before dark," Mama said without looking up.

"I will!"

She bounded down the steps and out to the sidewalk, her sneakers slapping the concrete as she made her way toward the field near the highway.

The neighborhood boys were already there, gathered in the dusty lot across from a cluster of apartment buildings. Phyllis stood off to the side, watching them take turns at bat, clumsily hitting balls into the outfield. Some couldn't hit at all.

They couldn't hit a barn if it were three feet wide, she thought.

"Can I play?" she asked, stepping closer.

Michael turned, already scowling. "No!"

"Why not?"

"Baseball's for boys," he snapped. "Why don't you go to the park and play softball with the other girls?"

"I don't like softball," she said flatly. "If Angelo were here, he'd let me play."

"Well, he's not," Michael shot back. "So scram."

She held her ground but said nothing. Deep down, she wondered why Angelo wasn't there. He usually never missed a game. He was one of the best hitters in the neighborhood — smooth, effortless. He didn't show off, didn't need to. Maybe that's why he'd always treated her with respect.

Back on the field, the pitcher tipped his cap, signaling a fastball. Michael stepped up to the plate, gripping the bat with too much confidence.

Phyllis squinted, studying his stance. He didn't have it.

The pitch came in. Michael swung — and missed.

She bit her lip, stifling a giggle.

Another pitch. Another swing. Another miss.

He had one chance left.

"Strike three! You're out!" the catcher barked.

Phyllis couldn't help herself. She smirked.

# Chinese Laundry

In the center of the tenement buildings was a square courtyard strung with clotheslines on pulleys, stretching from metal poles to apartment windows. Outside, kimonos and work shirts flapped in the wind. Some hung across fire escapes, others drooped from the lines like surrendered flags.

Sometimes, the pulley slipped off its winch, and someone had to climb out a window to fix it. Even in winter, wet laundry was hung outside on sunny days, though it often froze stiff before it could dry. Jeanette laughed at how pant legs turned rigid and could stand in the corner like ghostly figures.

She often sat at the windowsill, watching stray cats prowl the courtyard below, ears twitching as they searched for scraps. When the wind blew through the cracks in the windows, it made a soft moaning sound. Sonny wasn't around, and Jeanette was bored. So, she grabbed her coat and walked around the block to visit Jin and her little sister, Lai.

They lived behind their parents' Chinese laundry shop. In the back room, their mother sat in a wooden chair surrounded by piles of clothes, darning socks or hemming pant legs. White steam curled up from the pressing boards where their father ironed men's tailored shirts, each one crisp and exact. Once finished, the shirts were wrapped in brown paper and tied with a string. To pick up their laundry, customers had to present a slip of paper with Chinese characters scrawled across it. That was the rule. Without it, there was no way to find the matching bundle.

"No tickee, no shirtee!" they'd say with a shrug.

The neighborhood kids—Irish, Jewish, Italian—often mocked their accent, mimicking what they called "Pidgin English" and laughing when they left out pronouns or linking verbs.

*****

As the coldest days of winter waned, Jin's family began preparing for their spring festival, Yuan Xiao. According to the Chinese calendar, it was the Year of the Horse. The laundry shop, usually quiet and focused, now buzzed with a kind of joy. Jin's parents, who rarely spoke more than necessary, sang softly while they worked.

In the back room, Jeanette helped Jin and her family wrap dumplings. They sat around a low table, folding thin dumpling skins around ground meat, vegetables, and spices.

At first, Jeanette's dumplings fell apart—filling spilling out from the sides. She frowned at the mess.

"Here. I show you," Jin's mother said gently, dipping her fingers into a bowl of egg whites. "Must use egg. Keep together."

She brushed the edge of the dumpling skin, folded it neatly, and sealed it tight.

Jeanette copied her, and this time, the dumpling held. Jin's father gave a small, approving nod — rare from a man who barely showed emotion.

"Vewy good," Jin's mother smiled. "We make you part of family."

Jeanette beamed. Few outsiders were ever invited to the celebration, but Jin's family welcomed her as an honored guest.

"Can I bring my cousin Sonny, too?" she asked.

"Yes, of course," Jin said. "He's welcome."

Jeanette stepped out of the shop with a grin and ran straight into her older cousin, Ronnie.

"What were you doing in there, playing with the chinks?"

She froze. "They're not chinks. They're Chinese."

Ronnie scoffed. "Well, we don't want them here. They should go back to China."

Jeanette planted her feet and put her hands on her hips. Her eyes narrowed in defiance. "They have just as much right to be here as you or me."

Ronnie sneered. "Maybe I'll tell your father. I bet he'd be mad. You might even get punished."

"You say one more word," she growled, "and I'll pop you."

Ronnie leaned in, taunting, "Nah nah nah — Jeanette plays with ch — "

Before he could finish, Jeanette balled up her fist and socked him square in the nose.

The clotheslines in the courtyard came down to make room for a big tent. Paper lotus flowers and dragons stretched from one side of the yard to the other, swaying gently in the breeze. Rows of delicate paper cutouts—animals, flowers, and mythical figures—hung from windows, fastened in place with rice glue. Each symbol told a story from folklore or legend.

Above the courtyard entrance was a large peach cutout, and in the entryway stood the images of two fierce Chinese soldiers, arms crossed, eyes glaring.

"What does the peach mean?" Jeanette asked Jin.

"There's a giant peach tree in the spirit world," Jin said. "Two gods guard it."

Red lanterns with gold lettering swung along the former clotheslines. Most had the single character *fu*, but some carried longer phrases.

"In China, we write wishes on the lanterns and send them up to heaven," Jin explained. "It's kind of like when you blow out birthday candles."

"Can we make a wish?" Jeanette asked.

"Of course." Jin handed Jeanette and Sonny a small slip of paper and a pencil. They scribbled their wishes, folded the paper, and tucked them into the lanterns.

"Why are they red?" Sonny asked.

"For happiness and good fortune."

"What did you wish for?" he asked Jeanette.

"If I tell you, it won't come true."

Sonny grinned. "I bet I could guess."

"No!" Jin jumped in. "That's bad luck!"

Inside the tent, platters of food were laid out across long tables. Whole fish swam in pools of dark, savory sauce, their bodies draped in ribbons of Chinese cabbage and slender green onions. Jeanette had only ever eaten chow mein. She took a cautious bite of the fish — salty, oily, unfamiliar.

Another platter held a roasted chicken, its head still attached, the long neck curled, beak open, and one eye socket hollow. Only the feet were missing, but they floated in a giant pot of soup nearby. Jeanette and Sonny scrunched their noses.

Then Jeanette spotted the dumplings.

"I helped make those," she said proudly.

"They look good," Sonny said, eyeing the tray. "What's in them?"

Jin smiled. "Some have cow liver. Some have tuna belly."

Sonny's eyes widened. "Oh! They *look* delicious, but... I'm full."

Laughter rippled through the tent as the adults tried to tempt him with more delicacies. Jeanette stuck to the spring rolls — safe and familiar. A tray of meatballs caught her attention.

"I didn't know you ate Italian food," she said.

Jin's father chuckled. "Meatball? No Italian! Shandong cuisine. First made in 221 BC. Call 'Four-Joy Meatball.'"

Jeanette wasn't so sure. For as long as she could remember, meatballs simmered on her mother's stove, steeped in tomato sauce and served over spaghetti. *Did they invent that, too?* she wondered.

Stringed instruments and flutes played in the background as the adults shared stories about the Year of the Horse. Even the children joined in, spinning hand drums attached to bamboo sticks. Tiny balls on strings smacked the drumheads in rhythm as they spun them between their fingers.

Near the fire pit, a group of men stood burning money.

Jeanette gasped.

"Don't worry," Jin said. "It's not real. Just paper money. For ancestors."

Children gathered around the dessert table, eyes wide. A platter of twisted dough glistened with sugar, and Jeanette's mouth watered. She'd seen something like it at a street vendor on 8th Street — but her Sicilian mother, loyal to zeppole, never stopped to buy them.

Jin grabbed three. "Dragon tail," she said, handing one to Sonny and another to Jeanette. "Most popular."

Jeanette bit into the golden dough — soft, puffy, sugary heaven. She let it melt in her mouth before swallowing. She reached for another, but the plate was empty — only a dusting of sugar remained.

They moved on to the persimmon cakes. Jeanette ate two before Jin's father raised an eyebrow.

"Eat too much persimmon — get bad stomach."

Jin's younger sister, Lai, sat on their father's lap as he peeled a small, golden fruit.

"What is that?" Jeanette asked.

"Golden tangerine," he said. "*Gam kwat.*"

"You mean kumquat?" she asked.

"No. *Gam kwat,*" he said with a smile. "Grow in Guangdong. Ship here for feast."

Jeanette looked at Jin, who whispered, "It's a kumquat." She rolled her eyes. Jin's parents shook their heads. She was becoming too American.

Later, Jin's father gathered the children around to tell them a story.

"Long time ago," he began, "emperor invite all animals to party. Say, 'Order you arrive, will be noted.' Horse too scared pass cemetery. Hesitate. Close eyes, run full speed. Horse come seventh. That why horse is number seven in zodiac."

Jeanette listened wide-eyed, her mouth slightly open. The sky had turned deep indigo.

While others in the neighborhood welcomed the new year by banging pots, the Chinese celebrated with *bao zhu*—firecrackers. Jeanette and Sonny knew them as the loud pops their uncles lit on the Fourth of July. They didn't know the Chinese invented them.

Jin told them firecrackers were used to ward off evil spirits. A man lit the fuse on a long stick, lifted it high into the air, and sent sparks flying. The lanterns, now glowing softly, floated up into the night sky.

Sonny and Jeanette held hands and watched their wishes rise with the glowing lights.

Later, Jeanette clutched her stomach and groaned. "I knew I shouldn't have eaten so many persimmon cakes."

# Twenty-three Skidoo

Each morning, the bread deliveryman pulled his truck into the courtyard and rang his bell. Windows flew open as baskets filled with money were lowered to the ground by a rope. He'd trade the cash for a loaf or two of fresh, hot bread, still warm from the ovens on 86th Street.

But Giuseppe preferred to walk to the bakery himself, especially on Saturdays, when the scent of bread wafted through the neighborhood like a siren's call.

"Luci, wake up. It's Saturday!" Jeanette whispered with excitement.

She loved Saturdays—not just because there was no school, but because she got to spend more time with her cousin Sonny.

Luciana rubbed her eyes and grinned. The girls followed the aroma of fresh-brewed coffee into the kitchen. Phyllis was already seated at the table, and Mariella helped Mama at the stove. A brown paper bag filled with warm rolls sat in the center of the table. Jeanette reached in and grabbed the biggest one. Even though the black poppy seeds always stuck in her teeth, she loved the texture and the crunch.

She slathered it with butter until it dripped down the sides.

"I wish every day were Saturday," Luciana sighed. "I hate school."

"You girls don't know how lucky you have it," Giuseppe said as he buttered a roll. "I never made it past fifth grade."

Jeanette's eyes widened. "Why not, Pop?"

"In Sciacca, the teachers were strict," he began, leaning back in his chair. "If you talked in class, they whipped you with an olive branch."

He chuckled to himself. "One day, I was too chatty. Mr. Frisco called me to the front of the class and told me to hold my hands out. I kept pulling them back. That made him furious, so instead, he whipped my back. I ran all the way home."

He looked around the table, smiling at the memory.

"My mother was ironing my father's shirt in the kitchen. She looked up and said, 'What are you doing home? You get back to school right now!' So I told her what happened and showed her the welts."

"What did she do?" Luciana asked, wide-eyed.

Giuseppe laughed. "She was furious. Dragged me right back to school. I thought I was in trouble."

"But she wasn't mad at you?" Jeanette asked.

"No. She marched straight up to Mr. Frisco and said, 'If you ever touch my boy again, I'll have my Mafioso cousins pay you a visit.' His face went white."

"Nonna sounds like a strong woman," Jeanette said. "I wish I could've met her."

"She was a lot like you," he said softly, brushing Jeanette's cheek with his hand.

"I bet Mr. Frisco never tried it again," Phyllis said.

Giuseppe grinned. "He never got the chance. I refused to go back. Every time my mother sent me off in the morning, I'd sneak home a few hours later. Finally, she gave up. She said, 'If you're not going to school, you're going to work.' So she sent me to help my father on his fishing boat."

He paused, eyes distant.

"I sorted shrimp into one crate and sardines into another. I was so small, I had to stand on a stool just to reach the barrels."

"Is that why you sell fish now, Pop?" Jeanette asked.

"Yes. I come from a long line of fishermen. Every morning, my father took his boat out to sea. When I was a toddler, I watched from the kitchen window as he left the port. In the evening, I'd see his boat return, trailed by seagulls waiting for scraps."

"Your family must've been rich," Phyllis said.

Giuseppe smiled. "It paid well—but it was hard, back-breaking work."

"Did your sisters have to go to school?"

"Yes. Caterina and Maria were smart cookies. Antonella—she was feisty, like you, Phyllis. Always getting into trouble. But your Aunt Maria… she was gentle. Like a lamb."

"Like Mariella," Jeanette said, glancing at her older sister.

Giuseppe nodded, his smile fading into a faraway gaze.

"Do you miss Sicily, Pop?" Jeanette asked gently.

"Yes," he said. "Very much."

"Maybe we can go someday. I'd love to see where you grew up."

"Perhaps," he said with a sigh. "Someday."

*****

Anna placed a large platter of scrambled eggs in the center of the table. Mariella poured the coffee, then turned off the stove and joined the rest of the family.

After breakfast, Luciana picked up her book and climbed out onto the fire escape. She loved the peace out there and didn't mind the crisp morning air. On weekends, she could finish two or three books without blinking. Books were her escape, her quiet companions—and she didn't miss the petty drama of school.

Jeanette was the opposite. She hated reading almost as much as she hated math. Her favorite class was choir. She loved to sing and perform in school plays, especially around Christmas or Easter.

"Luci, let's go down to the trolley tracks and crush pennies," she said.

Luciana looked up from her book, considering it. "Nah, I don't feel like it. Ask Phyllis."

"Oh, all right."

"Don't forget—you're supposed to go to confession this morning," Luciana called after her.

Jeanette went to find Phyllis but barely made it to the bedroom before her sister brushed past her in the hallway.

"Where are you going?" Jeanette asked.

"To play ball in the lots."

"Can I come?"

"Nope. Go play with the kids outside."

With a sigh, Jeanette dropped the pennies into her travel fund can. Then she grabbed her new Jacks from Cheap John's and headed off to find Sonny.

*****

By nine o'clock, all the kids in the neighborhood were outside. Some of the boys were elbow-deep in mud, busy making pies with crooked grins on their dirty faces. They didn't care about the mess—just the fun.

Even in winter, they preferred to be outdoors, especially after Christmas. Bundled in coats and mittens, they showed off new sleds, bikes, and roller skates—gifts left under the tree by Santa. Cousin Robert pedaled proudly on his brand-new tricycle, its brass handlebars gleaming in the sun. The older boys tried to talk him into giving up a turn, but Jeanette and Sonny were right there to chase them off.

Jeanette climbed the stairs to Sonny's apartment. The door was open. She heard his mother inside.

"Sonny, you need to go to confession. It's Saturday."

"Aww, Ma, do I have to?"

"Yes. And Jeanette will go with you," she added, spotting Jeanette in the doorway.

Jeanette didn't mind. As long as she and Sonny were together, even church was fun.

They teased and laughed on the way.

"Step on a crack," Jeanette chanted, "break your mother's back."

Sonny immediately tried to trip her up, forcing her to step on more cracks than she wanted. She shrieked and chased him off the sidewalk.

They passed a group of girls playing in a circle, holding hands and singing.

**"Bobby and Janice, sitting in a tree, K-I-S-S-I-N-G. First comes love, then comes marriage, then comes Janice with a baby carriage!"**

The girls burst into giggles.

Jeanette and Sonny exploded with laughter — until the meaning of the song settled between them. For a moment, the silence was awkward.

"You're it!" Sonny suddenly shouted, tagging her shoulder.

Jeanette chased after him and slapped his back. "No, *you're* it!"

They tore through the neighborhood, cutting across a field of wild clover nearly up to their waists. When they couldn't run anymore, they collapsed onto the ground, panting, eyes turned toward the blue sky.

"Do you think we'll ever have kids?" Sonny asked.

Jeanette opened her mouth to respond, but a voice cut through the stillness.

"Hey, you kids!"

A cop on the beat came charging toward them.

"This is private property! Twenty-three skidoo!"

Laughing, they jumped to their feet and ran until their sides ached.

When they finally reached the church, Sonny hesitated.

"You go, Jeanette. I'll wait out here."

"But what about communion tomorrow? Your mom's gonna be mad if you don't go."

Sonny shrugged. "I might be too sick to go to Mass." He flashed her an innocent grin.

*How could anyone stay mad at Sonny?* Jeanette thought.

She went inside. The line for confession was longer than usual. Luciana stood halfway up, and Jeanette squeezed in beside her.

When it was her turn, she pulled back the curtain and stepped into the small, dark booth. The air smelled faintly of incense. She knelt, folded her hands, and waited for the small screen to slide open.

"Bless me, Father, for I have sinned…"

Jeanette didn't feel like she had done anything *too* bad, but she admitted to teasing her little cousin and cutting in line.

The priest murmured a prayer in Latin and made the sign of the cross.

"Your penance is two Hail Marys and one Our Father. Go now, my child, and sin no more."

Jeanette slid into a pew, whispered her prayers, then dipped her fingers into the holy water at the exit and made the sign of the cross.

Sonny was waiting on the steps, smirking.

"So… are you absolved?" he asked.

Jeanette rolled her eyes.

"Let's sneak into the Loew's theater," he said. "*The Mummy's Hand* just came out last week, and I *need* to see it."

# Hop Scotch

As winter loosened its grip on New York, clothes once again flapped in the courtyard breeze. Little brown and white sparrows with gray underbellies perched on the laundry lines and electrical wires, chirping as if to announce spring's return.

Heads popped out of the tenement windows to see what was going on. From the third floor, Anna watched her two youngest daughters, Luciana and Jeanette, playing in the street below. Phyllis and Cousin Ronnie were pitching pennies against the brick wall.

"Can me and Luci play?" Jeanette asked.

"No," Phyllis said flatly. "Go skip rope or something."

"We did that already. We're bored," Jeanette whined.

"Well, go play ball. Or Potsy."

"What's Potsy?" Luciana asked.

Phyllis rolled her eyes. "Don't you girls know anything? Get some chalk. I'll show you."

Jeanette and Luciana ran upstairs, digging under the bed until Jeanette found the colored chalk in their school supplies.

"Got it!"

Back outside, Phyllis warned, "Don't touch my pennies. I'll be right back."

"Okay, girls," she said, kneeling on the sidewalk. "I'll draw the board while you find something small to toss—maybe a pebble."

Phyllis drew two large squares side by side. Beneath them, she added a single square, then two more side by side, another single square, and finally, a pair of squares at the end. She numbered them one through eight.

"We have our pebbles," Jeanette said, though she looked skeptical. "But this doesn't look like much fun."

"I'm not done," Phyllis said, brushing her hands together. "Now listen. Luci, you go first. Toss your pebble into square number one."

Luciana threw her pebble, but it bounced and landed outside the square.

"Missed. You lose a turn. Jeanette, you try."

Jeanette tossed her pebble, and it landed right in the center of square one.

"I did it!" she yelled.

"Now hop on one foot into each square—except the one with the pebble. Don't step on the lines. When you get to the end, turn around, hop back, and pick up your pebble without losing your balance."

Jeanette bounced her way to square eight and back, grabbed her stone, and stepped out, beaming.

"Now throw it into number two. Same rules. You keep going until you mess up, then it's Luci's turn again."

Satisfied they'd picked up the rules, Phyllis returned to pitching pennies with Ronnie.

Jeanette and Luciana played on, and soon a small crowd of girls gathered around, eager to try. Even a few boys joined in—including Ralph, who lived next door to Cousin Dickie. Ralph waited patiently for his turn, but before he could go, a sharp voice rang out from above.

"Ralphie! I need you to run to the store and get me a bag of flour."

"Gol-lee, Ma," Ralph groaned, stomping his foot.

A small bundle of coins wrapped in brown paper fell from the second-floor window. He caught it midair.

"And bring me back the change!"

"I'll be right back," he muttered, then ran off.

When he returned, panting, he held up his pebble. "I didn't get a turn yet!"

"You have to wait," Jeanette said. "It's Lorraine's turn."

The sun was beginning to set, and Ralph fidgeted, afraid he wouldn't get to play. Finally, just as it was his turn, the window creaked open again.

"Ralphie! Time for your bath!"

"Ah, Ma! Can't I stay out a little longer?"

"You get up here this minute, or your father will deal with you when he gets home."

"I'm coming," Ralph mumbled. He threw his pebble into the gutter in frustration.

"Ralphie's gotta take a bath," Dickie teased.

"Shut up!" Ralph snapped, shoving him to the ground.

"You leave my cousin alone," Jeanette warned. Dickie might've picked on the younger kids, but he was family—and family stuck together.

*****

It was the day before Easter, and Jeanette and Sonny could hardly contain their excitement. Word had gotten out—though it wasn't supposed to—that all the kids were getting live baby chicks. They weren't meant to know, but Sonny had heard the soft chirping coming from the laundry room. Curious, he'd snuck over to take a peek, only for his father to catch him in the act.

"Out of here, Sonny," he said, waving him off. "It's a surprise."

But it was too late. The secret was out—and the anticipation made it nearly impossible to think about anything else.

# Pane di Pasqua

Easter was Jeanette's favorite holiday, more than even Christmas. She loved the pastel-colored eggs, the scent of spring flowers Mama arranged for the table, and most of all, the Easter baskets.

Each year, all four girls got one—even Mariella and Phyllis, who were practically grown. Four wicker baskets sat in a row on the sideboard, filled with chocolate bunnies and jellybeans, each wrapped in shiny cellophane—pink, yellow, green, and blue. The temptation to rip into the wrapping was overwhelming, but Luciana couldn't bring herself to do it. She gently peeled back a corner and peeked inside, her eyes wide with delight when she spotted her favorites.

Just as Jeanette was about to dive into hers, Mama called in from the kitchen.

"Not until after breakfast."

Giuseppe took his place at the head of the table and looked around. "Where's Phyllis?"

"She went to the park," Jeanette answered. "One of the Little League teams is playing today."

"On Easter?" Giuseppe frowned.

"Not everyone's Catholic," Anna reminded him, setting down a basket of warm rolls.

Mariella placed a platter of scrambled eggs beside the bowl of bright, hard-boiled eggs the girls had decorated the day before. Giuseppe dished out a few onto Jeanette's and Luciana's plates.

"Why do we eat so many eggs at Easter?" Jeanette asked.

"Because eggs are a symbol of spring and new life," he replied.

"They also represent Jesus coming out of the tomb—His resurrection," Luciana added.

Giuseppe smiled with pride. "That's right, Luci. In Sciacca, we used eggs in almost every Easter dish."

"What was your favorite, Pop?" Jeanette asked, her voice eager.

"My mother made a dish called *Taganu D'Aragona*. She'd layer a big pan with pasta, ground beef or sausage, and cheese, then pour in a dozen whipped eggs on top. Once it was baked, she'd flip the pan upside down. Came out perfect every time."

He closed his eyes for a moment, savoring the memory. "I sure do miss Sicilian cooking. My sister Maria probably kept the tradition going."

"I thought your sister was Aunt Adelle," Jeanette said.

"She is. But I'm talking about my other sister, Maria. The one who stayed in Sciacca."

"I didn't know you had a sister in Sciacca," Luciana said. "Tell us about her."

"The last time I saw Maria, she was newly married and expecting her first baby. After I came to America, we wrote letters for a while... then, I don't know—we just stopped. Life got busy. The last I heard, she had nine children. Eight boys and one girl."

"Nine?" Jeanette gasped. "That's a lot of babies!"

"I love babies," Luciana said dreamily. "But I don't plan to have any. I want to become a nun and join the convent. Nuns don't get married, you know."

Giuseppe smiled softly. "We'll see, Luci. You're only twelve. You may change your mind."

Luciana had been named after their mother, Anna. She was born with a condition that kept her eyelids fused shut. The doctors had warned she might never see. But after weeks of prayer, the hospital called with a miracle—her eyes had opened. Though she would always need thick glasses, she wasn't blind, as they had feared. From that day on, they called her Luciana, after the patron saint of the blind. She took her faith seriously and often spoke of dedicating her life to helping others.

"Pop," Jeanette asked quietly, "do you miss Sciacca?"

Giuseppe let out a breath. "Yes, I suppose I do."

"Can we go there someday? You could see your sister again."

"It's very far and very expensive," he said. "We'd have to travel by boat."

Jeanette lit up. "That sounds exciting! We can start a Sciacca fund!"

She dashed off and returned a moment later with an old tin she'd once used to store treasures she and Sonny found while scavenging. The faded label read *8*

*O'Clock Coffee.* She cut a slit in the plastic lid with a butter knife. "This will work perfectly. I'll save money from chores. And maybe some birthday money, too."

Giuseppe chuckled and reached into his pocket. "You're my adventurous girl."

He dropped a nickel into the can. It clinked against the bottom.

"There. Now we've officially started saving for Sciacca."

Jeanette beamed.

"Now eat your breakfast," he added, "because Mama and Mariella need the kitchen to start our Easter feast."

*****

Holiday meals were an all-day affair. In a world of uncertainty, food was the one thing the family could count on. It brought everyone together, no matter what.

There was always pasta and braided loaves of bread, each baked with a pastel-colored Easter egg nestled in the center. Pies filled the table—some stuffed with ricotta and glazed with egg, others made with rice and citrus, called grain pies. A lamb shank simmered in tomato sauce for hours, tender enough to cut with a fork.

Nonna was the family baker. All her old Sicilian recipes were stored neatly in her head, and she never shared them with anyone—except Mariella. Her first granddaughter had inherited her passion for baking. Mariella was by Nonna's side whenever the mixing bowls came out. While Nonna measured ingredients by instinct, Mariella insisted on using cups and spoons, determined to make everything just right.

A long table for the adults stretched wall to wall in the dining room, while a smaller table in the living room was set for the children. The rule was "seen but not heard," but none of the kids minded. They had each other. Sonny always saved the seat next to him for Jeanette.

"Sa bininica, Nonna," the children said in greeting. Nonna kissed each one on the cheek and handed them a gold-foil-wrapped chocolate bunny.

The wine flowed, and the food came in waves— first the pasta, then roasted lamb and salad. After the main course, Mariella brought out the marzipan lambs and the pastries she and Nonna had baked all week. Their reputation preceded them. Butter cookies dipped in chocolate and coated with rainbow sprinkles melted in your mouth. Every Italian pastry imaginable filled the trays—cannoli, sfogliatelle, pignoli, and more.

Uncle Alberto was the first to have a little too much wine. He jumped up from his chair and belted out "Lazy Mary," spinning around the room as he danced, causing the kids to burst into laughter.

In one room, the adults played cards, tossing in spare change as they sipped tiny cups of espresso laced with anisette. They picked at bowls of fruit and nuts, always present at the card table.

In the other room, the children played with their baby chicks and nibbled on chocolate. Their Easter baskets remained on the bookshelf, untouched — at least for the moment. No one wanted to tear the shiny cellophane.

"I see jellybeans!" someone whispered.

"Mine has Peeps."

"Look — there's a marshmallow rabbit!"

"I'm not opening mine until Christmas," Dickie declared.

"Not me," Jeanette said boldly, tearing through the cellophane and reaching for a chocolate-covered marshmallow egg.

Wrappers began to pile up on the floor as the cousins joined in like a feeding frenzy — Ronnie, Kathy, Joanne, Robert, Sonny, Lorraine, Regina, and Vinny.

"Let's give our chicks a bath," Sonny said, eyes gleaming.

A trail of kids followed him into the bathroom.

"The sink's too small," Lorraine pointed out.

"We'll use the washing machine," Sonny said confidently.

He turned the faucet and let the basin fill with water. One by one, the kids lowered their fluffy yellow chicks into the tub.

But suddenly, the water started to swirl.

"Stop!" Jeanette shouted, eyes wide. The room erupted in screams.

Uncle Vinnie came rushing in just in time to shut off the machine. The basin stopped spinning. The chicks were safe and very clean.

# Summer Fever

Jeanette and Luciana were in the courtyard trying out their new hula hoops. As soon as the trend hit, every girl on the block had one — pink, blue, green, or yellow, each with white stripes that blurred as they spun.

After an hour of twisting and wobbling, Jeanette grew bored.

"I'm going to call for Sonny," she said, dropping her hoop. "Wanna come?"

"Nah. I've got one more chapter in my book," Luciana replied. "I think I'll just read today."

Jeanette headed over and knocked on Sonny's door.

"Sonny can't come out," Rosetta said, opening the door just enough to try and shut it again.

Jeanette stopped it with her foot. "Why do you have to be such a brat?"

Rosetta stuck out her tongue. "Sooonny! Your *girlfriend* is here."

Sonny appeared from his bedroom wearing brown knickerbockers, suspenders, and no shirt. His tousled black hair fell into his eyes, and he raked it back with his fingers.

"Shut up, Rosetta," he muttered. "Or I'll deck you."

Jeanette smiled. Just looking at him made her heart flutter.

"Hi, Sonny. Want to collect stuff for the junkman?"

"He *can't*," Rosetta chirped. "He has to get his summer haircut."

Sonny rolled his eyes. "Ignore her. Nobody's home upstairs," he said, tapping his forehead.

"I'm telling Mom!" Rosetta shouted as she stomped away.

Aunt Evelyn came out of the kitchen, drying her hands on a dish towel. "What's going on here?"

"Jeanette wants Sonny to be a rag-picker!" Rosetta whined from down the hall.

"Rag-picker? What did I tell you about going through other people's garbage?" Aunt Evelyn snapped. "I won't have my son running around the streets like a beggar."

"Gol-lee, Ma…" Sonny groaned.

Then she turned to Jeanette. Her voice softened, but not by much. "Sonny's getting his haircut and going shopping. He'll see you later."

She opened the door a little wider, as if to usher Jeanette out. Rosetta stood behind her with a smug look on her face. Jeanette wanted to punch her. If they weren't cousins, she might have.

Jeanette could feel Aunt Evelyn's eyes on her as if she was trying to read her mind. There was something about her aunt's gaze—sharp, suspicious. Jeanette couldn't explain it, but she sensed she wasn't liked. Maybe because she teased Rosetta, or maybe because she took up too much of Sonny's time.

"I'll call for you after my haircut," Sonny said.

"Okay. I'll be waiting."

*****

At the start of every summer, Uncle Vincent set up a chair in the courtyard. He was the family barber, and one by one, he clipped the boys' hair down to size. They got haircuts all summer long until school started again. By mid-morning, the pavement was covered in little mounds of brown clippings.

On hot days, the sidewalks radiated heat like stovetops. Even the fruit man's horse moved slowly, straining to pull the wagon of watermelons, grapes, and apples.

Now and then, someone opened a Johnny pump and turned the hydrant into a fountain, sending streams of water into the street. Kids ran barefoot through the spray, squealing with delight. It was the only real way to cool off—except for the lemon ices sold from a cart in front of the bakery. They came in pleated paper cups, sticky-sweet juice dripping through fingers and onto the pavement. The icy treat hit the spot—at first—but always left them thirstier afterward.

The cousins stayed outside all day, chasing one another through the neighborhood, playing games in the street. No one went home until their mothers leaned out the windows and called them in for supper.

Women sat in clusters outside the building, fanning themselves and gossiping in hushed tones about the neighborhood tramps with their teased hair and low-cut blouses. Whispers carried on the breeze — speculation about who was cheating on whom, whose daughter was headed down the wrong path, and which wife had bruises that weren't from bumping into furniture.

"Did you see Tessie?" Evelyn asked. "Her cheek's swollen."

"That husband of hers is going to kill her one of these days," Giovanna muttered, shaking her head.

"I heard he's connected," Angela said. "He keeps her in diamonds and designer clothes. I guess that's the price she pays."

"I would *never* stand for my daughters going with such low lives," Anna declared. She wasn't too worried — Mariella was working hard at the bakery, Phyllis was more interested in sports than boys, and Luciana and Jeanette were still a few years away from thinking about romance.

Laughter from children filled the warm night air as they played hide-and-seek in the courtyard, their voices echoing between the buildings. Occasionally, the high-pitched wail of a fire truck sliced through the sounds of play. Then came the unmistakable melody of Mister Softee's ice cream truck. A stampede of children ran back to their parents, begging for change. If one gave in, the others usually followed.

"These kids," someone said. "They don't know how lucky they have it here in America."

Uncle Joey rounded up the kids and took them to the corner store, handing each a quarter. Jeanette came back with four candy bars and five cents' worth of penny candy. Sonny bought three candy bars and two boxes of Boston Baked Beans.

Jeanette wrinkled her nose. "I don't know how you eat those."

Later that night, when the streets quieted and traffic thinned, Uncle Alberto and Uncle Joseph lit a fire in the middle of the street. They struck a match to a pile of crates and paper scraps, building a bonfire so the kids could roast marshmallows on long twigs they'd collected from the alley.

The moon hung full and bright in the sky. It felt like magic.

Uncle Joseph introduced his new girlfriend, Genovese. She was elegant, with soft curls and red lipstick. Jeanette thought she looked like a movie star.

"Are you going to get married?" Jeanette asked, eyes wide.

Uncle Joseph grinned, and Genovese held up her hand. A diamond ring sparkled in the light of the streetlamp.

"Oh, that's beautiful," Mariella said. "I can't wait to have a church wedding someday."

Eventually, the night wound down. Parents began rounding up sleepy children, dragging them upstairs one by one. Before they left, Uncle Joey handed out another quarter to each kid.

"He must be rich," Jeanette whispered, tucking her coin into her pocket.

Back inside, she dropped the quarter into the Sciacca can and climbed into bed. She and her sisters shared a cramped bedroom with two small beds. Mariella and Phyllis slept in one. Luciana and Jeanette shared the other.

Though they slept side by side, Jeanette and Luciana rarely spoke at night. They were opposites in almost every way. Jeanette was sociable and energetic. Luciana was quiet and devout, often found praying at Our Lady of Guadalupe Church. Her poor eyesight made her more withdrawn, and she preferred reading and reflection over noise and crowds.

Through the open window, the thunder of elevated trains shook the walls, the screeching wheels making the bed springs vibrate. Jeanette winced, pulling the sheet over her head.

In the next room, she could hear Nonna's labored breathing.

Nonno and Nonna had given up their own apartment after diabetes and other health problems made it impossible for them to live alone. Anna and Giuseppe gave them their bedroom and moved into the living room, where they slept on a Castro Convertible—a couch by day that unfolded into a bed at night.

Almost every Italian immigrant household had one. The Castro Convertible was the miracle solution for cramped city apartments—and the invention that made Bernard Castro, once a poor Sicilian immigrant, a very rich man.

*****

Every Tuesday night, neighbors gathered on the apartment building rooftop to watch the fireworks show put on by the local brewing company. It was a weekly ritual, something everyone looked forward to.

The roof was known as *Tar Beach*. During the day, tenants lay out blankets in the blazing sun, the thick smell of melting tar rising beneath them. Some residents tended rooftop gardens — wooden boxes sprouting tomatoes, peppers, even a few scraggly grapevines winding up makeshift trellises.

It was also a hangout for teenagers, a place just out of reach from prying adult eyes. They lit cigarettes behind the garden beds, passing them around while dreaming up wild ideas for adventures in the city below.

They took turns tossing pebbles off the edge, trying to hit the electrical pole. Sometimes they filled balloons with water and waited for an unsuspecting target to walk below before letting them drop.

Between each building, there was a five-foot gap — just wide enough to be dangerous. Daredevils would take a running start and leap from rooftop to the next. Everyone had heard the story about the little boy who missed and fell to his death, but most kids figured their parents made it up to scare them.

And maybe they had.

# Brownstone

Giuseppe and Anna found a duplex around the corner on a quiet, tree-shaded street. The houses were connected two by two, each with its own set of stone steps leading up to a small front landing, the neighbors called a stoop.

On the side of the house, a narrow garden was framed by a low wrought-iron fence. In its center stood a plaster statue of the Blessed Mother, draped in a blue robe, her hands pressed together in prayer. She was surrounded by blooming forsythia — the official flower of Brooklyn. Statues like hers dotted the block, almost identical to one another, and some residents lit small candles around them at night, creating a gentle glow of devotion after sunset.

Giuseppe cleared a patch of earth for vegetables, but his pride and joy was a young fig tree, grown from a clipping he had carefully smuggled in from Sciacca. He tended it lovingly, pruning it back each year to keep it from growing too tall.

The new flat had four rooms: a living room, a kitchen, and two small bedrooms. From the kitchen window, Anna could see her sister Giovanna's apartment just across the alley. It was close enough for the two of them to call out to each other without leaving home.

*****

On Saturday morning, Jeanette woke to the sound of the junk man's wagon rattling through the neighborhood, calling out for unwanted treasures. The sun was still low in the sky, and the pavement hadn't yet begun to burn beneath the rising heat.

She peeked out the window and spotted Mariella walking to work at the bakery, her starched white apron crisp and clean, for now. By noon, it would be dusted with flour and stained with jelly and chocolate custard.

Minutes later, the sharpening man came rolling down the street, calling out to the neighbors. Everyone had a side hustle in the neighborhood — sharpening knives, selling clothes, peddling pots and pans. Nobody needed to go shopping. If you waited long enough, what you needed would come to you.

*****

One Saturday, Jeanette and Luciana sat on the stoop, folding sheets of pink, blue, and yellow tissue paper into accordion pleats. Using bobby pins to fasten the centers, they pulled the layers apart to make paper carnations.

In the distance, they heard hoofbeats clattering down the cobblestone street.

"The pony man!" Jeanette shouted.

They burst through the front door and ran to their father.

"Pop! The pony man's coming—can we have a ride? Please?"

Giuseppe lowered his newspaper and smiled. "Go get your sister. Two pennies each for the ride and one for the photo."

Anna frowned from the kitchen. "Giuseppe, that's a waste of money."

He shook his head gently. "Let them have a little fun."

Then he reached into his pocket again. "Luciana, take this paper sack. See if the pony leaves a little trail. My garden could use the manure."

"Aw, Pop, do I *have* to?"

"I'll do it!" Jeanette grabbed the bag. "I'm not afraid of a little horse poop."

Giuseppe chuckled. "That's my girl."

The girls raced outside, calling after the ponyman.

By the time they caught up, another child was already in the saddle. They waited their turn patiently, admiring the pony. His name was Chestnut. His coat was a glossy light brown, with a dark mane and tail, and he wore a shiny leather bridle trimmed in silver.

Jeanette reached out to stroke his nose and looked into his eyes, wondering if he was tired of carrying kids up and down the block all day. But his eyes were calm—gentle, even—and she decided he didn't seem sad at all.

"Okay, girls. Your turn," said Bob, the ponyman.

"You go first," Jeanette told Luciana. Bob helped her onto the saddle. But as Jeanette watched, she noticed something in her sister's expression — something somber, almost lonely.

"Can we ride together?" Jeanette asked.

"I don't see why not," Bob said. "Chestnut can handle it."

He lifted Jeanette up behind her sister, and the pony strolled slowly down the block. With no other kids waiting, Bob let them ride a little longer than usual.

"This is almost as good as reading," Luciana said.

When the ride ended, Bob helped them down.

"Can I take some manure for my dad's garden?" Jeanette asked, holding up the paper bag.

"Of course," he smiled, pinching her cheek. "Help yourself."

It was messy work, but Jeanette kept her promise.

*****

Later that day, Jeanette and Luciana jumped rope in front of the stoop. A few girls from the block wandered over, watching from the side and whispering among themselves.

"Can we have a turn?" one of them asked.

Jeanette's stomach turned when she recognized the voice. Cindy — the schoolyard bully — was the last person she expected to ask nicely for anything.

Every day at recess, kids gathered in the small, stone-paved schoolyard. Cindy was always there, waiting to pounce on someone new. One day, it was a quiet, overweight boy who'd just arrived from Sicily. He barely spoke English and looked lost as he shuffled through the crowd.

Cindy pounced.

"When'd you get off the boat?" she jeered.

"Leave him alone," Jeanette said, stepping between them.

Cindy narrowed her eyes. "Do you want a knuckle sandwich?"

"Try it," Jeanette said, standing her ground.

Cindy cocked her arm back — but before she could swing, Jeanette grabbed a handful of her curly blonde hair and twisted until Cindy dropped to her knees.

"I think you owe this boy an apology."

Tears welled in Cindy's eyes. The boy stood nearby, stunned.

Jeanette twisted a little harder.

"Sorry," Cindy muttered.

Jeanette let go just as the bell rang. Cindy ran off.

"Gee," the boy said. "No one's ever stood up for me before."

"*Come ti chiami?*" Jeanette asked.

"Michael."

"Be more careful next time, Michael."

"*Grazie.*"

From that day forward, Cindy never bothered Jeanette again. And now, here she was, wanting to play jump rope.

Jeanette hesitated, then handed her the rope. "Okay. You can try it."

She watched as Cindy jumped, a little awkwardly, but without malice. They'd never be best friends — but they weren't enemies anymore either.

*****

Every Sunday, Mariella, Phyllis, Luciana, and Jeanette walked together to ten o'clock Mass. Luciana, always devout, knew every part of the service by heart — even the Latin.

Anna stayed home to start the gravy. It was tradition: after church, the whole family gathered at Anna and Giuseppe's for Sunday dinner. The house filled with the joyful noise of laughter, conversation, clinking dishes, and the high-pitched squeals of children chasing each other through the hallway.

The meal always began with antipasto, followed by steaming bowls of pasta or plump, handmade ravioli stuffed with ricotta — Jeanette's favorite. Crusty loaves of Italian bread lined the table, ready to soak up every drop of sauce.

*****

One month before the birth of Uncle Joseph's first child, Nonna passed away from complications of diabetes.

"If it's a girl," he vowed, "I'm naming her Phyllis. After Ma."

Everyone in the family, it seemed, had a Phyllis. Anna had given the name to her second daughter. Uncle Alberto followed suit. And now Uncle Joseph would too. To keep them all straight, they started calling the newest one "Baby Phyllis."

Anna and her sister Giovanna wore black for an entire year. At the mere mention of their mother's name, they would lower their heads and murmur that she had been *a saint among women.*

Nonno died soon after. The doctor said liver failure, but Anna believed it was his broken heart. He was never the same after she passed.

# Cherry Bomb

The Fourth of July was a big deal on their street. Families spent months planning for it, pulling out their best dishes and treasured family recipes.

American flags swayed from every Brownstone, a proud display of patriotism. But the Italian flag wasn't forgotten either — hung just as proudly, a nod to where they came from. First-generation seniors wore their finest clothes, while their children and grandchildren kept cool in shorts, T-shirts, and Keds.

Playpens lined the sidewalks for the babies, while older children ran wild up and down the block. Long tables stretched across the street, barricading traffic at both ends. Red, white, and blue paper tablecloths flapped in the breeze, held down by platters and silverware. Every household brought a covered dish, eager to show off their cooking skills, especially those who owned a barbecue. The scent of charcoal filled the air, the black briquettes turning ashy around the edges, signaling that hamburgers and hot dogs were just moments away from sizzling on the grill.

Mariella had taken over the baking that year. Without Nonna, it was all on her shoulders. She kneaded dough and decorated cookies with tiny American flags. Her cake stood tall, piled high with whipped cream and sprinkled with red and blue candies.

Phyllis perched on the stoop, listening to the Dodgers game on the radio. Always the sports fanatic, she didn't care much for sweets — unless they came wrapped around a pack of baseball cards. She tossed the stick of gum straight in the trash. The cards were all she wanted. Her collection was impressive.

Jeanette sat beside her, listening to the old folks swap stories about neighbors who had moved away and newcomers they didn't quite trust yet. She kept glancing down the street, wondering why Sonny was late. Maybe his mother was holding him up.

Eventually, she saw him, Rosetta trailing behind, trying to keep up.

"What took you so long?" Jeanette asked.

"My mom wouldn't let me leave without her." Sonny jerked his head toward his sister.

Rosetta didn't look too happy about it either, but she clung to her brother's side like a burr.

"Well, I guess we're stuck with her. Let's go find something to eat."

"I want a hot dog," Rosetta said.

"Don't talk, or we'll leave you right here," Sonny warned.

"I'll tell Mom," Rosetta shot back. "And you'll be in a heap of trouble."

Sonny rolled his eyes. "Fine. Let's go get a hot dog."

The moment Aunt Evelyn and Uncle Carlino arrived, Jeanette and Sonny bolted, ditching Rosetta without a second glance.

Later that night, the sky lit up with Roman candles and skyrockets. Firecrackers snapped in the distance, making the neighborhood dogs cower and whimper.

Jeanette and Sonny waved sparklers through the air, drawing glowing circles until the sparks fizzled out. The younger kids watched enviously from the sidelines—they weren't allowed to hold them. The metal got too hot.

*****

The next morning, Jeanette and Sonny roamed the street in search of unpopped firecrackers. Most were duds, but they still contained a little gunpowder. They'd cut them open, pour the powder into a pile, and set it on fire. There was no bang—just a slow sizzle. Still, it was something to do.

# Coney Island

It was a scorching hot day. Anna peeled the red rind off the bologna and placed two slices between thick slabs of white bread for each sandwich, wrapping them carefully in waxed paper. She and her four daughters set off for the train station, bound for Coney Island to spend the day. Jeanette was thrilled to be going to the beach, but disappointed that Sonny couldn't come along.

The train rattled along the tracks, and Jeanette noticed a girl about her age sitting across from them with her mother. She was a little plump, with a thick, long, curly brown cascade of hair. They exchanged glances for a while.

"Aren't you in my English class?" Jeanette asked.

"Yes." The girl nodded. "I'm Dorothy."

"I thought you looked familiar." Jeanette stood and slid into the seat beside her. "I'm Jeanette."

"I know. I've seen you around school."

As the train hummed toward Coney Island, the girls chatted, while Anna struck up a conversation with Dorothy's mother, Camilla. When they stepped off at Stillwell Avenue, Jeanette could already hear the screams from the Cyclone as it plunged ninety feet toward the earth.

"Wouldn't it be amazing to ride that?" she asked Dorothy.

"No way," Dorothy said. "I hate roller coasters. I'd rather go on the Wonder Wheel. At least you're safe in a cage."

As they passed through the tunnel to the boardwalk, the scent of corn on the cob mingled with the salty ocean air. Jeanette breathed it in deeply. Her father had once told her the secret to perfect Coney Island corn—add a cup of milk and sugar to the water. The milk made it tender, the sugar sweet.

"I can already taste it," Dorothy said dreamily. "All slathered in butter and salt."

"I want a frankfurter," Phyllis said.

"What's that?" Mariella wrinkled her nose.

"Only the greatest invention since caviar! And it was invented right here in Coney Island."

Mariella frowned. "Sounds German to me."

"Enough about food," Anna said, patting the paper bag. "I packed lunch for us."

"Ahh, shucks," Phyllis muttered.

Once on the boardwalk, Jeanette caught sight of the carousel and perked up. "I hear the music. Can we ride it?"

"Don't you think you're too old for that?" Mariella teased.

"Never. I want to catch the gold ring."

"There's the thoroughfare," Phyllis pointed out.

"We're here for the beach," Mariella reminded her.

Jeanette slipped off her shoes. "I can't wait to feel the sand between my toes."

"Put those shoes back on," Anna warned. "Remember last time?"

Jeanette did. She'd gotten a giant splinter in her heel. Her father had to dig it out with a needle he'd held over a flame. It had terrified her, but she'd tried to be brave.

She slipped her shoes back on and ran to catch up.

From the boardwalk speakers, The Andrews Sisters crooned *Rum and Coca-Cola.* Jeanette strained to hear the waves beneath the music. Crowds swarmed in front of the ocean stairs. She stood on her tiptoes to glimpse the sea beyond the mass of umbrellas.

"Come on, Luci. Come on, Dorothy. Let's go swim!"

"Don't run ahead," Anna called. "There are hundreds of people here. We don't want to lose you."

The beach was packed — blankets spread just a foot apart. Mariella darted ahead to claim a spot.

Phyllis immediately disappeared toward the boardwalk. She was such a lucky duck, Jeanette thought. Tough than any boy. Nobody worried when Phyllis wandered off. But if Jeanette tried it, Anna would send out a search party.

"Let's go swim," Jeanette called again.

"Let me hold your glasses, Luci. You'll lose them in a wave."

"Oh, Mama. I won't be able to see."

"We can't afford new ones," Anna said. "Give them here."

Reluctantly, Luciana handed them over.

"Wait for me!" she cried, running to catch up.

The girls played at the shore, glancing now and then to make sure their yellow blanket was still in view. Vendors passed every few minutes—first the knish man, then the soda man, then the candy man. But the best was the ice cream man, who carried a silver box strapped to his shoulders.

Dorothy ran to her mother. "Can we get ice cream?"

Camilla frowned. "You just ate."

"I'm still hungry."

"Well, okay," she said. "Call him over. I'll buy for everyone."

Anna lifted her head. "That's very kind of you, but I can't accept—"

"Nonsense. We're celebrating new friends. My treat!"

"Is your family rich?" Jeanette asked Dorothy.

"I don't know. Maybe. My father works on Wall Street."

"That's cool," Jeanette said. "Maybe I'll work there too. That is—if I'm not a Broadway star."

"I heard you singing in the choir. You're terrific."

"It's getting late," Anna said. "This is your last chance to swim."

Jeanette devoured the last bite of her ice cream. "Owww. That hurts my head."

"They call that brain freeze," Dorothy laughed. "Let's go back in."

"You go ahead," Luciana said. "I'm going to read."

After a full day of sun and swimming, they folded the blanket and made their way toward the exit. Couples lingered beneath the boardwalk—girls in bikinis, guys in Speedos, tangled in shared blankets.

"What are they doing?" Jeanette asked.

"They're making out," Phyllis said. "Don't stare."

"I'm not!"

"You'd better never go under there."

"Don't worry. You won't catch me."

Phyllis laughed.

On a bench by the boardwalk, they sat to put on their shoes. Camilla pulled out a container of talcum powder and dusted Dorothy's feet. The sand slid off like magic.

"That's so clever," Jeanette said, doing the same.

"Hurry, or we'll miss the train," Anna said.

As they headed for the platform, Jeanette took one last look at the ocean and softly sang along with Vaughn Monroe: *There! I've Said It Again.*

Dorothy's stop came first—she lived farther away, on 71st Street and 16th Avenue. Her family was from Naples.

"They're all crooks," Jeanette's father had once muttered, though he never explained why.

The girls exchanged numbers and waved goodbye, promising to let each other know the next time they went back to Coney Island.

# Pennies from Heaven

Between Jeanette's twelfth and thirteenth birthdays, something shifted between her and Sonny. Without ever saying it aloud, they both knew — they belonged to each other.

Sonny sat on the stoop, waiting for her to finish her chores. He reached into his pocket and pulled out one of five cigarette butts he'd collected from the gutter. They were short and wrinkled, but each still had a bit of tobacco. He smoothed them out carefully and tucked them back into his pocket, along with a pack of matches he'd swiped from his father's dresser tray.

Jeanette burst through the front door, full of energy. "Where are we headed?"

"Let's go up to the roof," Sonny said. "I found some cigarettes. I want to try them."

Her eyes widened. "You want to smoke?"

"I just want to see what it's like."

"I heard once you get hooked, you can't stop."

"Uncle Joseph used to smoke, and he quit. Aren't you curious?"

"Well, maybe... but it might mess up my singing voice."

"One puff won't hurt."

Jeanette hesitated, then smiled. She'd do anything for Sonny.

They walked to his building and climbed the stairs. As they passed his apartment on the second floor, they could hear Rosetta's voice. The door was open. If she spotted them, she'd surely run and tattle. They tiptoed past, then quickly climbed two more flights and scrambled up the rickety wooden ladder to the roof. Sonny pushed open the heavy steel door.

Sunlight slanted across the rooftop, landing on Sonny's face and making his golden-brown eyes gleam. Jeanette had the same eye color as her father — plain brown. But Sonny and her sister Phyllis had inherited their striking eyes from their grandmother.

Sonny squinted against the glare and lit a cigarette butt. After taking a puff, he handed it to Jeanette.

She took a small drag and instantly wrinkled her nose. "That's nasty!"

Sonny laughed. "Yeah, I guess you're right." He reached into his pocket, pulled out a pack of Sen-Sen, and offered her a piece. The gum tasted like perfume, but it cleared the bitter taste from her mouth.

They sat on the edge of the rooftop, their hands loosely clasped. Across the alley, wild pigeons fluttered along the ledges. On one of the rooftops nearby, someone kept a coop with homing pigeons and chickens. A single rooster lived up there, too. He crowed every morning, loud enough for the whole block to hear.

The roof felt different during the day — noisy, exposed, and full of life.

"Don't stand so close to the edge," Jeanette said. "I don't want you to fall."

Sonny grinned. "Would you miss me if I did?"

"You know I would."

Jeanette looked down and spotted a penny stuck in the tar. She dug it out with her fingernail, then held it up proudly. "Let's go down to Mortie's and buy a pickle."

Old man Mortie smiled when they walked in. He already knew what they wanted. Shuffling over to the barrel, he opened the lid. "Everyone loves my pickles," he said.

Jeanette and Sonny leaned over the rim, watching the fat green pickles bobbing in the brine.

"That one looks good," Jeanette said.

Mortie poked around with a long wooden fork, trying to catch the one she pointed to, but it kept slipping away. He finally stabbed a different one. "Goyem," he muttered under his breath. They didn't know what it meant, but they could tell he was annoyed.

"That one's fine," Jeanette said quickly, even though it wasn't the one she wanted.

Mortie wrapped it in waxed paper and handed it over in exchange for the penny.

As they walked home, they took turns biting into the sour, juicy pickle. Their hands smelled like vinegar, and their hearts were light.

# Santa Rosalia

The annual Santa Rosalia Feast took over 18th Avenue during the last week of August. The festival, honoring Palermo's patron saint, also marked the unofficial end of summer. Streets were closed to traffic from 65th to 75th Street. Sparkling banners stretched across every intersection. Families in the apartments above the stores had a bird's-eye view from their fire escapes. When the music blasting from loudspeakers became too much, they slipped inside and shut their doors.

"Are you coming with us to the Feast?" Jeanette asked Luciana.

"Yes, but I'm waiting for Mariella to get home from the bakery. She asked me to go with her."

"Okay. I'm going with Sonny. I guess I'll see you there."

Sonny was already waiting on the corner when Jeanette arrived. Before heading to the feast, they retrieved their special stick from the alley — a long rod they used to fish for coins dropped through the subway grates.

"You got the gum?" Jeanette asked.

"Sure. It's in my mouth," Sonny said, sticking out his tongue.

They leaned over the grate, which vibrated with the rumble of a train deep below.

"There's a nickel," Sonny said.

"I think that's a whole quarter," Jeanette added. "Must've been a busy week."

Sonny pulled the gum from his mouth and pressed it to the end of the stick.

They usually spent their earnings at the penny store. Cheap John, the cranky old man who ran it, sold a little of everything, though not all of it cost a penny. Most of it was covered in dust, and the candy was stale. Now that they were older, they'd outgrown the babyish trinkets and stopped going.

That day, they managed to pull sixty-five cents from the grate and added it to the dollar Sonny had left over from Uncle Vinnie. They were sure to win a stuffed animal or a goldfish—and maybe even have enough left for zeppole or a ride on The Whip, their favorite. It whipped the cars around corners, and they always screamed in unison as it picked up speed.

The aroma of sausage and peppers led them to the games. Rows of colorful prizes lined the booths, and kids darted between them, laughter rising over the music.

They stopped at the spin-the-wheel booth to watch children place tokens on colored squares. Cheers erupted when the wheel spun and landed on the lucky number.

"Wanna try it?" Jeanette asked.

"Nah. Let's find a booth with better prizes."

"Look at that duck, Sonny — it's so cute. Think you can win it for me?"

"That one looks easy."

Sonny handed a nickel to the man behind the counter and received three rings — one red, one blue, and one green. His first toss, the red ring, bounced off and hit the ground. He aimed carefully with the blue ring and nailed it — a perfect toss that landed neatly around a pole.

"I want the duck!" Jeanette said excitedly.

"Oh, that's a two-ring prize," the man replied.

Jeanette's smile faded.

"I've still got one more shot," Sonny said. He focused, released the green ring, and it floated through the air, landing squarely on another pole.

"You won!" the man hollered, ringing a bell to draw a crowd.

"We'll take that duck now," Sonny said, grinning as he handed it to Jeanette.

"Oh, Sonny, thank you!" she said, hugging it to her chest.

They wandered through the festival, stopping at a booth lined with fishbowls filled with colored water.

"Let's try to win a fish," Jeanette said.

"They don't live long."

"I know — but they're fun for a week or two."

Sonny handed the man a nickel and received three ping-pong balls in return. Jeanette pitched the first one, but it bounced off the rim and vanished. Her second toss missed the table completely.

"No, silly. You have to throw it like this," Sonny said, taking the last ball. With calm focus, he lobbed it gently, landing it perfectly in a bowl of blue water.

The vendor scooped out the fish and poured it, water and all, into a plastic bag. "Here you go, missy. Put him in a tank when you get home — and don't forget to feed him."

"Feed him?" Jeanette asked, eyes wide.

Sonny chuckled. "Don't worry. I've still got fish food from last time."

They strolled on, the Wonder Wheel looming above them, stopping and starting as new riders boarded.

"Want to go up?" Sonny asked.

"Let's save that for last. If we time it right, we'll be up there when the fireworks go off."

"Good thinking. Hey, look — it's your sister at the skeeball tent."

Phyllis spotted them just as she rolled a ball. "Well, well. What are you lovebirds up to?"

Jeanette blushed. "Are you playing skeeball?"

"Yep, and you're just in time to see me win."

She rolled her next two balls — twenty points, then fifty.

"I win!" she shouted.

The man behind the counter pointed. "Pick a prize from row two."

Phyllis scanned the options but didn't seem interested.

"Jeanette, you can have it. I'm heading to the batting cage."

"Thanks!" Jeanette beamed and chose a big brown teddy bear.

"Now you've got two prizes," Sonny said.

Jeanette hugged the bear. "I'm going to name him Sonny."

"I smell something good."

"Zeppole?"

"Yep—and we've got just enough."

They found a woman in a greasy apron frying golden dough balls in a bubbling vat of oil. She placed a few into a brown paper bag and shook it with powdered sugar.

"Here you go, Sonny!" she said.

Jeanette and Sonny burst out laughing.

"How'd you know my name?" he asked.

She frowned. "What are you, some kind of wise guy? I live in your building. Now give me the dough."

Still giggling, they headed toward the Wonder Wheel.

They passed Luciana and Mariella at the church raffle booth, chatting with Father Herbert in his black suit and Roman collar.

"Hurry!" Sonny hissed. "If Father Herbert sees me, he'll ask why I wasn't in church—and Luciana might rat me out."

He grabbed Jeanette's arm and steered her past.

"Let's skip the Ferris wheel," he said. "We'll watch the fireworks from the roof instead."

They climbed to the rooftop and pushed open the steel door. The night air was thick with the scent of firecrackers and smoke. A low fog hovered in the sky, lit by bursts of red, green, and gold. They were alone.

Sonny's hand brushed Jeanette's. A shiver ran through her. They'd always been close, but this felt different. Sonny was fifteen now, his voice deeper. Jeanette had started wearing a bra, her body shifting into something new and unfamiliar.

She looked up at him, and he kissed her. Not like a cousin. On the lips.

Jeanette knew it was wrong, but she kissed him back. Her body tingled, her heart raced. She wanted him to kiss her again, but he pulled away. They stood in silence, watching the finale burst across the sky.

When the last spark faded, Sonny walked her home.

"I'll see you tomorrow," he said softly.

"Okay. Good night."

Jeanette stepped inside, then looked back before gently closing the door. She went straight to her room and placed the fish in a bowl of fresh water. Long after she said goodnight, she could still feel Sonny's kiss.

From that moment on, everything between them changed.

# Kissing Cousins

Jeanette lay in bed, staring at the ceiling, replaying the night before. Had Sonny really kissed her? Or was it just a dream? If it was, she didn't want to wake up. She wanted to stay there all day, suspended in that moment.

Voices drifted in from the kitchen. Her parents were up. With a sigh, she pulled herself from bed, more out of routine than hunger.

Giuseppe sat at the table, the *Brooklyn Eagle* stretched open in front of him, while Anna scrambled eggs on the stove.

"Says here La Guardia's not running for a fourth term," Giuseppe said. "Good. Maybe we'll get a Democrat this time. This O'Dwyer fella — he looks like he could get the job done."

Jeanette sat silently at the table, lost in her own world. Politics was the last thing on her mind.

The doorbell rang, and her heart leapt. Sonny.

She rushed to answer it, her pulse quickening. He stood there, casual, those warm brown eyes of his giving nothing away. She searched them for... something. But Sonny just smiled like always, and she felt too shy to bring up the kiss.

They headed outside. Brooklyn hummed with late summer life. Music floated from a street corner where a three-piece band played for tips. Kids danced on the sidewalk while parents leaned from apartment windows, tossing down coins.

Sonny grinned as they passed an organ grinder. "I like that one better."

Jeanette rolled her eyes. "Only because of the monkey."

She had to admit—the monkey *was* cute, dressed in a little red jacket and a pillbox hat, tipping it politely each time someone dropped a coin in the can. When the boys teased him, he'd hiss, sending them into fits of laughter.

They took a spin on the roundabout until they were dizzy, then stopped for lemon ice. Sharing it on the swings, they let the cold sweetness melt on their tongues and cool their flushed cheeks.

But as they walked home, Aunt Evelyn's voice rang out from an upstairs window.

"Sonny! I need you to watch your sister. Come upstairs."

"Can Jeanette come too?"

"No. Jeanette needs to go home. You can see her after dinner."

"I'll come by later," he said, dragging his feet as he turned toward the building.

Jeanette wandered home and played her father's old Sicilian records. She sang along, understanding more Italian with each verse. The music grounded her, but her mind kept drifting to Sonny.

After dinner, he returned. They walked for blocks, talking and laughing as the sun dipped behind the buildings.

"Let's go up to the roof," Sonny said. A warm breeze ruffled his hair.

Jeanette hesitated. "It's getting late. Maybe we should head home."

"Nah. No one'll miss us just yet. Come on."

She followed, heart thumping. There was no moon, but the stars gave off a faint glow, just enough to see their way, not enough to show she was blushing.

They stepped out onto the tar roof. The air was still, thick with city heat and unspoken tension. It felt like they were the only people in the world.

"Look, there's the Big Dipper," Jeanette said, pointing skyward.

Sonny came up behind her, so close she could feel his breath on her neck. Slowly, he wrapped his arms around her waist and turned her to face him. His lips touched hers, then deepened the kiss, his tongue brushing against hers. Jeanette's whole body tingled. She felt the world fall away until there was only that kiss, her heart pounding like a drum.

When they finally pulled apart, they stood silently, gazing at the stars until their necks ached.

"Let's lie down," Sonny said. "We'll get a better view of the constellations."

"We don't have a blanket."

He spotted a sheet pinned to a rooftop clothesline. With a mischievous grin, he freed it from the line and spread it out across the cool tar. They lay down together, the stars pouring over them like glitter.

"They feel so close," Sonny whispered. "Like we could touch them. Let's make a wish."

Jeanette closed her eyes. "Okay."

"What did you wish for?"

"That we could stay like this forever. Growing up is scary."

Sonny rolled onto his side, propping himself up on an elbow. "Growing up isn't so bad. Think of all the adventures we'll have."

"School's starting soon," she said softly. "Things will change. You'll be busy. You might not have time for me."

"I'll always have time for you, Jeanette."

He kissed her again, longer this time. Her lips tingled. Her breath came faster. It wasn't like when they used to run or play tag. This was something different—new, thrilling, and just a little terrifying.

They kept sneaking up to the roof night after night, watching stars, whispering secrets, kissing until their lips went numb. It became their quiet ritual, one they never spoke about during the day.

But everything was changing. And they both knew it.

*****

Summer was over, and there was a quiet sadness in the air. Still, Red Barber gave his play-by-play of the Brooklyn Dodgers every Saturday night, broadcast live from Ebbets Field. Most people called him the Ol' Redhead, but to Brooklyn, he was the voice of summer.

Phyllis was convinced the Dodgers would take the pennant. Everyone thought she was dreaming, given the team's rocky record—but somehow, they pulled it off.

"Well, he did it, Dodger fans," Red's voice rang out. "Jackie Robinson just connected—and brings the runners home!"

The Dodgers had swept the series. Brooklyn erupted in celebration. Even those who didn't care much for baseball pressed up to the curbs just to glimpse the victory parade. The Dodgers were the boys of summer, and for once, everyone was proud to call Brooklyn home.

Jeanette wasn't especially interested in baseball, but Sonny was, and he insisted they stay to watch the entire parade. She didn't mind. It was another excuse to be close to him.

After the last float passed and the cheering began to fade, Sonny tugged at her hand.

"Let's go up to the roof," he whispered.

They slipped quietly into his building, but before they made it up the stairs, Aunt Evelyn's voice cut through the hallway.

"What are you two up to?"

Sonny paused. "Just going to look at the stars."

Aunt Evelyn crossed her arms. "I don't think that's a good idea. Jeanette, it's time to go home. Sonny, I need you to help me with the dishes."

From that day on, Aunt Evelyn seemed to keep a closer eye on Sonny. She found reasons to keep him busy—babysitting, chores, errands. Jeanette could feel things shifting. Their secret rooftop evenings faded into memory. Her world was changing, piece by piece, and there was nothing she could do to stop it.

She spent the rest of the summer helping out at Aunt Giovanna's, babysitting her little cousins, Regina and Vinny. She taught Regina how to jump rope and lulled Vinny to sleep with made-up stories and soft lullabies. Every penny she earned went into the old Sciacca can she kept hidden under her bed.

By the time September rolled in, she had saved over a hundred dollars.

# Forever Friends

Jeanette and Luciana set their hair in pin curls and tied scarves around their heads the night before school.

"Summer's over," Jeanette said, tightening her scarf. "I'm glad. I'm finally in high school. They have so many plays I can audition for."

The two sisters squeezed into their small twin bed.

"When I graduate, I'm moving to Manhattan," Jeanette said dreamily. "I'm going to sing on Broadway. We'll be rich. Then I'll buy four new beds — one for each of us — so we'll all have our own."

"But I like sleeping with you, Jeanette. I don't think I'd like a big old bed all to myself."

Jeanette pulled Luciana into a hug. "I'll always be here for you."

"Promise?"

"Yes… I promise. We'll both marry wonderful men and have lots of babies. We'll live next door to each other so our children can grow up together."

"No… I'm going to be a nun."

Jeanette laughed softly. "You can be anything you want. Now let's get some sleep."

"Can I walk to school with you and your friends?"

"Of course."

"I love you," Luciana said sweetly, curling against her sister's back. "Good night."

Their parents' voices drifted in from the other room, rising and falling gently through the crack beneath the door. It was a familiar and comforting sound, like a lullaby that wrapped around them and sent them off to sleep.

*****

Jeanette combed her hair and swept the front up into a brown rhinestone-embellished clasp. Bobby pins littered the night table, and her clothes were strewn across the room. She slipped on her new saddle shoes — white with black trim — the ones her mother had bought just in time for school.

Following Mariella's voice into the kitchen, she found Anna at the stove frying eggs, but Jeanette was too excited to eat.

"I'll just take a banana," she said. "I'm meeting Laura at the corner. We're walking to school together."

She grabbed her new notebook and pencil case — with a built-in sharpener and a pink eraser — then called, "Come on, Luci. I don't want to be late."

Luciana jumped up, clutching her own notebooks. Jeanette couldn't wait to see Dorothy again — and Laura, of course, along with all the other girls she hadn't seen since summer ended.

Outside, they passed a cluster of screaming children clinging to their mothers at the school gate.

The women stood helplessly, tears streaming down their faces.

Jeanette remembered her own first day of kindergarten. One boy had cried so hard he wet his pants. It wasn't his fault — he'd raised his hand like the teacher said, but she was too busy to notice. Eventually, he lowered his hand in silence, and a dark puddle spread beneath his chair. The other kids had laughed, but not Jeanette. She'd felt terrible for him.

After morning attendance, the students were herded to the nurse's office for immunizations. Jeanette tried to be brave, but the sharp antiseptic smell and the tray of gleaming needles made her tremble. Her friend Laura's mother, Rachel, was the nurse on duty. She smiled when she saw Jeanette.

They'd met near the end of summer, and despite their differences — Laura was Jewish, lived in a house near the synagogue, and came from a family of professionals — they'd clicked right away. Jeanette had visited Laura's home once. Her bedroom alone was larger than Jeanette's entire living room, with a full-sized bed covered in a comforter printed with tiny pink roses. The scent of the room reminded Jeanette of a flower shop.

Rachel gently swabbed Jeanette's arm. "All done," she said, and Jeanette opened her eyes, surprised she hadn't felt a thing.

Laura's father was a doctor, and her mother a school nurse. They had plenty of money but little time. Laura's future had already been decided — college first, then medical school or law school. There was no discussion.

When the lunch bell rang, Jeanette pulled her brown paper bag from her locker and peeked inside. Tuna again. She loved the taste but hated bringing it to school. The oil soaked through the bottom of the bag, and the fishy smell lingered in her locker long after lunch was over.

Across the cafeteria, she spotted Sonny. Her heart lifted. She waved.

He waved back but turned quickly to rejoin his friends. He was popular now, more than ever. The girls adored him, and it wasn't hard to see why. His good looks had only sharpened with age. Jeanette missed him more than she wanted to admit. They'd shared everything once: games, lunches, secrets. But now, they barely spoke outside of holidays.

She thought about Aunt Evelyn. Maybe she'd seen something in the way they looked at each other — something she wanted to stop before it started. Jeanette was sure Sonny wouldn't have minded if things had turned romantic between them. Maybe he even hoped for it. But Aunt Evelyn had made sure they stayed cousins and nothing more.

# Broadway Baby

By autumn, the leaves had begun to fall, and the air turned crisp and thin. Still, the sun shone brightly enough to warm the afternoons. Jeanette tried to push thoughts of Sonny aside and threw herself into music. Whenever the school held a concert or play, she earned a leading role. It was the one place she felt completely herself.

One afternoon, one of her teachers asked to meet with her parents. When the day came, Jeanette sat nervously outside the office while the teacher spoke to them in private.

"Your daughter has a rare gift," the teacher said. "She has real potential. I strongly recommend she take formal voice lessons."

"Where is this singing school?" Giuseppe asked, cautious.

"It's in Manhattan," the teacher replied. "57th Street and Broadway."

"Manhattan?" He raised his eyebrows. "She'd have to take the train."

Jeanette burst in before he could say more. "You could come with me, Pop! Please? Singing is my dream."

Giuseppe hesitated, his eyes drifting to Anna.

She gave a small nod. "Let her try."

He sighed, then smiled. "Okay, Jeanette. We'll go on Saturday. I have to work at the fish market during the week."

Jeanette let out a squeal and hugged them both. Her heart soared. It was the first real step toward the future she imagined — one that stretched far beyond Brooklyn.

*****

On Saturday morning, Jeanette woke to the sound of the vegetable hawker calling from the street: "Insalata, pomodori, melanzane, mele!"

Her sisters were still asleep, so she tiptoed out of the room. She opened the front door and checked for the milk delivery. Two glass bottles stood waiting. Smiling, she carried them into the kitchen and poured herself a glass.

"Well, Jeanette," Anna said as she entered, tightening her robe, "this is a big day for you."

"I know. I'm so excited. But I don't want to cause you and Daddy any hardship."

"Nonsense," Giuseppe said, stepping into the room. "You have an opportunity to do what you love."

Jeanette and her father walked hand in hand to 62nd Street to catch the BMT to Times Square. It was a rare chance to have her father all to herself.

The sun tried to break through a cloudy sky, but the winter wind whipped around the corners. Jeanette pulled her coat tighter as bits of paper swirled along the gutters like tiny tornadoes.

In Manhattan, the tall buildings shielded them from the wind. A wave of warm air rose from the subway grates as they passed. Inside the building, they rode the elevator up to the twenty-seventh floor and checked in at the front desk.

Giuseppe sat in the waiting room as Jeanette practiced scales with the pianist, his chest swelling with pride.

They made the trip every Saturday, no matter how bitter cold. After each lesson, they'd stop at a street vendor for a hot knish — Jeanette liked hers plain, while Giuseppe slathered his with mustard. As they ate, Jeanette gazed up at the skyscrapers, thinking, *Brooklyn feels like a different world.*

*****

One day, Jeanette's coach invited a talent scout to hear her sing. Giuseppe was allowed to sit in during the audition, perched quietly in a folding chair at the back of the studio.

Jeanette stood center stage, chose "The Best Things in Life Are Free," and waited for her cue. When she sang, the studio seemed to hold its breath. The scout was impressed and asked if she would perform on his radio show the following Saturday.

Word spread through the neighborhood like wildfire. Those who had a radio planned to tune in. Those who didn't make arrangements to join someone who did, whether it was a Zenith, a Phillips, or an RCA.

On the big day, Jeanette and her father arrived at the station. She wore a crisp white blouse with a gray skirt, the top buttons undone just enough to give her a touch of Hollywood glamour. Her cheeks were pinched pink, her lips bright red. She didn't want to seem like just another Italian girl from Brooklyn — especially not with the prejudice Sicilians still faced.

"We're all God's children," Nonna used to say. But even so, kids still called her names. Jeanette held her head high, refusing to let anyone make her feel less than she was.

"Well, hello, Miss Jeanette," said Tommy, the studio technician. "I've got the music all set up. There'll be a short commercial between songs. Ever been in a radio studio before?"

"No, this is my first time."

"I'll walk you through it." He led her into a dim little room with a window and a microphone. "Think of this like a telephone. It picks up *everything*, so don't talk or sing until I give you the cue."

Jeanette's eyes sparkled with wonder. "I hope I can do this. My stomach's full of butterflies."

"Don't be nervous. Just sing like you always do."

He placed the headphones on her head and stepped out. Through the window, Jeanette watched him flip switches. The red light blinked. *Stand By*.

Then came the voice of the announcer: "We are pleased to welcome an exceptional young singer to our studio. She's a local girl with the voice of an angel. Please welcome Jeanette Corrao, performing Vera Lynn's *Blue Moon*."

The light changed. *On the Air.*

Tommy signaled, and Jeanette took a deep breath. She closed her eyes and imagined singing to Sonny.

Back in Brooklyn, Sonny and Rosetta sat in front of the radio with Aunt Evelyn and Uncle Carlino. Anna and her daughters were at Aunt Giovanna's with the cousins, all listening in. Even little Vinny, who remembered Jeanette singing him to sleep as a baby, waited in hushed anticipation.

When the music ended, Jeanette opened her eyes, momentarily disoriented by the silence.

"That was Jeanette Corrao," the announcer said. "She'll return with another song after a word from our sponsor."

The red light turned green.

"You did great," Tommy said through the intercom. "Just relax. I'll cue you again soon."

Jeanette could hear the commercial playing in her headset. Then the red light flashed again.

"Once again, we are pleased to present Jeanette Corrao with *You Made Me Love You*."

This time, she felt more at ease. *I could get used to this,* she thought as her voice filled the room once more.

When the segment ended, the announcer said, "Join us next week when we'll welcome Romanoff and his violin."

Before she left, Tommy handed her a 78-rpm vinyl recording of the performance. She clutched it to her chest like a treasure.

Back in her bedroom, Jeanette played the record over and over, letting her own voice fill the room, proof that her dreams might just be within reach.

# Turkey Talk

A big Thanksgiving dinner was planned, and the whole family would attend. The kitchen table overflowed with cakes and pies, the smell of nutmeg and cinnamon filling the air.

Jeanette looked forward to seeing her cousin Sonny. But when Uncle Carlino and Aunt Evelyn arrived with only Rosetta tagging behind, her heart sank.

"Where's Sonny?" Anna asked.

"Oh, he's coming," Aunt Evelyn replied. "I sent him to deliver a ricotta pie to the man in the next building. His wife passed last week. Poor soul is all alone."

"You should've invited him here," Anna said. "We can always make room for one more."

Then the front door opened, and Sonny stepped inside, the cold air rushing in behind him. Jeanette's face lit up like a Roman candle, her heart thudding in her chest.

"Hi, Jeanette. Happy Thanksgiving," he said with a soft smile.

"You too," she replied. "Sit here—I saved you a seat."

It felt like old times as they teased and laughed their way through dinner. After dessert, with the adults busy playing cards and sipping coffee, Sonny leaned close.

"Meet me on the roof," he whispered.

"What about your mom?"

"She's busy chatting. She'll never know."

"Okay."

"I'll go first. Wait ten minutes, then sneak up the ladder."

No one noticed when Jeanette quietly left the table.

Up on the roof, Sonny tossed pebbles across to the next building, lost in thought. When he heard her footsteps, he turned too quickly and let a rock slip from his fingers, watching helplessly as it plummeted to the sidewalk below. He winced, hoping it hadn't hit someone.

Jeanette shivered under the cloudy night sky. The moon glowed through a frosty haze.

Without hesitation, Sonny wrapped his arms around her. "I've missed you," he said and kissed her. Their warm breath mingled in the cold air.

"We probably shouldn't do this," Jeanette whispered, though she didn't pull away.

"Why?"

"My mom says it's not... culturally acceptable."

"We're not brother and sister. In some countries, it's common for cousins to marry."

"Marry?"

Sonny met her eyes. "We belong together. I know you feel it too."

"I do. But what about our families? What would people say?"

"I don't care what they say. We'll talk to our parents — we'll make them understand."

They stood together in the silence, watching the hazy Manhattan skyline. The pigeons cooed from nearby ledges.

"I wish we could stay up here forever," Jeanette said.

"Me too."

Then Sonny surprised her. "I want to come to Manhattan with you next Saturday for your singing lesson."

\*\*\*\*\*

The following Saturday, they met on the corner and took the train together. After Jeanette's lesson, they wandered the city streets, pretending they lived there. Sonny had three dollars in his pocket, and he was determined to treat Jeanette like a star.

"Let's go to Katz's Deli," he said. "My treat."

"Really? That place is famous."

They transferred trains and walked a few blocks. Inside, Jeanette gazed at the photos lining the walls.

"Someday, my picture will be up there too," she said dreamily.

"I know it will," Sonny replied.

Afterward, he took her out for a chocolate soda. Instead of sitting across from her, he slid into the booth beside her.

"Shove over," she teased.

Sonny just grinned and moved closer.

"You're such a tease," she said.

He reached over and tucked a strand of hair behind her ear. His fingers sent a chill down her spine, and she kissed him.

"Have you told your mom yet?" she asked.

"No. But I'm going to have a talk with her tonight."

"I'm going to the movies with my sisters. Come by afterward."

\*\*\*\*\*

That evening, Sonny sat down with his mother. The conversation didn't go as he'd hoped.

"You're what?" Evelyn snapped.

"I love Jeanette. We want to be together."

"She's your cousin!"

"That doesn't matter —"

"It does matter! I won't have my son caught up in some incestuous relationship!" she shouted, reaching for the phone. "I'm calling Anna."

Anna's hand trembled as she hung up the receiver. Giuseppe looked up from his paper.

"You look like you've seen a ghost."

"That was Evelyn. She says Jeanette and Sonny are sneaking up to the roof... and they think they're in love."

Giuseppe closed his eyes. "Don't be too hard on her."

"They're cousins!"

"I know it's taboo here, but it's not so uncommon back in Sicily."

"Stop with the old-country logic. This is America, and cousin coupling is frowned upon. I won't allow it."

"Okay," he said gently. "We'll talk to her when she gets home."

*****

Jeanette came home beaming from the movie, *The Ghost and Mrs. Muir,* still playing in her mind. Her sisters chattered beside her, but she grew quiet when she saw Anna's face.

"Jeanette, we need to talk. Sit down."

Giuseppe tried to intervene, but Anna was already in motion.

"Aunt Evelyn called."

Jeanette's stomach dropped. She sat with her hands folded in her lap.

"Did you kiss Sonny on the lips while you were on the roof?"

"It was only once," she lied.

"Well, it has to stop. He's your cousin."

"We're in love."

"Nonsense. You're too young to know what love is. And even if you weren't—he's your *first* cousin."

"But Pop said—"

"Pop said what?"

"That cousins marry all the time in Sicily."

"Well, this isn't Sicily. This is Brooklyn. And here, it's unacceptable."

Tears welled in Jeanette's eyes. She dabbed at them before they could fall.

"From now on, no more roof. No more sneaking around. Stay away from Sonny."

Jeanette nodded but had no intention of obeying.

Anna sighed. "I should've seen it coming. You two have always been inseparable."

"Is Sonny in trouble?"

Anna softened. "You know your Aunt Evelyn. What do you think?"

Jeanette's heart ached. She could still feel his kiss. And no matter what her mother said—no matter what the neighbors whispered—she wasn't ready to let go.

# Seven Fishes

Christmas Eve — *La Vigilia* — was the Feast of the Seven Fishes, and it was Giuseppe's time to shine in the kitchen. After a long day at the fish market, he came through the door with bags of clams, mussels, shrimp, crabs, squid, and fresh fish. He put on his apron and got to work, filling the kitchen with the scent of the sea and the promise of celebration.

Everyone was in the holiday spirit — everyone except Jeanette. She tried not to let it show, especially around her mother, who seemed to be watching her more closely these days. Jeanette missed Sonny terribly.

Still, she agreed to go caroling with Laura and Dorothy. A thin layer of ice hid beneath the fresh snow on the sidewalks, and the girls linked arms to keep from slipping. Brooklyn was dressed up for the season. Though the shop windows were frosted with cold, tiny colored lights still glowed along the edges, giving everything a magical shimmer.

When they returned, the smell of roasting chestnuts greeted them. Christmas was the only time Giuseppe made them, cutting small crosses into the shells before placing them on a tray in the oven. As they roasted, the cuts opened to reveal the soft, warm centers. Jeanette and her friends sipped hot chocolate and huddled by the stove, watching Mariella carefully decorate *petit fours* and arrange trays of *dolce*.

"All I ever get at home is Entenmann's," Laura said, wide-eyed as she piled her plate high with Italian pastries.

"What did you girls sing?" Giuseppe asked.

"*The Twelve Days of Christmas,*" Jeanette replied.

"Ah, *La Festa dell'Epifania!*"

"Epiphany?" Laura asked.

"Yes," Giuseppe nodded. "It's the celebration of the Three Kings, twelve days after Christmas. Some call it Little Christmas."

"Like in the song?" Jeanette asked. "*On the twelfth day of Christmas, my true love gave to me…*"

"Exactly."

"Is that why people go caroling?" she asked.

"There's an old legend," he said, warming to the story. "After Jesus was born, Mary and Joseph had to flee to Egypt. King Herod wanted to kill the baby. The people didn't know where he was, so they went house to house singing songs of joy, hoping to find him."

"I never heard that before," Jeanette said.

"There are many traditions you don't know. For instance, in Sciacca, there's no Santa Claus."

"No Santa Claus?" she said, stunned.

"No. Children don't receive gifts on Christmas. Instead, on the eve of Epiphany, a woman named *La Befana* fills the stockings of good children with treats. The bad ones get a lump of coal — or a stick."

"She sounds a little like Santa."

"Except she came first. *La Befana* rides a broomstick, not a sleigh. She wears a black shawl and visits all the children in Italy."

"Was she a witch?"

"Some say so. But her story is sad. The wise men asked her for directions to Bethlehem, but she turned them away, too busy with housework. Later, she changed her mind and followed the bright star, hoping to find the child. She never did. And so, to this day, she visits every home, leaving gifts just in case the Christ child is there."

"Why does she sweep the floors?"

"Some believe she's sweeping away the old year to make way for the new. In Sciacca, we used to break dishes at midnight!"

Jeanette laughed, thinking of all the times she and Sonny had blown penny tin horns and made noise outside as the clock struck twelve. Italian Christmas music played softly from the radio, and the sweetness of the moment was pierced by a pang of longing. Sonny and his family weren't coming this year.

She tried her best to hide her sadness. But when no one was looking, she slipped the gift she'd bought for Sonny from under the tree and tucked it away in her dresser drawer.

*****

One week later, it was New Year's Eve. In Brooklyn, that meant only one thing—midnight pots and pans in the street. Jeanette sat on the stoop waiting for the ball to drop. She glanced up at the rooftop and saw the shadows of a few figures. Sonny must be up there.

She ached to be beside him—to put her arms around him and kiss him as they once had under the stars.

She closed her eyes, her breath visible in the cold night air. The city rumbled in celebration around her.

"Happy New Year, Sonny," she whispered.

Her heart called for him in silence.

# Silver Star

After Christmas's festive lights were taken down and packed away in attics, basements, and closets, the city streets looked bare and gray. Jeanette counted the days until spring.

Soon, the sun glistened after each rain shower, melting away the last remnants of ice and snow. The trees were still bare, but tiny buds swelled along the branches, promising leaves to come.

Now old enough to walk alone, Jeanette made her way to Dorothy's house on 71st Street. She passed the street cleaner as it rumbled along, its large circular brushes sweeping away the litter from the day before.

Parked at the curb near Dorothy's building was the Silver Star Ravioli truck—Jeanette's favorite. The frozen ravioli came in sheets with perforations along the edges. Anna always let her snap them apart when they had them for Sunday dinner.

Dorothy sat on the stoop, working on a weaving loom—square, with prongs on every side. Using colorful elastic bands from the dime store, she stretched pink ones across the frame, then used a crochet hook to weave white loops through, forming a square. They rarely made enough for a full quilt, but potholders were always a hit. Jeanette loved matching colors and inventing designs.

Across the street, under the El, the park was alive with spring. Benches lined the sides, where older men and resting mothers watched their children play behind the wrought-iron fence. Little ones tumbled on monkey bars and raced down slides. Minor leaguers tossed balls on one side, and mothers wheeled baby carriages along the other.

Jeanette and Dorothy swung on the swings, laughing and dreaming. Overhead, the elevated train clattered past on its way to Coney Island or Manhattan. A few older boys strutted across the seesaws.

"My father says they're hoods," Dorothy muttered. "Best not to talk to them."

Her warning was cut off by the sudden wail of sirens. A squad car rolled to a stop, red lights flashing. Mothers grabbed their babies and scattered.

"Hands up! Don't move!" a voice barked through the loudspeaker.

One boy stepped forward. "What's this about, Officer?"

"Shuddup and raise your hands," the cop snapped, cuffing the boy and his friends. In moments, the police had them in the car and were gone.

The girls sat quietly on the swings, still swaying.

"It's getting dangerous to live in Brooklyn," Dorothy said.

"Yeah," Jeanette agreed softly. "But I'm moving to Manhattan someday."

*****

On her way home, Jeanette spotted Sonny at the corner with his friends. Their eyes met, and his smile spread wide. Jeanette ran into his arms, and they held each other for a long moment.

"You have a mustache," she said, touching the faint shadow above his lip.

His smile faded.

"I have to tell you something," he said. "Let's go for a walk."

"What's wrong?"

"I'm leaving Brooklyn in the fall."

"What? Where?"

"My mother's sending me to college in Boston. She has family there who offered to pay my tuition and let me live with them."

"College…" Jeanette whispered.

"It's a great opportunity, but I won't go if you don't want me to. I can get a job with my cousin in the sanitation department."

"Don't be silly. You'd never be happy as a garbage man. Maybe not at first, but eventually, you'd wonder what might've been. You'd resent me for it, and I couldn't live with that."

"I could never resent you, Jeanette. I love you."

"I'll never love anyone the way I love you," she said, tears stinging her eyes. "But your mother will never accept us."

They walked home in silence, their footsteps quiet on the familiar sidewalks.

"We could go up to the roof," he said softly. "If you want to."

Temptation tugged at her heart. She wanted one more kiss. One last moment. But what good would it do?

"No," she whispered. "I don't think it's a good idea."

He walked her to her door. Their hug was awkward — too long and not long enough.

"You're home late," Anna said as Jeanette entered. "Don't you have school tomorrow?"

"No. It's a holiday," she replied. "But I'm kind of tired. I think I'll go to bed."

Giuseppe looked up from his chair, concerned. But Jeanette was already heading down the hall.

Her sisters weren't home, so the bedroom was quiet. She closed the door, walked to the window, and lifted it, letting in the cold twilight air.

Then, like a balloon slowly deflating, she let out a long, shuddering breath — and sobbed until her chest ached.

# Nice Italian Girls

Jeanette stretched in bed. It was Brooklyn Day — a public holiday — and there was no school, which meant the rare gift of sleeping in. A delicious aroma drifted into the room, pulling her from under the covers. She heard voices in the kitchen and dragged herself out of bed.

The women in Jeanette's family were gathered around the Formica table, sipping coffee and nibbling on crumb cake dusted with snowy white sugar. Coffee and cake were a ritual in their house, especially after dinner, but on holidays, it started early.

Her sisters chatted about their futures and the kinds of husbands they imagined for themselves. Mariella, the oldest by eight years, was the most traditional. She yearned to be a homemaker. Even her clothing said as much — long, elegant dresses with buttons down the front and a belt cinched at the waist.

The conversation shifted to upcoming family events. Uncle Joseph's son — also named Joseph — was being christened, and Cousin Ronnie's wedding was set for next month. The reception would be held at Gennaro's banquet hall on 13th Avenue.

"I want a big wedding," Mariella said, eyes dreamy. "With a satin dress and a veil of flowers."

"I met someone special Friday night," she added. "His feet are long, and he trips over his shiny black shoes—but I think he's cute."

"What's his name?" Luciana asked.

"Vincent. He's taking me to the movies next Saturday."

"Is he Sicilian?" Anna asked. "Nice Italian girls marry Italian men."

"Yes, his family's from Palermo. He's so handsome—and he works in a bank."

"Ha! Palermo?" Phyllis scoffed in her usual sarcastic tone. "Home of gypsies and thieves. You sure he's not a loan shark?"

Phyllis, the loudest and most opinionated of the sisters, never held back. She dressed like a tomboy—baggy pants, sweatshirts, and her ever-present Brooklyn Dodgers cap pulled low over her dark curls.

"Where did you meet him?" Luciana asked shyly. She was the preppiest of the four, always in Bermuda shorts and spotless white Keds.

"At the church dance," Mariella said. "You girls should come with me next Friday night. You might meet Mr. Right."

"Yeah, some Italian bum fresh off the boat, looking for a new mommy," Phyllis said. "No, thanks. I'm going to marry a Jew. They treat their wives like queens—and they're big breadwinners. Now *that's* security."

Jeanette sat quietly, sipping her coffee, soaking it all in. She admired her older sisters and enjoyed these coffee klatches. But in her heart, if she couldn't marry Sonny, she didn't want to marry at all.

While her sisters dreamed of diamond rings, recipes, and respectable husbands, Jeanette dreamed of stages, spotlights, and singing in grand halls. She wasn't much of a cook like Mariella, and she hated cleaning. No—her path would be different.

As the sisters sat around the table, each lost in her own world of dreams, Jeanette's gaze drifted to the window. Somewhere beyond the rooftops and avenues of Brooklyn, her future was waiting.

# Wedding Bells

Mariella had finally proven herself in the kitchen and was allowed to help make bread for the bakery. She lifted the first ball of fluffy white dough from beneath the cloth where it had been rising. Rolling it flat with a wooden pin, she cut it into six equal parts and shaped each into a ball. These would become poppy-seed rolls. *Fifty more to go,* she thought, wiping the sweat from her brow.

Mr. Moretti and his wife kept Mariella busy. After finishing the rolls, she grabbed a tray of pastries from the refrigerator and arranged them neatly in the display cases. Just as she was stepping back to admire her work, the bell over the door jingled.

A tall young man in his late twenties walked in. He had a narrow face, strong jaw, jet-black hair, and a disarming dimple when he smiled.

"Can I help you?" Mariella asked.

"I'll take two sfogliatelle," he said.

She pulled out a small box and carefully placed them inside.

"Anything else?"

"Yes—two cannoli and a couple of chocolate custard pasticcotti."

"I think we'll need a bigger box," Mariella said with a smile, transferring the pastries. "That'll be sixty-five cents."

"Just charge it to my father."

"Your father?" She raised an eyebrow. "And who might that be?"

"Antonio Moretti, of course." He leaned against the counter, amused by her surprise.

"You must be *Antonio*," she said, blinking.

He laughed. "The prodigal son returns."

"When did you get back from Sicily?"

"Yesterday. I slept all morning. Long flight, you know."

He glanced at her slowly, appreciatively. "You're even more beautiful than my father said. I guess I'll be seeing a lot of you."

Mariella blushed under the weight of his sparkling blue eyes, a little caught off guard.

"Since you work here and all," he added with a wink.

"Oh—yes, of course."

Antonio picked up his box and headed up the stairs to the apartment above the bakery. Mariella watched him go, mesmerized. *Gosh, he's good-looking,* she thought.

Every Friday night, Vincent took Mariella dancing. He often came by the bakery to walk her home. But Mariella didn't feel the same way about him—she wished she did. She kept hoping her feelings would change. Eventually, she knew she had to be honest.

One Friday, the moment she saw Vincent waiting, she knew it was time. She gently told him it was over. He was devastated.

After that, she saw Antonio more and more. He always stopped to talk when he passed through the bakery.

"You look lovelier every day," he'd say.

One day, he lingered a little longer. "How about catching a movie at the Loews with me sometime?"

"I'd love to."

They started seeing each other. Mariella couldn't explain it — Antonio made her feel something Vincent never had. She felt bad for hurting Vincent, but not enough to stop seeing Antonio.

Occasionally, she spotted Vincent standing across the street, watching the bakery. She wondered if he was waiting to catch a glimpse of her and Antonio together. It made her uneasy. She wasn't sure what he might do if they ran into each other.

One afternoon, she took a tray of bread from the oven and set the golden loaves on the cooling rack behind the counter. As she finished, she glanced out the bakery window and froze.

Vincent and Antonio were face-to-face on the sidewalk.

Her stomach twisted. She held her breath, expecting the worst.

But instead of throwing punches, the two men shook hands.

Relieved, she blinked in disbelief as Vincent turned and walked away.

Antonio stepped into the bakery.

"What was that all about?" she asked. "Was he bothering you?"

Antonio laughed. "Not at all. At first, he was a little hot, but then he realized we were in the same first-grade class back in the day. Some older kid picked on him, and I gave the guy a bloody nose. He remembered. Said he always liked me for that."

Mariella raised an eyebrow. "What did you say to him... about us?"

Antonio grinned. "I told him we were engaged."

Her jaw dropped. "*What?*"

"Yeah. But only if you say yes. Otherwise, I'm a liar."

She blinked once, then again. Her heart did a somersault.

"Yes," she said breathlessly. "Oh — *yes.*"

*****

Jeanette and Phyllis walked through the front door and immediately sensed something was up. The whole family was gathered in the living room, buzzing with excitement.

"What's going on?" Phyllis asked.

"Mariella's getting married!" Luciana squealed. "Isn't it wonderful?"

Mariella beamed and held up her left hand. A small diamond sparkled as it caught the light. "Antonio proposed."

"Yay!" Jeanette clapped her hands. "We're going to have a wedding! Can I help you pick out your dress?"

"I'm going to wear Mama's wedding dress," Mariella said, "but I'm sure there'll be plenty of other things you can help with before the big day. I'd be honored if you'd sing at the reception."

"Of course! Pop and I wouldn't miss a chance to perform — right, Pop?"

Giuseppe nodded proudly. "There will be plenty of singing and dancing. It's a time for joy in this family."

Phyllis folded her arms. "Did you and Mama already know about this?"

"Yes," Giuseppe said. "Antonio came by last week to ask for Mariella's hand."

Anna chuckled. "Your father made him sweat it out a bit before saying yes."

"I wasn't worried," Mariella said with confidence. "Antonio's a good man — and he comes from a respectable Sicilian family."

Anna's smile faded slightly as emotion crept into her voice. "I'm happy for you, *figlia mia*. But I'll miss you."

Luciana's eyes widened. "Wait… are you moving away?"

"Don't worry, cupcake." Mariella reached for her youngest sister's hand. "We're getting an apartment right around the block on 18th Avenue. I couldn't imagine living far from all of you."

"Are you still going to work at the bakery?" Luciana asked.

"For a while," Mariella said. "At least until we start a family. Antonio doesn't mind me working — as long as I'm home in time to cook dinner."

"Speaking of food..." Phyllis said, scanning the kitchen. "Has anyone thought about what we're having for dinner?"

Mariella and Anna exchanged wide-eyed looks. In all the excitement, dinner had completely slipped their minds.

"We still have some leftover pasta," Mariella offered.

"Nonsense!" Giuseppe said, standing up. "This is a celebration! Let's go out. How about that little Chinese place around the corner?"

Everyone agreed, and the family buzzed with renewed excitement as they gathered their coats and headed out.

*****

Antonio's parents insisted on a large wedding. With over two hundred relatives and friends, there was no other way.

Giuseppe scratched his head. "How am I supposed to organize something that big? We can't fit everyone in our house."

"Don't worry," Antonio's father said. "We'll cover the reception hall, and my wife will take care of the table arrangements. We'll even make the cake. You just handle the food and champagne."

Giuseppe brightened. "That, I can do. My brother-in-law Aldo will supply all the fish."

\*\*\*\*\*

Antonio and Mariella exchanged vows before a crowd of family and friends that spilled out through the church doors. Mariella's gown looked as fresh and radiant as the day her mother wore it to marry Giuseppe. When the newlyweds stepped outside as husband and wife, grains of rice rained down in joyful celebration.

At the reception, a bucket of iced champagne adorned the center of every table. Each place setting featured a delicate bundle of candy-coated almonds wrapped in lace and tied with a white bow.

Jeanette sang for the couple's first dance. When she finished, the room erupted in applause. Guests praised her beautiful voice and were moved by the heartfelt performance.

Mariella was now Mrs. Moretti.

# Hooky

One year later, Mariella left her job at the bakery and spent her days pushing a baby buggy up and down the Avenue. Baby Janine was adored by all her aunties, especially Jeanette, who often volunteered to babysit. She kissed the baby's cheek, then linked arms with her two best friends and headed off to school.

"Let's hang out at Lenny's Pizza Parlor," Laura suggested.

Jeanette enjoyed Laura's company, even if she was a bit of a bad influence. Dorothy usually kept them grounded, but not always.

"Then we can sneak into the movies," Dorothy added. "*The Heiress* is playing at Loew's. You know, with Olivia de Havilland and Montgomery Clift." She fanned herself with her notebook and gazed at the sky. "He's so dreamy."

"I don't know..." Jeanette said, uncertainty written across her face.

"Oh, come on," Laura nudged. "It'll be fun."

"Alright. But if my cousins see me, I'm dead."

Laura laughed. "If your cousins spot you, that means they're ditching too."

Lenny's was packed with teenagers, mostly older boys who had dropped out of school and hung around scoping out girls. They tried hard to look cool: slicked-back hair, tight jeans, snapping gum, and combs whipped out every ten minutes. They rode motorcycles and wore black leather jackets over white T-shirts with cigarette packs rolled into the sleeves.

Jeanette and her friends slid into a booth while Dorothy rummaged through her purse for jukebox change. *He's a Real Gone Guy* spilled from the speakers. Dorothy's gaze drifted toward the guys on the stools. One of them had a cigarette tucked behind his ear. He caught her eye and smiled crookedly. She quickly looked away.

"That's Frank," Laura whispered. "His father's connected."

"Connected?" Jeanette asked.

"You know — the Mafia."

"Really?" Jeanette couldn't help staring at Frank's wavy black hair. "He kind of looks like Dean Martin."

"He's got swagger, that's for sure — and a bad rep. He's not like the squares at school."

"I don't think squares are so bad," Dorothy said. "At least their lives don't revolve around causing trouble. Now, are we getting pizza or what?"

Before they could place their order, a young guy in a sauce-stained apron approached the table carrying a whole pie.

"This is from that guy over there," he said, nodding toward Frank.

Frank smiled.

"He said to get you girls whatever you want. Want sodas?"

"Sure," Laura said. "I'll have a vanilla Coke."

"Egg cream," Dorothy added.

"Same," said Jeanette, sneaking another glance at Frank. "Maybe we should invite him over."

"No way," Dorothy warned—but it was too late. Frank was already heading toward their booth.

"Thanks for the pizza," Laura said, but Frank's eyes were on Jeanette. He slid in beside her.

"I haven't seen you around," he said. "New to the neighborhood?"

"Not at all. I've lived here all my life."

"Huh. Hard to believe I missed a face like yours. You must've been hiding."

Jeanette blushed. "I spend a lot of time in Manhattan. I'm going to be a singer."

"Beautiful *and* famous?" he grinned. "How old are you?"

"Eighteen," she lied.

Dorothy shot her a warning look.

"We're heading out, Frank!" his buddies called. "Let's go!"

Frank stood, still smiling. "Maybe I'll see you around."

He followed his friends outside. Engines roared as they mounted their Harleys and Indians and took off down the street.

Jeanette watched him go. He was three years older and in another league entirely. Still, she wondered if she'd ever see him again.

# Bliss

Jeanette still spent time with Laura and Dorothy after school. The three of them walked arm-in-arm up and down the avenue, skipping, laughing, and sharing a single ice cream cone between them. Playing hooky had been exciting at first, but Jeanette was beginning to lose interest. Her focus had shifted to her singing career, and she'd even landed a regular spot performing at the weekly church dance.

Each afternoon on their walk home from school, they passed a group of boys lingering on the corner — cracking jokes, striking poses, trying hard to look cool. Among them was Robbie, who lived in the same building as Sonny, though his apartment was all the way at the end of the row.

Robbie had taken a liking to Dorothy, and their innocent flirtation became an excuse to linger longer on the corner. Since Dorothy wasn't allowed out past eight, Laura often invited her for sleepovers so she could spend more time with Robbie without getting in trouble.

Jeanette wasn't interested in the boys. In fact, their loud, teasing banter only made her miss her cousin Sonny more. Still, she smiled politely and tried to stay social for Dorothy's sake. When she was ready to go home, Laura and Dorothy would walk her to her door before heading back to the corner, where they stayed long after the streetlights flickered on.

*****

Ever since Dorothy met Robbie, she has spent nearly all her free time with him. She was so smitten, she tried to set Jeanette up with Robbie's friend, Nicolas — but Jeanette wasn't interested.

One afternoon, the phone rang.

Luciana poked her head into the bedroom. "Some guy — Nicolas — is on the phone for you."

Oh no, Jeanette thought. Dorothy always joked about giving him her number, but she hadn't believed she'd actually do it.

She walked to the kitchen and picked up the wall phone. "Hello?" she said cautiously into the receiver.

"Hi, is this Jeanette?"

"Yes."

"I got your number from Dorothy. We're all going to Coney Island today, and I was wondering if you'd like to come along."

"I don't think so."

"Ah, come on — it'll be fun. Dorothy and Robbie are coming, and another couple is coming too. We're all meeting at the pizzeria."

Jeanette was about to use her usual excuse — that she had chores to do — but before she could cover the mouthpiece, her mother chimed in from the other room. "Yes, I think you *should* go to the beach with your friends."

Jeanette froze. Nicolas definitely heard that.

She didn't have to guess why her mother suddenly approved. Ever since the situation with Sonny, Anna had been eager to fix her up with someone more "appropriate."

Jeanette sighed. "Okay. My mom says I can go."

"Great! Meet us under the train station on the corner in an hour."

After she hung up, Jeanette went to her room and pulled out her new bathing suit. She had begged for a bikini—it was all the rage—but Anna had been adamant. *"Just because there's a song about an itsy-bitsy, teeny-weeny, yellow polka-dot bikini does not mean my daughter is parading around in one."*

So she settled for a one-piece in a bold floral print. In front of the mirror, she studied her curves—her full bosom, long legs—and decided the suit was cute, but not enough to win her the Miss Coney Island crown. Not that she wanted her picture plastered on city buses and subway stations anyway.

At the pizzeria, Dorothy greeted her with open arms, clearly happy she'd come. The three couples jumped on the train and headed to Coney Island.

The beach buzzed with life—transistor radios played doo-wop and rock 'n' roll, mixing with the shrill calls of lifeguards. *"Too far out!"* one shouted. *"Away from the rocks!"*

Jeanette stretched out on the warm sand, letting the sun soak into her skin. To her surprise, Nick turned out to be a sweet, funny guy. And despite her initial hesitation, she continued to date him.

*****

On a warm summer night, Jeanette walked alone to the park. She tried not to look at the couples strolling hand in hand or kissing beneath the streetlamps. But each glimpse was a quiet ache. They only reminded her of Sonny — of the way he used to hold her, the way he kissed her. She tried to summon the feeling, the warmth of it, but the memory was beginning to fade.

Word had spread: Sonny had met a girl in Boston. They were engaged.

*How could he forget me so quickly?*

Anger rose in her chest, sharp and bitter. But beneath it was something softer — understanding. She knew the pressure he'd faced, the heavy hand of family expectation. Defying his mother would have meant a deep, possibly permanent rift. And how could she hold it against him when her own mother had refused to accept what they had?

Maybe it wasn't entirely their mothers' fault. They were both American-born, raised on inherited fears that a love like theirs would lead to shame — or worse, children, born broken. That warning had been repeated so often that it became truth. And neither of them had found the courage — or the science — to refute it.

Still, none of that softened the sting.

It wasn't the engagement that cut the deepest. It was how she'd found out. Not from Sonny himself, but in whispers, in someone else's passing remark. After all they'd shared, he hadn't even said goodbye.

# Out to the Ballgame

The auctioneer's voice cracked as he held up a Lou Gehrig card.

"Eight bucks," David shouted.

"Eight bucks? This card is rare, sir."

"All right, ten," he huffed.

A man in a blue shirt and a grimy baseball cap barked, "Fifteen bucks."

"I have fifteen. Do I hear sixteen?" the auctioneer called out.

David raised his hand.

"Sixteen," the auctioneer confirmed, his eyes darting toward the man in the cap.

The man shot David a glare. "Idiot," he muttered under his breath.

*Whack!* The gavel came down. "Sold for twenty."

Reaching behind him, the auctioneer grabbed the next item. "This one's from the same collection. They're usually sold as a pair, but the series is long out of circulation."

*Babe Ruth!* That was the one Phyllis had come for — a prized piece from the 1933 DeLong set. She sat forward, clutching her purse. Nineteen dollars was all she had.

"Ten bucks," the man in blue shouted again.

"Twelve," David called out.

"Thirteen," Phyllis chimed in, her voice clear and steady.

David turned in surprise. She was young, with curly auburn hair and almond-shaped eyes that sparkled with purpose.

"Fourteen," he said, watching her.

"Sixteen!" Phyllis stood, raising her voice with conviction.

"I have sixteen. Do I hear seventeen?" the auctioneer called.

David began to lift his hand — but hesitated when Phyllis caught his eye, daring him to challenge her.

"Eighteen," she said firmly, her gaze never wavering.

"I have eighteen. Do I hear nineteen?" Silence. "Going once... twice... Sold!"

Phyllis let out a slow breath, her relief visible.

David smiled and leaned in. "You're a little vixen," he said. "I hope you've got the rest of that set."

She grinned. "All I had was nineteen bucks. You could've outbid me."

"Why do you want it?"

"I've always been a Babe Ruth fan," she said. "I've collected most of the series. They should've kept them together. That jerk didn't have a clue."

"You've got spunk. I like that." He paused, then asked, "Hey, want to grab a soda?"

"Sure," she said, then added with a raised brow, "But first, I need to know your name."

"David. David Gordon."

"That's Jewish, right?"

"Guilty. And you — I'm guessing Italian?"

"You'd be right. My name's Phyllis."

"So, Phyllis... a true baseball fan?"

"All my life."

David smiled. "Maybe you'll let me take you to a game one Saturday."

She lit up, then composed herself. "That would be nice."

"Great. Let's get that soda — and maybe your phone number too."

\*\*\*\*\*

For their first date, Phyllis and David went to Ebbets Field. The Yankees were playing the Red Sox, and Phyllis had to pinch herself. She could hardly believe it — here she was, sitting in the stadium she'd only ever imagined while listening to games on the radio.

The announcer's box jutted out from right-center field, perched beneath a towering twenty-foot scoreboard. Two tiers of bleachers wrapped around the diamond like eager arms. The outfield wall was a riot of color, plastered with eye-catching ads — the striped and polka-dotted Botany Tie ad, the bold red of the Coca-Cola sign, and others fighting for attention in a blur of commercial cheer.

Their seats were just above the dugout — close enough to hear the crack of the bat, the bark of the players, and the rhythmic murmur of the crowd. Below, kids and curious adults knelt at the bottom of the double-exit doors, peeking through gaps for a better view. But none lingered too long. A patrolling officer tapped heads and toes with his billy club, and before long, a new crop of eager faces popped up in their place.

The crowd loved to razz the umpires. Whenever a questionable call was made, the stadium organ would blast *Three Blind Mice* to roaring laughter. And when an opposing batter struck out, it played: *The worms crawl in, the worms crawl out, into your stomach and out your mouth.*

Phyllis beamed at it all. Her senses were alight, her heart buzzing with the thrill of it.

During the second inning, a batter cracked a towering fly ball. It hit a sign in the outfield that read, *Hit Sign, Win Suit!*

"Oh! He's going to get a free suit," Phyllis said, eyes wide with excitement.

David chuckled. "Ahh, it's nothing. Just a gimmick. They'll give him an ill-fitting, cheap suit off the clearance rack."

Phyllis laughed, loving his dry humor almost as much as the game.

When the Red Sox clinched the win, David whooped and clapped.

"So, you're a Sox fan, huh?" she asked, raising an eyebrow.

"Guilty," he said with a grin. "I'm from Massachusetts. I've always rooted for the Sox. Please don't hold it against me."

She smirked. "I'll try not to — but just remember, you're in Yankee territory."

As they walked out of the stadium, Phyllis thought to herself: *So this is what it feels like — dating a nice Jewish boy.*

David was a sports journalist, sharp and quick-witted, but charmingly humble. When friends asked who the mystery man was, Phyllis just smiled and refused to say. Some things, she thought, were better kept secret — at least for now.

\*\*\*\*\*

Six months later, Phyllis surprised everyone by announcing their engagement.

David was the ideal husband — attentive, funny, and just as baseball-obsessed as she was. On weekends, they lounged in the park or watched Dodger games together. Even during her pregnancy, Phyllis still insisted on hitting balls that David pitched to her in the field behind their house.

One bright Saturday morning, the sun spilled through the windows as Phyllis stirred, feeling a little off.

"You sure you're up for this?" David asked as they walked to the park.

"I'm fine," she said with a grin. "Just a little achy. A few swings and I'll feel better."

But after just two pitches, she dropped to her knees.

"Phyllis!" David rushed to her side, panic in his voice. "Are you all right?"

She looked up at him with a weak smile. "I think the baby's coming."

David didn't waste a second. He helped her to the car and raced to the hospital.

Three hours later, Phyllis delivered their first little Dodger fan—a healthy baby boy.

The whole family came out to Long Island to meet him. Aunts, uncles, cousins—they all gathered around, cooing and fussing, declaring him the cutest baby boy they'd ever seen.

And Phyllis, exhausted but glowing, held him close and whispered, "You've got your daddy's eyes… and your mama's swing."

# Luciana's Secret

Now that everyone had moved out, the house felt empty. At least Jeanette still had Luciana.

"Hey, Lu, want to go see a movie?" Jeanette asked one afternoon.

"I'm going to the library," Luciana replied, slipping on her coat.

Jeanette raised an eyebrow. "You've been spending a lot of time there lately, haven't you?"

Luciana hesitated, then leaned in. "Can you keep a secret?"

Jeanette grinned. "Always. Spill it."

"Well… there's this boy in my class. He's the smartest student in school. He reads tons of books and goes to the library every Saturday morning."

Jeanette's eyes lit up. "Oh my goodness, Luci — you have a crush!"

Luciana blushed. "What good does it do me? All the girls are crazy about him."

"What's his name?"

"John. He's quiet, kind of shy. The only time I can get him to talk to me is when I ask what he's reading. I even wrote down the title of one of his books and read it at the library, just so we'd have something to talk about."

Jeanette laughed. "That's dedication!"

"I told him I'm an avid reader."

"You are!" Jeanette said.

"He told me maybe he'd see me there one Saturday."

Jeanette gave her a playful nudge. "Hey, what happened to your plan of becoming a nun?"

"I still want that," Luciana said thoughtfully. "But you have to be eighteen to join a missionary program overseas. I've got three more years to decide."

"Well," Jeanette said, "I don't think a date or two would hurt in the meantime."

"You think he'll ask me?"

"Let's improve your chances."

Luciana looked skeptical. "What do you mean?"

"A makeover," Jeanette said, already pulling off her sister's glasses. "A little eye shadow, some lipstick—he won't know what hit him. But first, we have to do something about those clothes."

Luciana looked down at her outfit. "What's wrong with my clothes?"

"No offense, but you look like a schoolteacher."

"I don't have anything fancy."

"You can borrow my red sweater. And I have a skirt that'll fit you perfectly."

Jeanette was practically buzzing as she got to work. She pulled Luciana into her room and sat her at the vanity.

"Let's do something with your hair. An updo will make you look more sophisticated."

"I don't know…" Luciana said hesitantly.

"Come on, live a little. You'll be the only girl in high school without a boyfriend if you keep playing it safe."

Luciana let Jeanette fuss over her, though she stiffened when the red lipstick appeared.

"Where did you get that?" she asked, eyeing the tube suspiciously.

"I borrowed it from Laura," Jeanette said. "Don't worry. I'm not going to make you look like the town tramp. Red lipstick is all the rage."

Jeanette applied it carefully, then handed her a tissue. "Now blot."

She stepped back to admire her work. "Hmm. One problem—those glasses. Can you see without them?"

"Only if I don't mind walking into a wall."

"Then I guess they stay."

"Can I look in the mirror now?"

Jeanette turned the mirror toward her.

Luciana gasped. "Wow! Is that me?"

Jeanette smiled. "Almost there." Then her gaze dropped to Luciana's feet. "Wait—you can't wear loafers. We need dressier shoes."

Luciana frowned. "Where am I supposed to get those?"

"Mariella left a bunch of shoes in the closet when she moved out. I borrow them all the time."

Luciana looked alarmed. "That's not a great idea. She'll be mad if she finds out. And besides, her feet are smaller than mine."

"We'll put them in a brown paper bag. You can change when you get to the library. Mariella will never know — I promise."

Reluctantly, Luciana slipped on a pair of black patent leather heels and tried walking across the room.

"They're too tight," she winced.

Jeanette waved a hand. "Don't worry. Your feet will stretch them out."

*****

Luciana spotted John as soon as she stepped into the library. He was at his usual table near the back, hunched over a thick novel. She took a breath, smoothed her borrowed skirt, and walked past him.

"That's a great book," she said casually. "I read it last month."

John looked up, surprised. "Really? I'm enjoying it, but you're the first person I've met who's read it." He paused, then added, "Do you want to sit here?"

He pulled out the chair beside him.

"My name's John McCrery."

"I know," Luciana said, smiling. "You're in my English class."

John nodded, then returned to his reading. Luciana opened her book, though her eyes barely skimmed the pages. Just being near him made her chest flutter with anticipation.

Every so often, he'd pause and ask her opinion on a passage. She answered thoughtfully, giving an honest critique. Before long, they were deep in conversation, debating the central themes, disagreeing over character motives, and laughing quietly at the author's quirks. The hours slipped by until a librarian called out, "Five minutes until closing!"

John stood and gathered his books. "That was great," he said. "You're the first person who's ever challenged me on that book in a good way. Can we meet again—maybe Wednesday?"

"I'd love that."

"Great. Then it's a date."

Luciana tried to contain her excitement as she rose from her chair. At the door, she turned to glance back. John was still at the table. He lifted his hand in a friendly wave. Blushing, she waved back and stepped into the night.

She skipped up the street, her smile bright enough to light up Times Square.

When she got home, Jeanette was waiting by the window.

"Well?" she asked, arms crossed but grinning. "What happened?"

Luciana beamed. "It worked. John asked me out on a date."

From that moment on, Luciana seemed to change overnight. The girl who once dreamed of becoming a nun now had a boyfriend. And though she still went to the library every Saturday, she stopped talking about missions and novitiates.

Jeanette could only smile. Love had a way of rewriting even the most carefully laid plans.

# Fly Me to the Moon

It was Friday night, and Jeanette's first stage performance at the church dance. She paced by the window, glancing outside every few minutes. Laura and Dorothy were late picking her up, and her nerves were mounting.

She slipped on her favorite black dress, the one with rows and rows of turquoise ruffles peeking out from beneath the skirt. Sweeping her hair up, she secured it with a barrette, then rummaged through the closet for her black open-toed heels with the ankle straps — saved for only the most special occasions.

Standing in front of the mirror, she studied her reflection. Even without makeup, she looked older, more confident, more like the woman she hoped to become. *If only I had some mascara.* Anna didn't allow makeup, but Jeanette still had the red lipstick she borrowed from Laura, tucked secretly in her purse.

Growing impatient, she checked the clock again. *Where are they?*

Finally, the doorbell rang. Jeanette threw on a sweater, tying it loosely over her shoulders, and headed to the living room. Giuseppe was in his chair, glued to a wrestling match. He didn't notice her until she bent down and kissed the top of his head.

He looked up and smiled, taking in her outfit. "You look so pretty. You'll have all the guys in love with you tonight."

"I'm going to be with my new boyfriend, Nicolas, so I don't think I'll have any problems, Pop," she said with a grin.

"Come on, Jeanette!" Laura called from the doorway. "We have to meet the guys at the pizzeria."

Anna poked her head out from the kitchen. "Have fun, but don't stay out too late. Tomorrow is Janine's christening."

"I'll be home early, I promise, Mama."

The three girls clip-clopped down the block, their heels clicking against the pavement.

"These garters are cutting into my thighs," Dorothy muttered, tugging at her stockings.

At the pizzeria, the boys were already waiting, and soon the three couples walked arm-in-arm toward the church gymnasium.

"Are you nervous about singing tonight?" Nicolas asked.

Jeanette shook her head. "No. Something strange happens to me when I get on stage. It's like I become someone else—someone special. I'm singing a Vera Lynn song."

"I love Vera Lynn," he said. "Did you know her real name was Vera Margaret Welch? She was born in England."

Jeanette smiled. "Yes, I know all about her. Someday, I'll be just as famous. Then I'll change my name, too."

*****

The dance was already in full swing when the girls entered the auditorium. The room buzzed with energy — teenagers milling about, couples slow dancing under dim lights, others lingering near the punch bowl, giggling and whispering.

Jeanette and Dorothy checked their coats as the band played a dreamy instrumental. They made their way through the crowd toward the front of the stage. As the song ended, the announcer's voice came through the microphone.

"Now we have a real treat for you tonight, ladies and gentlemen. An extraordinary talent from right here in town — you may have even heard her on the radio. Please welcome Jeanette Corrao, singing *Taking a Chance on Love!*"

A smattering of applause rose as Jeanette stepped onto the stage. She scanned the crowd for Luciana and John but didn't see them. Among the sea of teenage faces, one stood out: Frank — the guy who had once sent over a pizza at Lenny's. He was leaning against the wall, arms crossed, watching her intently.

Jeanette stepped to the microphone, took a deep breath, and began to sing. Her voice floated through the room, rich and confident. When the final note lingered in the air, the auditorium erupted in applause.

The band picked up the tempo, and the dance floor quickly filled.

Frank stayed in place, waiting for the right moment. When Jeanette stepped down from the stage, he made his move, slipping through the crowd and cutting off her path.

His eyes sparkled. "Would you like to dance?"

Jeanette hesitated. "I'm here with someone... I don't think that'd be a good idea."

"It's just a dance," he said with a shrug.

She glanced at the crowd, then back at him. "All right. But just one."

The music was fast-paced and lighthearted, and they kept a polite distance. It all felt harmless — until the tempo slowed and the band began to play *When I Fall in Love* by Nat King Cole.

Jeanette turned to leave, but Frank gently caught her arm. "One more," he said, lowering his voice.

Across the room, Nicolas was watching. His face reddened as he pushed through the crowd.

"Get your hands off my girl, asshole."

Frank turned, unbothered. "What did you say?"

"I saw you grab her," Nick said, stepping in close. "Back off."

"You don't own her," Frank snapped, his jaw tight and fists clenched.

"C'mon," Jeanette whispered urgently, tugging Nick's arm. "Let's just go."

But neither boy backed down. The crowd shifted around them, parting to make room as the tension built.

Before fists flew, a commanding voice cut through the noise.

"Break it up, you two," Father Murphy warned, stepping between them. "I won't be having any brawls here tonight."

Nick exhaled sharply and slipped his arm around Jeanette's shoulder, leading her away.

The band, undeterred, launched into a lively tune, and the crowd surged back to the dance floor.

"Boy, that guy was a jerk," Robbie muttered. "He was cruisin' for a bruisin'."

"I could've taken him," Nicolas said, chest still heaving. "But I didn't want to ruin the night for everyone."

Dorothy tugged Jeanette aside. "We need the little girls' room," she said, dragging her away from the group.

"Wasn't that the guy from the pizzeria?" she asked once they were alone.

Jeanette nodded. "Yeah. Frank. He's not that bad. I kind of like him."

Dorothy gave her a sharp look. "Don't let Nicolas hear you say that."

"Why? Nicolas doesn't own me."

Dorothy studied her face. "You've got it bad, Jeanette. I can see it in your eyes."

They rejoined the group, and Robbie pulled Dorothy onto the dance floor. Nicolas turned to Jeanette.

"Want to dance?"

She shook her head. "I'm feeling a little tired. Would you mind if we just went home?"

"Sure," he said, trying to hide his disappointment. "If that's what you want."

"I just need to get my coat."

As she reached the coat-check counter, Jeanette felt someone behind her. She turned — and there was Frank. Without a word, he slipped a folded piece of paper into her hand. She tucked it quickly into her pocket and turned away.

From across the room, Nick saw the exchange. His fists clenched again.

"What did he want *now*?" he asked as she returned.

"He just wanted to apologize," Jeanette lied. The last thing she wanted was another scene.

Later that night, Luciana was already in bed when Jeanette got home. She slipped off her shoes and leaned on the doorway.

"How was your date?" Luciana asked sleepily.

Jeanette sighed. "It was all right, I guess. But I saw Frank again — remember him? From the pizzeria? He's so dreamy."

Luciana sat up a little. "He is good-looking, but… he drinks too much. I've seen him sneaking liquor into the dances."

Jeanette rolled her eyes. "Don't be a prude. Everyone drinks at church dances."

"Maybe… but I still don't trust him."

Jeanette sat on the edge of the bed. "Why weren't you and John there tonight?"

"He wasn't feeling well," Luciana said quickly, though it wasn't the full truth. She didn't want to tell Jeanette that John didn't like dances, or that he thought Frank was bad news, too.

For now, she kept that to herself.

*****

Luciana and John had planned to attend the dance with another couple, but he bailed at the last minute. That afternoon, they sat in a candy store sipping chocolate egg creams, but Luciana felt completely out of place. John barely looked at her, like she wasn't even there.

Even after they got engaged, she found herself waiting by the phone for calls that often never came. The excitement she once felt had turned into gnawing doubt. Suspecting something wasn't right, she began wandering the streets of Brooklyn, hoping—half-hoping—to catch him with another girl. But John was elusive, always just out of reach.

It wasn't long before her suspicions narrowed in on Gilda.

Luciana's cheeks burned as she watched the way Gilda giggled at everything John said, casting sideways glances to see if Luciana noticed. She did. Gilda knew he was her fiancé, but clearly didn't care.

She seemed to enjoy the tension, basking in the discomfort she caused. Henry, Gilda's boyfriend, sat beside her, completely unaware. Or maybe just too kind to say anything.

Luciana, however, couldn't look away. She watched John's eyes — how they lingered too long, how he smiled too easily. In that moment, she knew: he wished he were with Gilda instead.

She brooded the whole way home, arms crossed, her jaw tight.

"What's wrong?" John finally asked.

Luciana stopped walking and turned to face him. "The whole time, all you and Gilda did was flirt. While poor Henry and I just sat there. It's not the first time, either. She's trying to steal you from me, and you're letting her."

John's brow furrowed. "Why are you acting like this? Gilda wasn't trying to do anything."

"There you go again — defending her." Her voice trembled. "Why don't you just admit it? You have a crush on her."

"You're being ridiculous."

"She's not a nice person, John. And I don't want to go to the dance with her tonight."

"I can't tell her not to come," he said, folding his arms.

Luciana stared at him for a long moment. "Then go without me."

"Maybe I will," he snapped, and turned away, walking off down the street.

Luciana stood frozen on the sidewalk, fighting back the sting of tears. Somewhere between the chocolate egg cream and the bitter goodbye, she realized she was no longer the girl in love with the boy from the library.

# Facets of Light

Luciana hadn't heard from John since their fight about Gilda. Days passed in silence, but the ache didn't fade. Hoping for answers — or maybe closure — she walked to the candy store where they used to meet.

There he was, standing out front, hands stuffed in his pockets.

"I've been thinking about our conversation the other day," he said quietly. "I'm sorry."

"It's okay," Luciana replied, though her voice lacked conviction. "I shouldn't have overreacted. I guess I was just... jealous."

John looked down at his shoes. "You had a right to be," he said after a pause. "We should've told you sooner. We didn't want to hurt you."

"We?" Her chest tightened.

"Gilda and I... we have a lot in common."

*I knew it.* The confirmation stung, but it wasn't a surprise. Luciana had sensed it long before he admitted it. Gilda had always liked John — she wore plunging necklines, too much blush, and batted her lashes shamelessly whenever he was around. And he'd fallen for it.

Luciana, like most Sicilian women she knew, had been raised to take care of her man. She cooked his favorite meals, ironed his shirts, and made herself small to fit his moods. But the more she gave, the more he pulled away. It had become a vicious cycle—her devotion met with his growing indifference.

She stared at him, blinking back tears. "Is it because Gilda will have sex with you, and I won't?"

John hesitated, then looked her in the eye. "No... but that's part of it."

Luciana didn't hesitate. She slid the engagement ring from her finger and placed it firmly in his hand. He looked down at it, turning the diamond until it caught the light, then slipped it into his pocket without a word.

Luciana turned and walked away, her heart cracking with every step. When she got home, she went straight to her room and cried—but silently. No one saw her tears. She tucked the pain deep inside, where no one could find it.

And just like that, the dream she once had of love with John McCrery was over.

***** 

To Jeanette, it felt like everyone was in love—except her.

Even Dorothy was getting married and had asked Jeanette to be her maid of honor. She accepted with a smile, but her heart ached with the quiet loneliness she couldn't quite admit.

Laura, on the other hand, had caused quite a stir in the neighborhood. She'd gotten into trouble with a boy from school—a college-bound type with no intention of settling down. When she refused to put the baby up for adoption, her parents were horrified. But Laura stood her ground. Her child might be illegitimate in the eyes of the world, but to her, little Luca was a gift from heaven.

Each day, she strolled him down the avenue in his carriage, her chin lifted high. She kept her eyes straight ahead, ignoring the gasps and whispered judgments that followed her like a shadow.

Jeanette adored the baby. She cradled him whenever she visited, inhaled the sweet scent of powder and milk, and dreamed of having a child of her own one day, with the right man.

Nick was sweet, dependable, and thoughtful — but something inside her said he wasn't the one. Her heart wasn't stirred by his kindness the way she imagined it should be. She reached into her purse and unfolded the small slip of paper she had kept hidden for weeks.

Frank's number.

She stared at it, then slowly dialed. The phone rang three times.

"Yeah, what is it?" a man's voice barked.

Jeanette blinked. "Frank?"

"Who the hell is this?"

Before she could answer, the line went dead.

She stood there, stunned, the dial tone humming in her ear. "He hung up on me!"

A moment later, the phone rang. Hesitantly, she picked it up.

"Hello?"

"Jeanette?" It was Frank.

"Why did you hang up on me?" she asked.

"I didn't. That was my brother, Vincent. He was drunk."

"Oh…" she paused. "I think I remember him."

"Yeah. Vinny gets crazy when he drinks. Always starting senseless brawls. I'm sorry he was rude."

"That's all right," she said softly.

"Hey, me and a few buddies are heading to Luna Park at Coney Island tonight. Want to come?"

"I've never been there at night."

"You're in for a treat. Coney Island's like a wonderland after dark — the lights, the music, the smell of popcorn and sea air. It's something else."

Jeanette smiled. "That sounds magical. I'd love to."

"Great. I'll pick you up around six."

After she hung up, Jeanette sat in silence for a moment, her fingers still wrapped around the receiver. Her thoughts drifted to Vincent. She could still hear the anger in his voice, the roughness. It left her unsettled. *What made him so angry?*

But she pushed the thought aside. Tonight, she was going to Luna Park with Frank.

And maybe, just maybe, something magical really *could* happen.

# Fortune Teller

Giuseppe opened the front door to find Frank standing on the stoop, holding a bouquet of flowers.

"Good evening, Mr. Corrao. My name's Frank. I'm here to pick up Jeanette."

Giuseppe eyed him from head to toe before reluctantly stepping aside. "Jeanette!" he called over his shoulder. "You have a visitor."

As Frank stepped into the hallway, Giuseppe studied him. "Are you Italian, Frank?"

"Yes, sir."

"What part of Italy's your family from?"

"They were born here. They're American."

Giuseppe narrowed his eyes. "And their parents?"

"My grandfather came from Naples."

Giuseppe clicked his tongue, unimpressed.

Anna, wiping her hands on a dish towel, appeared in the doorway. She had heard every word.

Jeanette rushed in, breathless. "Flowers? Oh, Frank, thank you."

"Make sure you bring my daughter home by ten o'clock," Giuseppe said, arms crossed.

"Don't worry, Mr. Corrao. I'll get her home safe."

Giuseppe gave a tight nod as he watched them leave. Turning to Anna, he muttered, "I don't like that boy."

Jeanette sensed her father's disapproval but pushed the feeling aside. She slipped into Frank's car — and, in some way, into his world.

"This is a real treat," she said. "I've never seen Coney Island at night."

Frank smiled and parked. They walked through the tunnel onto the boardwalk, where carnival lights glittered and music drifted on the breeze. His friend Jimmy was waiting.

"We were about to give up on you," Jimmy said. "Where've you been?"

"Had to run an errand for my father. You remember Jeanette, don't you?"

"Yeah — you're the singer from the church dance." Jimmy turned to the girl beside him. "This is my girlfriend, Beth."

"It's nice to meet you," Jeanette said.

"Likewise, I'm sure," Beth replied, eyeing Frank. "What happened to Sue?"

Frank's expression tightened. "Shut your mouth if you know what's good for you."

Beth laughed. "I meant Stella. And where are Stella and Sal?"

"Sal said they'd meet us later," Jimmy offered.

"I thought he got arrested last week," Frank said.

"Yeah, but his uncle got him off."

Jeanette recalled the article her father had read in *The Brooklyn Daily Eagle* — a piece about a man named

Anthony Gambino and the city's rise in organized crime. *"They ought to lock them all up and throw away the key,"* Giuseppe had said, tossing the paper aside.

A chill crept through her, but she told herself Frank wasn't like that.

The dazzling lights of Luna Park pulled her back into the moment. Frank took her hand as they strolled along the boardwalk. The Cyclone rattled overhead. Screams from the plunging coaster riders drowned out the tinny music from nearby speakers. In the distance, the Parachute Jump sent people drifting gently to the ground like falling leaves.

"I went on that during the World's Fair," Jimmy shouted. "It's great. Let's ride it!"

Beth hesitated. "It looks scary."

"I'm not scared," Jeanette said, raising her chin. "I'll go."

Jimmy and Beth were strapped into one seat; Frank and Jeanette into another. As they were hoisted high above the park, Jeanette's heart pounded. She wasn't sure if it was the height or how close she was to Frank. When the parachute released, they floated down in slow, sweeping circles, landing softly on the springs below.

"My legs are shaky," Beth said, laughing nervously. "Glad we did it, but I'm done with rides."

They wandered the boardwalk, bought cotton candy, and passed a vendor hawking hot dogs.

"I'm starving," Beth said. Jimmy pulled out his wallet and ordered.

"Want one?" Frank asked Jeanette.

"Yes, I'd love one."

"Two dogs and two orange pops," he told the clerk.

"That'll be sixteen cents. Mustard and kraut's over there."

As they ate, Jeanette's eyes landed on a mechanical fortune-teller booth—a mannequin gypsy with wild hair, gold chains, and glowing eyes sat behind the glass, her hand dealing cards in slow, robotic motions.

"We should see what she says," Jeanette said. "It's only a quarter."

"That one's fake," Jimmy said. "There's a live fortune-teller further down the boardwalk."

"Let's try her," Frank said.

Beth frowned. "I don't believe in that stuff. It's witchcraft. Playing with the devil."

"Oh, come on," Jimmy teased. "It's just for laughs."

"I'll go," Jeanette said.

As they neared the striped tent, the barker's voice boomed. "Come one, come all! Madame Lavinia sees all! Will you be rich? Will you find true love?"

Frank peeled a dollar from a thick roll secured with a rubber band. "Two, please," he said.

"One person at a time," the barker said, motioning Jeanette inside. "Have a seat. Madame Lavinia will be with you shortly."

She sat alone in the dimly lit tent. Three candles flickered on a small round table, casting shadows across the hourglass, a deck of tarot cards, a teacup, and a cloudy crystal ball.

The curtain rustled. Madame Lavinia entered, her long skirt swishing as she sat across from Jeanette.

"So, you wish to see the future?" she said, voice low and thick with mystery. "You may ask three questions. Only three. Give me your hand."

Jeanette offered her palm. The woman traced the lines gently, her brows tightening.

"I see… women in your family."

"Yes. I have three sisters. And my mother."

The fortune-teller dropped her hand and turned to the crystal ball. She rubbed it slowly, and white flakes swirled inside like a snow globe.

"I see romance," she said, peering into the glass.

"Yes. I just met someone. Will I marry him?"

"You will marry this man... but—" Her expression shifted. "I see another woman. She is waiting… at a train station. Her hand is pressed to her chest. She's in pain."

The gypsy abruptly covered the ball with a cloth.

Jeanette's stomach tightened. "Wait—I still have two questions."

"I'm sorry. I cannot continue."

"What did you see?" Jeanette whispered. "Please. Tell me."

"No. It is too terrible. You must leave. I'll return your money. Go now."

Staggering into the night air, Jeanette found Frank waiting.

"I think I'm going to faint," she said, grabbing his arm. "Take me away from here."

# Lundy's

Jeanette's family wasn't thrilled about her dating Frank. Though he was Italian, his father carried a reputation that made people uneasy. Everyone in the neighborhood knew he had his hands in the numbers racket and other gambling ventures. No one spoke about it openly, only in hushed whispers over coffee and biscotti. He'd never served real time, but his name was tied to repeated arrests—Prohibition violations, racketeering, and shady dealings that seemed to float just under the surface of the law.

That night, Giuseppe sat in his armchair, waiting. He heard the low rumble of Frank's car pull up and parked himself near the front door. With four daughters, he'd had his fair share of late-night encounters with suitors—and a lifetime of instincts about men.

The front door opened softly. Jeanette tiptoed inside, startled when her father's voice broke the silence.

"Who is this Frank?" he asked, arms crossed. "You seem to be spending a lot of time with him."

"Oh, Pop!" Jeanette gasped and clutched her chest. "You scared me. I didn't know you were still up."

"When my daughter is out with a bum, I don't sleep."

"He's *not* a bum," she shot back. "He's just a guy from the neighborhood. I met him at Tony's Pizzeria. He goes to the church dances, for heaven's sake."

Giuseppe's brow furrowed. "What happened to Nicolas?"

"Nicolas?" Jeanette rolled her eyes. "He's... boring."

"I suppose Frank isn't? Why do you have to get mixed up with someone like him? I've always told you — *never* date a man tied to the mob."

"Frank isn't his father," Jeanette insisted. "He's kind. Thoughtful. He listens to me."

"He sees things, Jeanette. He hears things. You grow up in that world, it leaves a mark — whether you want it to or not."

"Pop, you're judging him without even knowing him. Don't believe everything you hear. Frank's not like that."

Giuseppe stared at her for a long moment, then sighed and looked toward the kitchen, where Anna was drying dishes.

"There's something off about that boy," he said quietly. "I can't put my finger on it, but I don't like it."

\*\*\*\*\*

"He'll steal your dreams," Jeanette's mother, Anna, warned — but it was exactly Frank's mystery that compelled her.

Still nursing a heartache over Sonny, Jeanette couldn't resist the thrill of a new romance. Frank wrote her poems in slanted cursive, took her places she'd never been, and made her feel like the center of the universe. The girls in the neighborhood noticed, too. All eyes were on Frank—and now, on her.

One afternoon, she waited anxiously by the phone, hoping no one else would answer. Her family couldn't stand Frank. The moment it rang, she darted for it.

"Some of the gang is meeting at Lundy's for clams," Frank said. "You want to come?"

"That's in Sheepshead Bay. I should ask my father—"

"Ah, don't be silly," Frank cut in. "You're not a baby. He'll never even know."

She hesitated, then gave in. "All right."

"I'll swing by in an hour."

The moment Frank's horn tooted from the curb, Jeanette jumped up to leave.

"Why doesn't he come to the door like a gentleman?" Phyllis asked.

Jeanette fumbled for a response. "It's no big deal."

"If you're not careful, he'll turn you into a *puttana!*" Phyllis snapped.

"Watch your mouth," Giuseppe warned sharply. "Jeanette isn't that kind of girl."

Frank honked again, more impatient this time. Jeanette hurried out, slid into the passenger seat, and barely had time to close the door before Frank puffed on his Camel, flicked it out the window, and said, "I have to make a quick stop."

He turned down a desolate street lined with low, dark warehouses and parked. "Wait here. I won't be long."

Jeanette watched him slip into a side door and return minutes later carrying a large box. He popped the trunk and stowed it away without a word.

"Okay," he said with a grin. "Now the rest of the night's ours."

At Lundy's, they waited on the veranda for Sal and his girlfriend, Stella. Sal pulled up in a gleaming candy-apple red Corvette.

"Hey, Sal. Nice wheels," Frank said.

"Gift from my uncle," Sal smirked.

"Man, all I've got is this old Ford. But someday, I'm trading it in for an El Camino."

Sal nodded toward Jeanette. "Who's the lovely lady?"

"This is Jeanette," Frank said. "We've been seeing each other for about a month."

"No wonder we haven't seen you at the pizzeria lately."

"Hi, Jeanette," Stella said warmly. "Nice to finally meet you."

"Yes, I've heard a lot about you," Jeanette said politely.

They were seated at an outdoor table. Stella ordered steamed clams with drawn butter. Jeanette considered the same, but Frank beat her to it—raw clams on the half shell.

She stiffened.

"You've never had 'em raw?" Frank asked, amused.

"I've had fish. Cooked."

He chuckled, squeezing lemon over two clams, adding cocktail sauce. "Watch and learn." He slid one toward her, then tipped his own into his mouth, teeth scraping the shell.

Jeanette braced herself, closed her eyes, and swallowed.

"It's an acquired taste," he grinned, handing her another.

By the end of the meal, Jeanette was proud she hadn't gagged. Maybe she was stronger than she thought.

"Let's sneak into the Brooklyn Fox," Sal said. "I hear Murray the K is spinning rock and roll all night."

They walked to their cars. Frank's engine sputtered and groaned but refused to start.

"Damn it!" He smacked the steering wheel. "I just cleaned the carburetor and replaced the filters."

Sal leaned out of his Corvette. "Hop in. We'll come back later and get it running."

Frank opened the back door for Jeanette. The scent of fresh leather filled her nose, but it was quickly overpowered by the cigarette smoke as Sal and Stella lit up in front.

Frank struck a match, lit his Camel, then offered her one.

"I shouldn't," she said, hesitating before taking a drag. It burned. She coughed and handed it back. "It's probably not great for my singing voice."

They were two blocks from the Fox when a flash of red lights cut through the night, followed by a blaring siren. A patrol car whipped around them, forcing Sal to veer to the curb and slam on the brakes.

An officer approached, gun hand poised. "Keep your hands on the wheel. Don't move."

Jeanette crouched low in the back seat.

Frank leaned over. "Don't worry. I won't let anything bad happen to you."

"Out of the car," the officer ordered. "All of you."

Jeanette stepped out, trembling. The air felt suddenly cold. She stared at the pavement, heart pounding, and remembered her father's warning—*I don't want my daughter dating a hoodlum.*

\*\*\*\*\*

Jeanette continued to see Frank, though their nights out grew fewer and fewer. More often now, they spent evenings at his house, upstairs, in his room, with the door closed. He no longer talked about taking her dancing or sneaking into late-night movies. He just wanted to lie back on his bed, a drink in his hand, the radio playing low in the background.

Ever since he got his draft notice, something in Frank had changed.

He laughed less. Drank more. He no longer saw his friends much, and when they did stop by, he brushed them off. Even Sal.

"Come on, man," Sal had said one night, standing at the bottom of the stairs. "We're all heading to the boardwalk."

"Not tonight," Frank called back, not even bothering to come down.

Jeanette watched it all unfold—the restlessness, the frustration simmering beneath his skin. He wouldn't talk about the draft. Every time she tried to bring it up, he shut down.

"You think I want to go fight someone else's war?" he muttered one night, staring at the ceiling. "My father pulled strings to keep me out this long. Guess they finally caught up with me."

Jeanette sat on the edge of the bed, unsure how to comfort him. She hated seeing him like this—closed off, angry, drifting. But she also couldn't ignore the growing distance between them. Sometimes, when he looked at her, she wondered if he even saw her anymore.

He reached for his bottle, took another swig. "They ship me out next month," he said, voice flat. "So, don't get any ideas about forever."

Jeanette nodded slowly, her heart sinking.

She had fallen for Frank because he made her feel alive, seen, and wanted. But now, in the soft light of his room, with a haze of cigarette smoke curling toward the ceiling and a half-empty bottle on the nightstand, she wondered if she was falling into something else entirely.

Something she couldn't save.

# Phrases of Love

From time to time, the radio station called Jeanette in to fill open airtime. Her clear, soulful voice and effortless stage presence caught the attention of several music directors.

One afternoon, during a rehearsal, a stranger appeared. He stood silently at the back of the room while Jeanette sang, arms crossed, eyes fixed. She noticed him but didn't falter—instead, she gave it everything she had.

"Who is that?" she whispered to her teacher as the final note faded.

"That's Allen Goldberg," her teacher said, glancing over. "A big-time Broadway producer. Every now and then, he drops by to scout talent."

Jeanette's breath caught as Goldberg approached.

"Who is this lovely creature?" he asked, eyes never leaving hers.

"This is Jeanette, one of my most gifted students," her teacher replied.

"You have a beautiful voice," Goldberg said. "How long have you been singing?"

"Since I could talk, I guess," Jeanette said, still catching her breath.

"Ever thought of doing it professionally?"

"Yes—it's my dream. I've even sung on the radio a few times. I loved it."

"How old are you?"

"Almost eighteen."

"Well," he said with a slight smile, pulling a card from his coat pocket, "call me the moment you turn eighteen. I want you to audition for a new Broadway show."

He handed her the card. Jeanette stared at it in awe. She felt like she had to pinch herself—this was the kind of break she'd only dared to dream about.

That night, she told her father first. Giuseppe, who rarely showed enthusiasm, smiled softly and gave her a nod of approval. Then she rushed to Frank's house to share the news.

He was in his room, slouched on the bed, sipping from a silver flask he kept hidden beneath it. The smell of liquor hit her before she even crossed the threshold. His eyes were bloodshot. Something was off, but she was too elated to let it weigh her down.

"I have good news," she said brightly, pulling the business card from her purse. "I met a producer today—Allen Goldberg. He wants me to audition for a Broadway show!"

Frank squinted at the card and snatched it from her hand.

"Who is this guy? Probably just wants you on the casting couch."

Jeanette recoiled. "That's not true. He's a respected director. He thinks I have talent."

"I don't want my girl hanging around the city with some fast-talking showbiz creep."

"I'm not hanging around. I'm *working*. I'm finally getting my chance."

"No," he said firmly, gripping the card tighter.

"Frank—give it back," she said, her voice rising.

"You're not doing this," he muttered—and tore the card in two.

Jeanette gasped. "What did you do?" She grabbed the ripped pieces, trying to fit them together in her shaking hands. "You can't stop me from singing!"

"I can stop you from throwing away your future."

"No—you're the one dragging me down!" she shouted. "I've had enough of your jealousy. I'm going home."

She stormed toward the door, but Frank leapt up and blocked her path. His face was red, his breath thick with alcohol.

"Let me out," Jeanette said, pushing against his chest. He didn't budge.

"Frank," she warned, panic creeping into her voice. "Let me out!"

"Don't go. Just listen—"

"Help!" she cried out. "Somebody—help!"

A knock rattled the door. "What's going on in there?" came his mother's voice.

"I want to leave!" Jeanette cried.

"Frank! Let her go!" his mother snapped.

Frank hesitated, torn. Then, silently, he stepped aside. Jeanette rushed past him, and there stood his mother, small and pale, her face etched with worry. She looked as if she'd seen this side of her son before.

"I'm sorry…" the woman whispered.

But Jeanette didn't stop. She burst out of the house and ran all the way home.

Upstairs, she closed her bedroom door behind her and collapsed onto the bed, sobbing into the pillow.

Moments later, the phone rang.

Anna knocked gently. "Frank's on the phone."

Jeanette sat up, face streaked with tears. "Tell him I'm not home."

"You sure?"

Jeanette nodded. "Yes. I never want to see him again."

*****

The next day, Giuseppe opened the front door to find Frank on the stoop holding a bouquet of flowers.

"What do you want?" he asked flatly.

"I need to speak with Jeanette."

Giuseppe didn't move. "Wait outside. I'll see if she wants to see you."

Frank nodded and sat down on the stoop, elbows resting on his knees. He lit a cigarette and stared out at the street.

From the upstairs window, Jeanette watched him. He looked sober. His tousled hair caught the breeze, and his broad shoulders seemed to sag under some invisible weight. Despite everything, her heart pulled toward him.

She came down the steps and stood beside him.

"I need to talk to you, Jeanette," he said, standing.

"I have nothing to say to you."

"I want to apologize." He looked her in the eye. "I didn't mean to frighten you. I'm ashamed of how I acted. Please… don't be mad."

"It's your drinking," she said quietly. "You get angry when you're drunk — and it scares me."

"You're right," he admitted. "I've been drinking too much. I haven't told anyone this, but… my mom — she has cancer. It's bad. She's dying. And I'm shipping out to the Army soon. I guess I've been falling apart."

Jeanette's expression softened. "Oh, Frank… I'm sorry. Your mom always seemed like a nice woman."

"She is. She's the most beautiful lady I've ever known — besides you."

Jeanette looked away, blinking back emotion. "She must think I'm terrible for running out like that."

"No," Frank said gently. "She likes you. She even asked if you'd come to dinner on Sunday. It'll be the last night I have with my family before I leave for basic training."

Jeanette hesitated. "All right," she said. "But no drinking. I mean it."

Frank gave a small, grateful smile. "No drinking. I promise."

But they never got to have that dinner.

Frank's mother passed away that Friday, losing her battle with cancer before they could say goodbye properly. Grief hollowed him out. With his bags packed and sorrow weighing on him, Frank said goodbye to Jeanette at the train station and boarded a train bound for New Jersey.

Two months later, a letter arrived. He'd been stationed in Michigan. Because of his natural talent for fixing anything mechanical, the Army had assigned him to the armored division's motor pool.

He signed off with a simple line: *"Don't forget me."*

Jeanette folded the letter slowly and tucked it into the box where she kept her keepsakes — the ones too full of feeling to throw away.

*****

Frank wrote poetic phrases of love in his daily letters, each one a heartfelt attempt to win Jeanette's heart. For him, writing came naturally. Beneath the tough, streetwise exterior, he showed the world was a tender, sensitive soul — a man full of longing and quiet vulnerability, desperate to be seen and loved for who he truly was.

"Isn't he wonderful?" Jeanette beamed, holding one of his letters as she read aloud to her sisters.

"He's a romantic guy," Mariella said with a soft smile.

Phyllis rolled her eyes. "Those are the ones you need to look out for."

"Oh, don't listen to her," Mariella teased. "She's just an old grump."

"I am not," Phyllis snapped. "I'm just saying — be careful. Frank's family isn't exactly respectable. Everyone knows his father's into illegal stuff."

"Frank isn't his father," Jeanette said firmly. "He's not like that."

She continued reading aloud, her voice lilting with excitement — until she suddenly stopped. Her eyes darted ahead, and she lowered the page.

"What is it?" Phyllis asked, narrowing her eyes.

Jeanette pressed the letter to her chest. "He's coming home," she whispered. "Frank's coming home on leave."

# Holy Calling

Luciana walked slowly down the center aisle of Our Lady of Guadalupe — the same aisle she once dreamed of walking in white to meet her future husband at the altar. Twilight spilled softly through the chapel windows, casting a warm glow across the rows of solid cherry pews. In the quiet, they seemed to breathe with her.

She paused before the image of the Blessed Mother, veiled in the smoky haze of incense and the golden shimmer of flickering candles. Her heart swelled. Gently, she kissed her fingertips and pressed them to the cool ceramic of Mary's robe. Then she bowed her head, made the sign of the cross, and stepped into the rectory where Father Herbert's office was tucked away behind a paneled door.

The old priest looked up from his papers, his eyes pale and watery behind thick glasses.

"Well, hello, Luciana," he said kindly.

"Hello, Father Herbert. I need to speak to you… about something important."

"What is it, my child?"

"I want to serve the Lord," she said, her voice steady but quiet.

Father Herbert smiled. "I'm sure you do that every day, Luciana."

"No, I mean full-time. I want to become a missionary nun. Like Mother Teresa. I want to help the poor, travel to other countries, and spread the Word of God."

He folded his hands. "I thought you were engaged to the McCrery boy."

"It didn't work out," she said softly.

The memory flared—John's laughter with another girl, the hollow ache afterward—and faded just as quickly. She had loved him, or thought she had, but he had chosen someone else.

Father Herbert studied her face. "Are you sure this isn't about him?"

"No, Father. I've wanted this since I was small. Even before John. It's always been in my heart."

"This is no small calling," he said gently. "You must give it deep and serious thought. Have you spoken to your parents?"

"Not yet," she admitted.

"There's a convent in Rome that trains missionary sisters. You'd need to travel there for the formation if your application is approved. Then, you'd likely be assigned to a mission in Africa or South America."

Luciana nodded eagerly. "Where do I get the application?"

"I have one right here," he said, reaching into his drawer. "But you'll need your parents' permission before you submit it."

Luciana took the crisp papers and held them to her chest like a fragile treasure.

That evening, she sat at the kitchen table and asked Jeanette to help her fill it out.

Jeanette looked at her little sister — still young, still innocent, yet somehow already carrying the weight of the world.

"Are you sure about this?" she asked gently.

Luciana nodded. "It's the only thing I'm sure of."

\*\*\*\*\*

Luciana waited until Sunday dinner to share her news. Lately, it was the only time the whole family gathered under one roof. Mariella, now eight months pregnant with her second child, had come with Antonio and little Janine, who was propped up on a stack of phone books at the table.

As everyone settled into their seats, Luciana folded her hands and cleared her throat.

"I'd like to lead the prayer tonight," she said.

Giuseppe looked up from his wineglass, surprised, but nodded. "Go ahead, Luci."

Luciana bowed her head. "Dear Lord, bless this food we are about to receive. Bless this family gathered here today. And please, Lord, bless the sisters in Rome who will read my application to join the convent. May they see my heart and grant me the chance to do Your work. Amen."

A hush fell over the table. Forks hovered mid-air. Janine giggled, unaware of the weight of her aunt's words.

Giuseppe and Anna exchanged a glance. They had always admired Luciana's devotion, but this was the first time she had spoken of it so openly. Anna's eyes glistened with unshed tears.

Giuseppe leaned back in his chair, exhaling slowly. "So… it's official, then?"

Luciana nodded. "Yes, Papa. I've applied to the missionary program in Rome. If I'm accepted, I'll go there for training."

"We always knew faith was important to you," Anna said quietly. "But I didn't realize you wanted to dedicate your whole life to it."

"I've thought about it for a long time," Luciana said. "It's what I truly want."

Her sisters weren't shocked. Luciana had dropped hints for years—collecting rosaries, copying passages from the lives of saints, spending hours volunteering at the church. Mariella gave her a knowing smile and reached across the table to squeeze her hand.

Giuseppe took a sip of wine, then set the glass down with a decisive thud. "If this is what you truly want, we won't stand in your way. In Sciacca, we took religion seriously. Everything revolved around the Virgin Mary."

He looked into the middle distance, remembering. "Once, some fishermen went out to sea. Days passed — no catch, just empty nets. Then one morning, they pulled up something heavy. They thought it was a tangle of seaweed, but when they brought it on board, it was a statue of the Blessed Virgin."

The room fell silent.

"They carried her into town," Giuseppe continued, his voice soft with reverence. "Placed her in the Basilica. From that day on, she was known as Madonna del Soccorso — Our Lady of Help. Every year, during the fishermen's feast, they parade her through the streets, thanking her for their blessings."

Luciana's eyes shone.

"Maybe that same Virgin is watching over you now," Giuseppe said. "And maybe she's guiding your path."

Anna nodded. "If this is your calling, Luciana, we'll support you. Just promise you'll write us when you get there."

"I will," Luciana said. "Every week."

They bowed their heads again in silence. And when they finally ate, the food tasted warmer, richer, seasoned with love, and a touch of something holy.

*****

Two months later, a cream-colored envelope bearing the seal of the Missionaries of Charity arrived in the mail. Luciana tore it open with trembling fingers.

She was in.

Excitement fluttered in her chest, chased by a ripple of nerves. She would miss her family deeply, but this was the path she had chosen. A holy calling, one few dared to follow.

Aunts, uncles, and cousins expressed surprise at first, but their pride soon shone through. In the weeks leading up to her departure, Luciana spent every moment she could with them, savoring the laughter, the dinners, the scent of Sunday sauce simmering in her mother's kitchen. She was keenly aware these days would become memories she'd carry like relics.

On the night before her flight, Luciana gently took down the dried palm from Palm Sunday that hung beside her bed. Folding it carefully, she tucked it into the corner of her suitcase—a simple case, light and easy to manage. Still, her brother-in-law, Antonio, insisted on carrying it to the car.

At the curb, her sisters embraced her one by one. Anna held her close, whispering prayers in Italian through quiet tears.

"I'll write every week," Luciana promised, her voice thick.

They stood in a cluster on the stoop, waving as the car pulled away. Luciana twisted in her seat to catch one last glimpse of her mother in the rearview mirror, growing smaller and smaller until Anna faded from view.

The airport terminal was a swirl of motion—suitcases wheeled across tile floors, children crying, announcements crackling over loudspeakers. When Antonio pulled up to the drop-off lane, Luciana turned to him.

"You can just let me out here."

"You sure you don't want me to come in?"

"No," she said gently. "This is something I need to do alone. Take good care of Mariella and the baby."

"I will. God be with you, Luci."

Luciana smiled and stepped out into the bustling crowd.

Inside, she spotted them right away: a group of twenty nuns in crisp white habits, waiting patiently by the gate. Their serene presence calmed her. Though she was still in street clothes, she stayed near them. Already, she felt like one of them.

When it was time to board, the sisters were seated together near the front. Luciana, assigned to a row in the back, found her seat beside a man by the window.

He looked Italian—thick dark curls, olive skin, a strong Roman nose.

He noticed the glance she cast toward the window and smiled. "Would you like to switch seats?"

"Oh—yes. That would be splendid," she said, rising as he slid over.

As the plane began to taxi, she tightened her grip on the armrests. The thrum of the engines vibrated through her legs. When the plane lifted into the sky with a sudden weightlessness, Luciana closed her eyes and whispered a Hail Mary.

"You okay?" the man asked kindly.

"I think so. It's my first time on an airplane."

"Ah, that explains it. I'm Luigi," he said, offering his hand.

"I'm Luciana."

"A beautiful name," he said. "What brings you to Rome? Visiting family?"

"No," she said, cheeks flushing. "I've been accepted into the convent at the Vatican. I'm going to become a missionary nun."

Luigi blinked in surprise, then nodded respectfully. "Then I should call you 'Sister Luciana.'"

"Not yet," she said, smiling. "But soon, God willing."

They shared a warm silence as trays of food were distributed down the aisle. Luciana picked at hers, too excited to eat. The tiny rolls and cubes of cheese reminded her of airplane meals she'd only seen in movies.

Luigi eventually pulled his fedora over his eyes and dozed. Luciana tried to sleep too, but the engines hummed like a lullaby she couldn't quite surrender to. Instead, she rested her eyes, her mind drifting to what lay ahead: the cobbled streets of Rome, the grandeur of St. Peter's Basilica, and the unknown country she would one day serve.

At last, she dozed off, rocked by altitude and dreams of a life just beginning.

*****

As the plane descended into Aeroporto Internazionale di Roma–Fiumicino Leonardo da Vinci, passengers stirred in their seats, stretching and retrieving their belongings from the overhead bins. Luciana sat still for a moment, gazing out the window. Rome stretched beneath her in a patchwork of ochre rooftops and winding streets—ancient, mysterious, and entirely unfamiliar.

She followed the flow of travelers through the terminal, clutching her boarding pass like a lifeline. At the carousel, her eyes quickly landed on her suitcase, marked by a red ribbon Jeanette had tied to the handle. A small act of love that traveled with her across the ocean.

"Got it," Luigi said, catching her bag before it passed. He hoisted his own worn leather case just in time, then turned to her with a gentle smile. "Rome is a big city, but you'll find your way. May your journey be safe."

With that, he disappeared into the crowd.

Outside, the warm Italian air wrapped around her. She joined a line of travelers waiting for taxis. When it was her turn, she handed the driver a slip of paper with the convent's address. The cabbie read it, nodded, and launched the car into traffic with barely a word.

A rosary swung from the rearview mirror, clicking softly with every turn. A tiny statue of the Virgin Mary clung to the dashboard. Luciana clasped her own cross and murmured a silent prayer as the car weaved through the chaos of Rome's streets.

They passed the Tiber River, domed cathedrals, and pastel-colored buildings bathed in the golden light of late afternoon. As the cab entered St. Peter's Square, Luciana's breath caught. The grandeur of the basilica loomed like something out of a dream.

The driver pulled around to a modest side building tucked in the shadow of the Vatican. She paid him with a few crisp lira notes and stepped out, suitcase in hand, just as the chapel bells began to toll.

The sound echoed through the square. Luciana turned in a slow circle, awed by where she stood.

She was far from home.

Yet something in her stirred — not fear, but purpose.

Though her family had softened with each generation in America, shedding old customs for new lives, the essence of who they were — the faith, the strength, the fire in their hearts — remained.

Jeanette's ribbon was still tied to the suitcase. The Blessed Mother watched from every street corner. And Luciana, the girl who once walked the pews of Our Lady of Guadalupe, had come to serve.

A new chapter had begun.

# Far and Away

During the war, American men had no shortage of work. Many pulled double shifts on the railroad or labored in ammunition factories. Even the women took up roles in textile mills, working long hours to sew uniforms, pea coats, and pack cartridges by the thousands.

At first, it was a blessing. After years of hardship, money poured into the neighborhood. Men cashed their paychecks, and women lined up at the butcher, no longer asking for soup bones. When the war ended, people were drunk with cash. The hum of prosperity echoed through the tenements. Horns blared as the wealthiest raced their new Fords and Chevrolets up and down 18th Avenue.

No one predicted that prosperity would be the very thing to unravel the family. Petty rivalries sprang up like weeds in a sidewalk crack. Who had the newest curtains? The best parlor furniture? The most stylish coat? Holidays became a blend of family togetherness and not-so-subtle competition.

As the children grew, many turned their backs on the grit and noise of Brooklyn. They moved to Long Island, Staten Island, or across the river to New Jersey — trading stoops and fire escapes for lawns and white picket fences. The family spread its wings, and with that flight, old traditions began to fade. There were no more Sunday dinners, no more weekday coffee klatches. Eventually, they gathered only for weddings and funerals.

Even Phyllis left Brooklyn. Her husband, David, a sports journalist with a promising future, accepted a transfer to *Newsday* on Long Island. They moved to a sleepy little town called Massapequa, tucked into the south shore. David's family helped them finance a modest country home with a wide bay window in the living room and modern appliances in the kitchen. It was quiet. Peaceful. Almost too quiet.

Unlike Brooklyn, the neighbors kept their distance. Yards separated homes like invisible moats. The streets stretched on for blocks, and a car was required to get anywhere. Phyllis learned to drive. David bought her a yellow Ford, and just like that, she slipped into suburban life.

*****

Frank was home on leave and couldn't wait to tell Jeanette everything about his life in the Army. He proudly bragged about his promotion to sergeant in the motor pool in Michigan. Every day they lounged on the beach, strolled the boardwalk, and at night went dancing or caught a movie.

One night, they went to a dime-a-dance joint. Frank wore his uniform—servicemen got a discount— and bought a strip of tickets. The orchestra struck up one of Jeanette's favorite songs, *They Can't Take That*

*Away from Me* by June Christy. She adored Christy's smooth, sultry voice and rise to fame with the Stan Kenton Orchestra.

When another serviceman asked her to dance, Frank's mood shifted. Though she assured him she was his girl, he sulked in the corner. Jeanette cut the dance short and returned to him.

Later, with Frank's best friend Jimmy and his new wife Beth, they drove to a lake house on land deeded to Frank's father by a debtor. The property sat beside a stable, and the owner sweetened the deal by offering use of the horses. They grilled hot dogs and watched the sun glint off the water. Frank seemed happiest when Jeanette was by his side.

He didn't want to waste a minute apart. His time home was flying, and the thought of returning to base without her gnawed at him.

"I wish I didn't have to go back to Michigan," he said. "All I do is think about you — and how some guy might steal you away while I'm gone."

"Don't be silly," she said, brushing his cheek. "No one's stealing me."

"I want you to be my wife."

Jeanette smiled. "I'd love that, Frank — but maybe we should wait until you're discharged."

"I heard the Army helps pay for housing if I'm married. We could have a small apartment off base. We could be together."

"I don't know what my parents would say..." Jeanette hesitated. The idea of leaving New York scared her, but the thought of living with Frank and starting a new life excited her more.

"Please, Jeanette. Marry me."

"I love you," she said quietly. "I'll talk to them tonight."

At home, she knew what was coming. Her mother, Anna, tried to reason with her.

"You're such a beautiful singer. You could have an exciting life. Why throw it all away?"

"I can still sing if I'm married."

Anna sighed. "This Frank seems jealous."

Jeanette thought of the Broadway producer's business card—how Frank had ripped it up—but kept the memory to herself.

Giuseppe shook his head. "These Neapolitan men... they treat women like dogs."

"Sicilians aren't saints either," Jeanette said. "The Black Hand was Sicilian. They'll cut off their own if crossed."

"Those are the bad apples," her father said, "driven by pride and greed. Most of our people are good."

"Please, Pop. I love him." Her voice cracked.

Giuseppe looked at Anna. "Maybe it's time we let go."

"But Michigan is so far away," Anna said softly.

"I'll come back every month," Jeanette promised. "There's a train—it only takes two days."

Tears welled in Anna's eyes. "I may not be here when you get back."

"Mama," Jeanette whispered, "Where would you go?"

"Dead!" Anna cried and rushed to her bedroom, refusing to speak of the wedding again.

But as the days passed, she softened.

One morning, Jeanette found her in the kitchen, washing dishes.

"You look tired," Jeanette said. "Let me help."

"No, your wedding's in two days. You don't want hands like mine—rough and red."

"Then let me dry." Jeanette grabbed a towel.

They worked side by side in silence.

"Mama… I'm sorry this upset you."

"I always thought your life would be different."

"I know. But everyone else has husbands and families. They all seem happy."

"Not everything is what it seems." Anna sighed.

"I'm sure everything will be all right. You'll see."

Anna looked at her with sad eyes. "I'm going to miss you terribly. But I want you to be happy."

"I am, Mama. Don't worry. I'll never stay away too long. We'll be back as soon as Frank gets out of the Army."

# Honeymoon

Jeanette married Frank at Our Lady of Guadalupe. They made a stunning couple — he looked sharp in his military dress uniform, and she was radiant in a flowing white gown. The train trailed six pews behind her like a whisper of dreams.

As the ceremony unfolded, Jeanette scanned the crowd of family and friends. She wondered if Sonny was there. She had mailed the invitation, but he'd never responded.

"If anyone has a reason these two should not be joined in marriage," the priest intoned, "speak now or forever hold your peace."

Jeanette closed her eyes and, for a flicker of a second, imagined Sonny standing up and shouting, *"Stop the wedding!"* But when she opened them again, it was Frank's face that met hers.

"I now pronounce you husband and wife," the priest said. "You may kiss the bride."

The organ rang out as the couple walked arm in arm down the white satin runner. Rice flew through the air. Jeanette lifted her arm to shield her face, still half-dreaming.

The reception was held at an elaborate banquet hall, paid for by Frank's father. Mariella's in-laws donated a three-tier cake adorned with pink sugar roses and topped with a tiny bride and groom. The room brimmed with relatives and the cheerful chaos of children.

Phyllis and David drove in from Long Island, bringing their baby son Alfred, who was dressed in a red, white, and blue romper with a tiny Dodgers cap perched on his head.

All of Jeanette's sisters were there, except Luciana, who had sent a letter from Rome. She regretted missing the wedding but wrote that she was adjusting well to convent life and learning Italian.

There was no time for a honeymoon — Frank had to return to Michigan the next day. So the newlyweds spent their wedding night in his childhood bedroom, just down the hall from his family.

When they entered, Frank removed his uniform and carefully hung it in the closet. Standing in his skivvies, Jeanette noticed how the Army had chiseled his frame — broad chest, defined muscles, narrow waist. He looked like a man sculpted by duty and discipline.

He walked toward her slowly, undressing her with reverent hands. Jeanette let the dress fall to the floor. As he lay her down gently, she closed her eyes and tried to push away the ache in her heart.

It should've been Sonny.

Frank kissed her, his breath laced with whiskey. As his hands moved over her, she turned her head slightly. He whispered, "C'mon. We're married now."

At first, his touch was soft. Her body responded with a strange mix of nervousness and desire. She arched toward him, wanting to believe in this moment. But then he grew urgent and impatient, pushing himself into her.

Jeanette cried out. Pain bloomed and faded just as quickly. Within moments, it was over.

Frank rolled onto his back and passed out.

From the thin walls, she heard his father and brother talking in the next room — loud voices, muffled Italian. She couldn't make out what they were saying.

Jeanette lay awake, staring at the ceiling. A dull ache settled inside her. She wondered if they'd heard everything — if they knew. She turned on her side, facing away from Frank, and waited for morning.

*****

The next morning, Jeanette kissed her family goodbye. She boarded the train with her new husband, leaving behind everything she knew for a strange land called Michigan.

Frank had made all the arrangements. An apartment awaited them off-base.

When they arrived in Detroit, a cab took them to their new home. Frank carried their bags up to a second-floor flat. It was smaller than Jeanette had expected — no frills, just a one-bedroom apartment with basic utilities and a worn-looking bed.

Frank had to report for duty early the next morning, but that night they stayed up late, whispering and laughing under the covers until they drifted off in each other's arms.

The next day, daylight streamed through the curtainless window. Jeanette opened her eyes to an empty bed. Frank had already left for the base. In the kitchen, she found a note beside a few folded bills.

*Buy yourself something nice. I'll see you tonight.* — *Frank*

Frank's days were long and grueling — drills, calisthenics, and crawling under barbed wire. Although he was assigned to the motor pool, the Army expected every man to be combat-ready. By the time he returned home each night, his muscles ached, and his uniform clung to him with sweat.

Jeanette stayed busy setting up their apartment. She missed her mother deeply but found purpose in cooking hearty meals and folding fresh laundry. She turned their modest space into something warm.

Still, the loneliness crept in, especially when Frank was sent away on training missions for days at a time.

"I get so lonely here," she confessed one evening. "I miss my family."

Frank considered letting her go home for a short visit, but the holidays were approaching, and the thought of being alone gnawed at him. Instead of comforting her, he changed the subject or brushed her off.

Every weekend, they attended dances on the base — social events hosted to boost morale. Jeanette loved dressing up, slipping into a new dress, and curling her hair. The music, the laughter, and the brief illusion of glamour lifted her spirits. But her beauty didn't go unnoticed, and Frank couldn't stand it when other men cut in.

Jeanette thought it was harmless fun. But when they returned home, Frank's resentment simmered.

One night, Frank emerged from the bedroom wearing only his pants. He lit a Camel, took a slow drag, and stared at her across the room.

"You've got every man on that base wrapped around your little finger," he snapped. "They all know who you are."

His eyes were dark with suspicion. She saw it—the way his jaw clenched, the way the worst possibilities played out behind his gaze.

"It's not like that," she whispered. "They're just dances."

He took a swig of scotch and stubbed out his cigarette, the ash curling against the edge of the tray.

Jeanette knew it was the alcohol talking, but it didn't make it any less frightening. He had promised he'd stop drinking, but the stress of Army life wore him down. What began as a nightcap had become a half-empty bottle at dinner.

He sat at the table, swirling the amber liquid in his glass as she stirred sauce on the stove.

"I miss my family," she said again, quieter this time.

"I don't want to hear about your goddamn family anymore," Frank snapped.

Her shoulders stiffened. The ladle slipped from her hand and clattered into the pot.

"I want to go home," she whispered.

"You *are* home!" he shouted. Then, without warning, he raised his hand.

She flinched.

But instead of hitting her, he hurled the glass against the wall. It shattered into a spray of sharp fragments. The scotch dripped down the plaster like a wound.

Frank stormed out of the apartment, slamming the door behind him.

Jeanette sank to the floor, her hands trembling. The sauce continued to simmer on the stove.

*****

Jeanette woke alone. The bed beside her was cold. Frank hadn't come home.

Sunlight filtered through the sheer curtain, falling across the small apartment's worn furniture and discolored linoleum floor. A wave of emptiness pressed on her chest.

This wasn't the life she had dreamed of. Not the stage, not a microphone in her hand. Just pots, laundry, and silence. Instead of a future in music, she had the thankless life of a soldier's wife, where days bled into one another with cooking, cleaning, and waiting. And at night, she dreaded the pull of the marriage bed and what came with it.

Late that afternoon, the door creaked open.

Frank walked in holding a bouquet of wilted daisies from the corner market.

"I'm sorry," he said, sheepish and unshaven.

Jeanette took the flowers but said nothing.

He expected her to melt, to accept his apology the way she had before. But when he reached for her that night, her body tensed.

"I'm not in the mood," she said, turning away.

Frank didn't listen.

He pulled her close in the dark, pressing against her, his weight heavy and unrelenting. She tried to push him off, but he was stronger.

"Stop!" she cried, but he kept going.

Afterward, she lay still, her back to him, her tears soaking the pillow. The room was thick with silence.

For days, she said nothing. Her eyes dulled. She moved like a ghost through their cramped apartment, speaking only when she had to.

Frank tried to make amends. He made dinner once, washed the dishes. But something had broken, and they both knew it.

Finally, one evening, he sat at the table and stared at his hands.

"All right," he said quietly. "You want to go home? I'll buy you a ticket."

# Train Wreck

With her bags packed and waiting by the door, Jeanette sat on the edge of the sofa, watching the clock tick. Each minute felt longer than the last. Frank was supposed to take her to the train station, but he was nowhere to be seen.

Finally, with just half an hour to spare, the door creaked open. Frank stumbled in, his eyes glassy, his breath laced with whiskey.

"Can't you wait until Friday?" he slurred, his tone more pleading than angry. "Just a couple more days."

Jeanette stood. Her voice was steady, but her heart raced. "No, Frank. My mother's expecting me."

His expression shifted to irritation, but he said nothing more. Grudgingly, he grabbed the keys and led her to the car.

The ride was tense. The car veered side to side, and Jeanette gripped the seat, silently praying they'd make it. Frank said nothing, lost in whatever fog gripped him.

When they arrived, he parked crookedly by the curb. Before she could open the door, he grabbed her hand.

"Jeanette," he said, eyes suddenly wet. "I'm sorry. I promise—I'll stop drinking."

"You've made that promise before."

"This time, I mean it."

She looked at him—really looked—and saw the boy beneath the bravado, scared and broken. But she couldn't let that be her reason to stay.

She turned her face just slightly, and his kiss landed on her cheek.

Without another word, she took her bags and boarded the train.

Inside, she found a window seat and sat down, letting out a long breath. As the train pulled away, she watched Michigan disappear behind her.

Two days. That's all it would take to get back to Brooklyn—to the comforting smell of her mother's sauce on the stove, the sound of familiar voices, and the safety of home.

By afternoon, the train was cutting through Ohio. Lake Erie glinted in the distance, catching the last of the sun. Jeanette pulled a sandwich from her bag and ate in silence. When the conductor announced dinner in the dining car, she declined and went to her sleeping berth instead.

Pulling the curtain closed, she curled into the narrow bed and pressed her cheek to the cool pillow.

For the first time in weeks, Jeanette felt a flicker of peace.

*****

By the following morning, the train rolled into Buffalo. Jeanette felt the familiar tug of home. She was back in New York. She leaned against the window and nibbled on a crisp red apple from the paper breakfast bag the dining car had provided, along with a packet of crackers and a carton of juice.

She smiled, imagining the Thanksgiving table, the smell of roasted turkey, her mother's ravioli, and the clatter of voices and laughter around the table. She'd be there just in time for dinner — home at last.

But fate had other plans.

A fatal train crash miles ahead brought everything to a halt. Emergency crews were clearing the wreckage. Her train sat motionless on the tracks for hours. By late afternoon, passengers were told they'd be delayed overnight.

There was no way to reach her family. No phones on the train. No telegram. Nothing but waiting.

*****

Back in Brooklyn, the Corrao house buzzed with holiday warmth. Anna and Giovanna worked side by side in the kitchen, stuffing the bird and basting it with melted butter. The scent of rosemary and garlic drifted through the house, mingling with the melody of *The Italian Hour*, which echoed from the living room radio.

"Jeanette will be starving when she gets here," Anna said, laughing as she sprinkled breadcrumbs over the stuffing. "She's probably been eating army food for months."

Suddenly, the music cut out. A crackling voice interrupted the broadcast.

"We interrupt this program for breaking news: a passenger train en route from Detroit to New York has been delayed following a catastrophic accident up ahead. Casualties have been reported—details to come."

The spoon dropped from Anna's hand.

"Giovanna…" she whispered. Her face went pale. "Jeanette. That's her train."

"Mama, wait—don't jump to conclusions—"

Anna's knees buckled. "Oh, God, no!" She collapsed onto the kitchen floor, clutching her chest, unable to breathe.

Giovanna screamed. "Papa! Help!"

Giuseppe rushed in. They carried Anna to the bedroom, her breath shallow, her skin clammy.

"Call Mariella. And Phyllis," Giovanna said urgently. "Tell them to come now."

*****

On Long Island, Phyllis was listening to the Dodgers game when the phone in the hallway rang. She called out for David to answer it. She could hear his voice, low at first, then rising with urgency.

She clicked off the game and walked into the hallway. "What's going on?"

David looked at her, his expression grim. "It's your mother. She collapsed. They're waiting for the doctor, but we need to get to Brooklyn. Now."

"Get the baby," Phyllis said, already grabbing her coat.

By the time they arrived, the doctor had come and gone. His face was solemn as he stepped out of the bedroom.

"I'm sorry. She's gone. She stopped breathing before I arrived."

"No..." Phyllis pushed past him and ran to her mother's side, crying out, "Mama!"

But she was too late.

The scent of roasted turkey still lingered in the air. But no one touched it. No one was hungry.

Except the children.

Aunt Genovese quietly filled a few plates. The children ate without understanding, their usual chatter replaced with a heavy silence.

Then came Uncle Vincent, carrying a cake from Ebinger's Bakery, his eyes bright with hope.

"Happy Thanksgiving!" he called, stepping inside — then froze.

The room was still. Faces somber. The truth hit him like a punch to the gut.

He dropped the cake, which splattered across the floor, and collapsed to his knees at Giuseppe's feet, sobbing uncontrollably.

Giuseppe, grief-stricken but composed, made the decision. "We'll have the wake here," he said. "In the house. Like we did in Sicily."

No one argued. No one had the heart.

# Sealed in Stone

The train didn't arrive until Friday morning. Jeanette had missed Thanksgiving, but she was grateful to be close to home at last. Her Uncle Vincent met her at the station, his face pale and drawn.

"What's wrong?" she asked, alarmed.

"I'm sorry," Vincent whispered. "Your mother thought you were in that train wreck. She collapsed on Thanksgiving morning. The doctors say it was a stroke."

"A stroke?" Jeanette gasped. "Where is she? I want my mother."

"I'm sorry, Jeanette." His voice broke. "Your mother is gone. The funeral is tomorrow."

"No... no!" The words clanged in her ears. The loss hit her like a tidal wave, crashing over her with full force. Jeanette sobbed the entire ride, clutching her uncle's arm.

"I never should have left," she wept.

"Don't blame yourself, Jeanette," he said. "None of this is your fault."

They pulled up to the Corrao house. Flowers were already filling the rooms—carnations, lilies, roses. The scent hit Jeanette hard, making her stomach turn. She leaned on Vincent as she walked into the living room and caught sight of the casket. Her breath caught in her throat. The room dimmed. She saw only her mother, still, serene, unreachable.

Then everything went black.

A vision rose through the darkness: Anna, radiant and golden, glowing like the sun. Nonna and Nonno stood beside her, smiling gently. The image shimmered, then faded. Jeanette opened her eyes to her uncle's face, waving smelling salts.

Mariella placed a cold cloth on her forehead. Phyllis helped her sip water. When she could finally stand, Jeanette moved to the kneeler before the casket. Giuseppe stood silently beside her, his hand resting on her shoulder, but she didn't acknowledge him. Her eyes remained locked on Anna's face. The mortician had done well, but the skin was waxen. Jeanette reached out and gently touched her mother's cheek. Cold.

The sisters gathered close before the casket. A passing train rumbled down New Utrecht Avenue, rattling the windows.

"What are we going to do without Mama?" Mariella whispered through tears.

"We still have each other," Phyllis said. "We have to stick together. That's what Mama would've wanted."

Suddenly, the front door opened. A figure stepped inside in a crisp black habit.

"Luci's home," Mariella whispered. She and Phyllis rushed forward.

"Luciana!" Jeanette cried. "We lost Mama." She clung to her sister's robes and wept.

*****

The entire family gathered at the cemetery, including Sonny.

When Jeanette saw him, she rushed forward and threw her arms around him. Emotion surged, and for a moment, she nearly kissed him.

But Sonny gently pulled back. "This is my wife, Jiao."

Jeanette froze. The woman beside him was beautiful, with long, silky black hair and coal-dark eyes. A swell under her dress revealed she was expecting.

"I didn't know you were married," Jeanette managed.

"You didn't get an invitation?" he asked gently.

"No... but I saw the picture."

The image flashed in her mind: Sonny and Jiao surrounded by both families, seated formally at the reception. Sonny's smile gave nothing away. She studied him now, searching his face for the boy she once loved, for some hidden feeling. His expression was kind, unreadable.

"I'm sorry it had to be under these circumstances," Jiao said softly.

"Yes," Jeanette replied. "And... congratulations."

Her eyes flicked toward Sonny's wife, her belly tight under the fabric. The name Jiao returned to her — lovely, dainty. She and Sonny had once pored over

Chinese name books on their rooftop, dreaming of the future.

Of course, he married someone like her.

She tried to be happy for him, but her chest ached.

Standing at her mother's grave, Jeanette felt Sonny and Jiao just behind her. She didn't turn around. She didn't want to hear them talk.

*****

Back home, Jeanette shut herself in her bedroom and pulled Anna's pillow into her arms. The lemon verbena scent clung faintly to the fabric. She pressed her face into it and wept.

She thought of the fortuneteller. Had she seen this coming in her crystal ball?

*It's my fault*, Jeanette thought. *If I hadn't married Frank. If I'd been home… maybe she'd still be alive.*

The memory of her mother's warnings echoed loud in her mind — warnings about Frank's drinking, his jealous streak. Warnings she had ignored. Now they became cement around her heart, hardening against Frank with every passing hour.

# Perseverance

Jeanette woke to the scent of bread browning in the oven.

*Mama!*

For a fleeting moment, she thought it had all been a bad dream. The familiar murmur of voices rose and fell from the kitchen, but Anna's voice was not among them. A hollow ache sank into her chest. Her breath caught, tight and dry in her throat, as the truth settled in.

Her mother was gone.

She buried her face in the pillow and sobbed until her eyes ached. When she finally lifted her head, she blinked—and saw someone standing at her bedside.

"Sonny," she whispered, stunned.

He held a breakfast tray. "I brought you something."

Jeanette sat up slowly. Her hands trembled as she reached for the fork, but her appetite had vanished. She pushed the food around the plate without taking a bite.

Sonny gently brushed a stray lock of hair from her forehead. "I'm here to make sure you eat something."

"I'm not very hungry."

"That doesn't matter. You've got to keep up your strength." He tore a small piece of bread, dipped it in butter, and brought it to her lips.

Jeanette let him feed her like a child, too drained to resist.

"Where's your wife?" she asked, barely above a whisper.

"She had to go back to Boston. I stayed behind." He looked at her closely. "You look like hell, Jeanette."

"I lost my mother," she said flatly.

"I know." He sat beside her on the edge of the bed. "Anna loved you more than anything."

"It's my fault." Her shoulders hunched. She turned her face away from him, ashamed.

Sonny placed a hand gently on her back. "That's not true. And you know it."

She didn't respond, but his words wrapped around her like a blanket. She wanted to believe him.

He pulled her into his arms. Jeanette clung to him, pressing her face into the front of his shirt. The steady beat of his heart calmed her. She inhaled the faint scent of shaving soap and starch. She raised her head and traced the curve of his lips with her finger.

They were warm. Soft. Familiar.

She longed to kiss them, just once, to feel something besides sorrow. For a brief second, she thought he might want the same. His eyes held hers.

Then, a voice called from the kitchen — his mother.

Sonny pulled away, gently tucking the blanket around her.

"Please," he said softly. "Pull yourself together —
for me."

And then he was gone.

Jeanette stared at the door long after he'd left. She
lay still as shadows shifted across the walls and
daylight disappeared. The voices in the kitchen
quieted. The house grew dim. Still, she didn't move.

But Sonny was right.

She had to pull herself together.

*****

Jeanette woke to the sound of laughter drifting in from
the kitchen. The voices of her sisters — Mariella, Phyllis,
and Luciana — mingled in cheerful conversation about
Cousin Ronnie's upcoming wedding.

She slipped out of bed and padded into the
kitchen, her hair still tousled from sleep. "I could use a
cup of coffee."

Mariella jumped up. "I'll make some."

Moments later, she returned to the table with
steaming mugs, a fresh loaf of bread, and a small bowl
of olive oil infused with garlic. The scent filled the
room, warm and familiar, pulling their father from his
comfortable chair in front of the television.

"I'm not going," Jeanette said, her voice quiet but
firm.

"What do you mean?" Phyllis asked, frowning.

"Just what I said. I'm not going to Ronnie's
wedding. You can all go without me."

No one spoke at first.

Luciana glanced down at the table. Her black habit hung stiffly from the bedroom door down the hall, a stark reminder of what lay ahead. In just two days, she would leave for her first assignment in Africa — Sudan — where she'd serve displaced children amidst political turmoil.

"We're going to miss you, Luciana," Jeanette said gently. "As soon as you're settled, send us the address so we can send you things."

Luciana smiled. "Like what?"

"I don't know... soap, coffee, whatever comforts they don't have."

Giuseppe let out a long sigh. "What's happened to our family? All my children are leaving."

"Not me, Pop," Jeanette said, meeting his eyes.

"Aren't you going back to Michigan?" he asked.

She shook her head. "No. Mama came to me last night. She told me not to go back."

A heavy silence settled over the table.

"What about your husband?" Giuseppe finally asked.

"He's jealous and possessive — just like Mama warned me. I've made up my mind. Besides, you need someone to take over for Mama. I can cook and clean. It'll just be the two of us, Pop."

Giuseppe studied her, pride flickering behind his tired eyes. Though he tried to hide it, a smile tugged at the corners of his mouth. Jeanette was headstrong, through and through — true Sicilian blood. Determined. Audacious.

He had raised her with Sicilian stories of loyalty, family, and faith—not to make her submissive, but to make her resilient.

# Dainty and Delicate

Boston was no different from Brooklyn. The sun still rose in the east and set in the west. Sonny trudged through his classes at Northeastern University, trying to focus on his studies to forget Jeanette. But no matter how exhausted he was, no matter how hard he slept, she came to him in dreams every night.

One day, the professor assigned a group project that required pairing up with another student. Sonny was matched with a quiet Asian girl who rarely spoke in class. On the first day, all he could get out of her was her name — Jiao. But Sonny never failed to break the ice. His smile alone could thaw the frost off a Boston sidewalk.

Before long, they were laughing and talking easily. He learned she was the youngest of three sisters, and that her parents — second-generation Americans like his — still lived in Boston. Though they were nearby, Jiao lived in the women's dorm. Her parents wanted her to learn to be independent.

"Would you like to go for pizza after class?" Sonny asked one afternoon.

"I'd love to," she said.

It became their ritual. After class, they'd stroll to Regina's for slices, then walk along the Fort Point

Channel to watch the boats. Sonny stole his first kiss there.

Sometimes, they lost track of time and had to rush back before curfew. Sonny always walked Jiao to her dorm and waited until she was safely inside. But one night, they were late. She made it inside with minutes to spare—but there wasn't enough time for Sonny to return to his own dorm before the doors were locked.

"Oh no… what are you going to do?" Jiao asked, alarmed.

"I'll sleep on a park bench," he joked. "Or maybe in the library—if I can find an open couch to crash on."

Jiao didn't laugh. "We can sneak you into my room. My roommate's away this week. No one will know."

"Really?" he grinned. "Think we can get away with it?"

"Here—put on my sweater and keep your head down."

They crept through the stairwell, racing up to the third floor. Jiao peeked around the corner to make sure the coast was clear, then waved him forward.

"Hurry!" she whispered.

Once inside, they couldn't stop giggling. The thrill of breaking the rules charged the air between them. Jiao threw her arms around him and kissed him again. They fell onto her bed.

Sonny had only been with one girl before—Kathleen, a bold neighborhood girl from Brooklyn. That summer before he left, she'd strutted past the stoop where he and his friends were hanging out. Her Irish green eyes locked onto his.

"She wants you," his friend Robert had said. "Go take a walk."

And he did. They ended up in the back seat of an old junked car in an alley, and twenty minutes later, Sonny emerged changed.

But now, with Jiao, it was different. Even though he tried to act like he knew what he was doing, he didn't feel experienced. Gently, he undressed her and slipped out of his own clothes. They made love for the first time in her bed.

Sonny closed his eyes, trying to push away thoughts of Jeanette. When it was over, he felt oddly triumphant—like he had passed some test, like maybe he was finally moving on. But he was surprised to find blood on the sheets.

"Haven't you ever…?"

"No," Jiao said softly. "I was a virgin. Or… I was."

Sonny kissed her forehead. "Thank you for trusting me."

He sneaked out of her dorm at dawn and headed back to shower and get ready for class.

From then on, when Jiao's roommate went home to Connecticut on the weekends, Sonny stayed over. They made love and talked through the night. Jiao told him about Chinese customs and her family. Sonny told her about Brooklyn—his friends, his parents, and Cousin Jeanette.

"You'd love my cousin Jeanette," he said, eyes glowing. "She's the smartest, most talented girl in Brooklyn."

"You really love her," Jiao said gently. "I can tell."

"She's my cousin," he replied too quickly, defensively.

"I see."

Sonny changed the subject. "Next week is the Fishermen's Feast. The Madonna Del Soccorso Society runs it. Want to come?"

"It sounds very Italian."

He laughed. "It is. One of the biggest Italian festivals. My parents are coming. I'd love for you to meet them."

"Do you think they'll like me?"

"Of course," he said with a smile — but deep down, he wasn't sure. His mother had never liked any woman who got too close to him. A lot of Italian mothers were like that — overprotective of their sons. She was no exception. Sonny never had to lift a finger at home. No laundry, no dishes, and a hot meal always waiting on the table. But that kind of love came with a price. His mother didn't easily share him with anyone.

*****

On the morning of the festival, Sonny and Jiao met his parents in front of the church. He had already broken the news to his mother about Jiao's background and had pleaded with his father to keep her in check. Still, Sonny knew better than to trust his mother's silence — it was never a guarantee of peace.

To his surprise, the day passed without incident. His mother kept her cool, smiling politely and making small talk with Jiao. It was unnerving. She was too composed, too pleasant — like she was humoring a fad she expected would pass. But her approval, or the illusion of it, only made Sonny more miserable.

Every time he looked at Jiao, he felt a pang of guilt. She was kind, gentle, and smart. But she wasn't Jeanette. And every time they made love, Sonny's heart ached. He was with the wrong person. He cared for Jiao, but he didn't love her — not fully. Not the way he still loved Jeanette. He knew what he had to do.

He had to end things with Jiao.

He had to go back to Brooklyn.

He had to find Jeanette.

But before he could say the words, Jiao sat him down one evening in her dorm room, her eyes wide and uncertain. She fidgeted with the hem of her sweater.

"There's something I have to tell you," she said quietly.

Sonny's heart thudded. He knew. Before she even spoke, he knew.

"I'm pregnant."

The words hit like a hammer. Everything in him collapsed inward. Jeanette faded into the background like a dream he could no longer touch.

# Sudan

The plane touched down on a remote airstrip in South Sudan. Heat shimmered off the tarmac as Luciana stepped out with three other nuns. A rusted jeep waited nearby, its tires caked with red dust. Their driver, a wiry man in fatigues, waved them over without a word.

They were taken to a makeshift landing strip a few miles from the camp, where the rhythmic thump of an approaching helicopter grew louder by the second. Wind and grit churned in the air as it descended, rocking wildly on its skids. Luciana clutched the metal frame of her seat despite the seatbelt digging into her waist. The rotor's roar consumed her prayers.

Once the blades slowed, two armed soldiers rushed forward to help the nuns climb down. Luciana's veil whipped around her face as they crossed the open field to the camp.

The refugee hospital was little more than a large tent held together with rope and willpower. Inside, there were folding tables and crude cooking grills along the sides. Chickens, goats, and stray dogs wandered in and out without notice. Two men, themselves displaced by the conflict, handled most of the cooking—usually chicken stew or boiled eggs, the only reliable food sources.

Twenty smaller tents dotted the dusty clearing. These housed the patients, volunteers, and the nuns. Luciana's tent had a dirt floor, two creaky bunk beds, and a cracked basin for washing. The latrine was a small hut covered in palm thatch with a splintered wooden door that barely swung shut.

Luciana boiled linens, scrubbed floors, rolled bandages, and changed beds. She held down trembling children as doctors stitched wounds or cleaned burns. Some cried. Some didn't. The silence of the youngest ones haunted her most.

After weeks without rest and days that blurred into one another, Luciana sat under the flickering light of a single oil lantern and wrote home.


Dear Jeanette,

I'm sorry I haven't written sooner, but we're in the middle of nowhere. The mail only comes once a month, if we're lucky.

It's hard to describe the conditions here. Most of the people have fled violence—women with starving babies, elderly men missing limbs, and far too many children who watched their parents die. They don't cry much. They've seen too much.

Sometimes I ask why God allows so much suffering. But I know the answer already. I'm not here to understand. I'm here to serve. It's not for me to question His will, only to do His work.

God loves us. We just have to keep believing that.

Love,
Luciana


Jeanette folded the letter and slipped it back into the envelope. For a long time, she sat staring out the window, clutching the fragile paper like a lifeline.

She admired her sister's faith, the strength it gave her.

But she couldn't feel it herself. Not anymore.

Since her mother died, God had gone silent.

Is He even real? She wondered. And if He is... why does He keep breaking hearts like mine?

# Courthouse Steps

After hearing of Anna's death, Frank reluctantly agreed it was best for Jeanette to remain in New York until he finished his service. He packed his belongings, moved back to the barracks, and quietly served out his time. Determined to change, he cleaned himself up, cut back on drinking, and avoided confrontation.

Eight months later, he was discharged. He was going home, back to Jeanette.

As the train carried him east from Michigan, Frank stared out the window, watching the landscape roll by in silence. His wallet was fat with Army savings, though he knew the money would disappear fast once he set things in motion.

The train jolted as it pulled into the station, snapping him out of his thoughts. Stepping onto the platform in his uniform, he noticed a few commuters nodding respectfully. He straightened his shoulders. His mother would have been proud.

But pride faded quickly. He wasn't sure how he'd face Jeanette — or her family — after everything.

Since she didn't know his exact arrival date, he figured he had time to ease back into civilian life. Jeanette still lived with her father. She had refused to move into his family home, and Frank hadn't blamed her. The bickering in his house had worsened since his mother passed. He needed a few days to regroup.

He stopped by his old friend's place.

"Hey Jimmy, I just got out last week. Thought I'd see my old drinking buddy." Frank grinned and held up a bottle of bourbon. The golden liquid caught the light.

Jimmy opened the door just wide enough to speak. "Beth doesn't allow hard liquor in the house," he said, glancing over his shoulder.

"You gotta be kidding me."

"I wish. She's pregnant again, and the baby's teething. We're running on fumes."

"Man, you've been busy."

Jimmy laughed, but his smile faded. "Another time, Frank."

The door closed. Frank stood there a moment, listening to the muffled sounds of children and laughter.

Four blocks later, he knocked on his father-in-law's door.

Giovanna opened it. Her expression changed the moment she saw him. "There's someone here to see you," she called toward the back room.

Jeanette entered and stopped cold. "Frank."

He smiled. "Aren't you happy to see me?" He stepped forward, arms open.

Jeanette didn't move. Her arms stayed pinned to her sides. Her expression was distant, hollow. "It's your fault. You killed my mother."

The words hit him like a slap. His chest sank as though all the air had left the room.

Giuseppe and Giovanna stood frozen in silence. No one had ever seen Jeanette like this.

"She doesn't mean that," Giuseppe said softly. "You can't blame him."

"But I do. If I had listened to her, she'd still be alive." Jeanette's voice cracked. "Now you're here to claim me? Go away, Frank. I never want to see you again."

Frank's eyes scanned the room, hoping someone would speak, defend him. But the only answer was the floor beneath their gaze.

He looked once more at his wife. She was unrecognizable. Then he turned and walked out the door.

Outside, the streetlamp cast a yellow glow over his car. Frank unscrewed the cap on his bottle and took a long swig. The bourbon was warm going down. Familiar. Comforting. Damning. By the time he'd emptied half, he was numb. The anger kept him upright, but he knew the truth. He had no one to blame but himself.

Inside, Jeanette sat at the kitchen table, her hands trembling.

"I'm sorry, Pop," she said at last. "But you always taught me to fight for what's right. And I don't think staying married to Frank is right. I've decided to divorce him."

She waited, expecting pushback. Divorce wasn't common among Sicilians, not even American ones.

Giuseppe barely raised an eyebrow.

"Did you hear me?"

"I heard you," he said. "Talk to David. He'll help you file. If you need money, I'll pay for it."

He paused, then added, "In the meantime, I'll talk to the church. Maybe we can get it annulled."

*****

Dressed in a dark blue suit, Giuseppe climbed the courthouse steps beside Jeanette. His shoes clicked against the stone as they ascended in silence.

"I'm sorry to bring shame to our family, Pop," she said softly, her eyes fixed on the doors ahead.

"Nonsense," he replied, patting her arm. "It's a new generation. Things are different from when I was young. I love you the same."

Jeanette nodded, grateful for his steady presence.

Inside the courtroom, her stomach twisted as she scanned the room, half-expecting Frank to appear. But he didn't. He hadn't filed an objection or even responded to the court summons.

The judge granted the divorce by default. It was over.

A strange emptiness settled in her chest—not regret, exactly, but the quiet sadness that comes when you finally close a painful chapter. She had never truly loved Frank, not the way she had loved Sonny.

"I'll never get married again," she whispered as they walked out of the building. "It's just you and me now, Pop."

Giuseppe smiled gently. "That's enough for me."

Back at home, reality set in. Jeanette needed a job. But what could she do?

Antonio and Mariella had offered her a place at the bakery, but she knew they couldn't afford another employee. They were only trying to help.

There was always the sewing factory around the corner — they were desperate for seamstresses to run the machines. But the thought of those sweltering sweatshops made her stomach turn. She remembered the clatter of needles, the smell of hot oil and fabric glue, the sticky heat of summer pressing down on your shoulders until it was hard to breathe.

She wouldn't last a week.

That night, she lay in bed with the covers pulled up to her chin. The room was dark except for the glow of the streetlamp filtering through the curtains. She closed her eyes and tried to picture her mother's face.

*What should I do, Mama?*

In her mind, Anna's lips moved.

*Go to Wall Street,* she whispered.

Jeanette opened her eyes, wide awake now.

Wall Street?

The words echoed in her mind — strange, unexpected, and somehow exactly right.

# Wall Street

Five months pregnant, Mariella tucked the blanket snugly around baby Janine and gently rocked the carriage. The infant fought to stay awake, but her eyelids soon drooped, and she went still. Mariella slipped a few slices of bread into the toaster and poured a cup of coffee for her father.

"I'm worried about Jeanette," Giuseppe said, cradling the mug in his hands. "She hasn't been the same since your mother passed. She barely comes out of her room. I had to force her to eat the spaghetti you brought over the other day. I don't know what we'd do without you."

"You know I'll always be here, Pop," Mariella said, rubbing her belly. "Once I have this baby, I'll step back from the bakery a bit. I can come by more often."

Soft singing drifted from the bedroom. A moment later, Jeanette emerged wearing a tailored red suit and matching pumps. Around her neck hung Anna's strand of pearls.

Giuseppe sat up straighter. "Good morning, Jeanette. It's good to see you up and dressed. Are you going somewhere?"

"I'm heading to Manhattan for a job interview," she said, adjusting her purse strap.

"A job? What kind?"

"They're hiring on Wall Street—clerical jobs. Some even offer training."

Mariella blinked. "Wall Street? That's for men."

"That's what *they* want you to think," Jeanette said. "But Phyllis has a friend who works there. They need receptionists, file clerks. It's a foot in the door."

Janine stirred and let out a cry. Mariella scooped her up and bounced her gently on her hip.

"Here, let me," Jeanette said, taking the baby in her arms. She cradled her niece and whispered lullabies until Janine quieted.

"You should go back to your husband," Mariella said softly. "Start a family. That's what you need."

Jeanette's smile faded. She handed the baby back.

"Just because you're happy baking cookies doesn't mean that's the answer for everyone."

Mariella looked stung. "I'm just saying—it's not going to be easy, working with all those men."

"Nothing worth doing ever is," Jeanette said. She kissed her father on the cheek and headed for the door, her heels clicking confidently against the floor.

\*\*\*\*\*

The idea of working in a male-dominated industry thrilled Jeanette.

She caught the subway at 79th Street and 18th Avenue and transferred at Lafayette to the number five train. Her red heels tapped nervously as she stood, crammed in with the morning crowd. Gripping the overhead strap, she swayed with the car's rhythm and adjusted her silk stockings, ensuring the back seams were perfectly straight. Before exiting at Wall Street, she smoothed her jacket and exhaled.

Morgan Guaranty Trust Company stood just a few blocks from the station. Inside the lobby, mirrors reflected the sleek leather furniture, making the space feel as if it were wrapped in water. She waited as the elevator creaked downward, stopping at each floor like a hesitant thought. When it finally opened, a pale man with a clipboard looked up.

"Ninth floor," she said.

He stared longer than she liked. Jeanette clutched her purse closer and kept her eyes forward.

The ninth floor buzzed with energy. Two long rows of desks faced the windows. At each one, sharply dressed men read newspapers, scribbled notes, or debated market trends in clipped, confident tones.

She ran a finger along the edge of an empty desk. The polish gleamed like glass.

"Can I help you?" A man in a charcoal suit stepped forward.

"Yes, I'm here for the receptionist position."

"You must be Jeanette."

"I was told to see Mr. Arnold."

"That's me," he said, offering a wolfish grin. His eyes scanned her from head to toe. "Nice legs."

Jeanette didn't flinch. "They get me where I want to go."

He barked a laugh. "Most women would have walked out by now. I like that you didn't. You'll hear worse than that around here—crude jokes, curses, innuendos. Any objections?"

"None," she said.

"Then you'll do just fine."

Mr. Arnold led her down the hall. Hanna will be finishing the week. She'll train you. You start on Monday. Nine to five, half-hour lunch. Twenty dollars a week."

A buzzer cut through the air. A voice over the intercom announced, *"The market is now open."*

The room exploded. Phones rang. Voices shouted. Brokers sprang into action.

Jeanette followed Arnold back to the reception area, this time noticing the thick glass wall that separated the floor from the front lobby. Behind the barrier, the suited men moved like agitated fish in a tank.

A tall, striking woman sat on a high stool. Her jet-black hair was pinned up with a large clip, and her almond eyes were rimmed in black liner. Her lips were bare—unusual, but elegant.

"Hanna, this is Jeanette, your replacement," Arnold said.

The woman stood, revealing a rounded belly. Jeanette understood instantly.

"It's nice to meet you, Mrs. Castaloni," she said.

"Relax, hon. Just Hanna. Everyone calls me that."

Arnold nodded and disappeared into his office.

"When's the baby due?" Jeanette asked.

"Not for four months, but I'm already showing," Hanna sighed, smoothing her blouse.

"Will you come back after the baby's born?"

"I wanted to. My mom offered to help. But Vincent—my husband—put his foot down. He's old-school Sicilian. Thinks a mother's place is in the home."

"I see," Jeanette said.

"Are you married?"

"Divorced."

A bell rang. Jeanette jumped.

Hanna grinned. "Don't worry—it just means one of the brokers closed a deal. They ring that stupid bell every time. You'll get used to it."

"I think it's exciting. I wish I were one of them, calling the shots."

"Nice dream, kid. But for now, let's get you answering the phones."

Jeanette caught on quickly. Within two hours, she had memorized the names and extensions of nine agents and recited the greeting with practiced ease.

At noon, the lunch bell rang, and the floor cleared.

"Where are they all going?" Jeanette asked.

"Upstairs. The men have their own break area with soft music and long lunches. We don't," Hanna said flatly. "Besides, someone has to answer the phones. Did you bring lunch?"

"No, I thought there'd be a cafeteria."

"There is. But you'll waste your whole break in line. Here—take half my sandwich. I can't stomach much these days."

"Thanks," Jeanette said, accepting the smaller half of the tuna on Wonder Bread.

After lunch, the floor came alive again. The same voice called out, *"Hit the phones, guys,"* and the brokers rushed back to their desks.

By 5:00, Jeanette was comfortable with the headset. Mr. Arnold returned and leaned over the counter.

"You have a lovely voice," he said. He turned to Hanna. "How'd our girl do?"

"Just fine," Hanna said with a smile.

Jeanette beamed. She floated down the street in the humid air, weightless.

Each morning after that, Jeanette arrived early, eager to prove herself. Within two months, everyone knew her name. Mr. Arnold raised her salary to twenty-four dollars a week.

That night, lying in bed, Jeanette stared at the ceiling. She thought of the singing career she gave up for Frank. On a whim, she ran to the closet and dug out an old purse. Inside, tucked in the lining, was a tattered business card.

Allen Goldberg – Talent Manager

She smiled.

Maybe the dream wasn't dead after all.

# Broadway Blues

In the morning, Jeanette gently smoothed the worn business card and taped its torn corner. The name still stood out in bold print: Allen Goldberg – Schultz Productions, W. 54th Street. She jotted down the address. It wasn't close enough for a lunch break visit, so she decided she'd go after work.

*Will the Broadway producer still remember me?*

That evening, Jeanette stood quietly at the back of a rehearsal theater, her heart quickening as she listened to the voices rising from the stage. There was a vibrancy to it—familiar yet distant, like hearing a melody from a former life.

Then she saw him.

Mr. Goldberg spotted her in the shadows and broke into a warm smile. During a break, he came down the aisle.

"Jeanette," he said, eyes twinkling. "You've grown into a fine woman. I'm glad you came to see me."

"I wasn't sure you'd remember me."

"Oh, I never forget a pretty face."

Jeanette hesitated, then said, "I know it's been a while, but you once heard me sing. You said I had talent. I'd still like to audition—if that's all right."

"I'm sure we can arrange something," he said, his eyes drifting lower than her face. "Come up to my office. We can talk privately."

Jeanette stiffened. "I only have a few minutes. I need to catch the train back to Brooklyn."

"Just a quick chat," he coaxed, already turning toward a staircase beside the stage.

She followed him, unsure. At the top was a small dressing room cluttered with costumes, wigs, and an old vanity lined with makeup jars and crumpled tissues. Goldberg closed the door behind them and locked it.

Jeanette's chest tightened. She took a step back.

"You've got potential," he said softly, drawing closer. "You play your cards right, you might have a whole new career."

She felt his breath too close to her ear. Her body tensed.

"I have to go," she said, stepping away quickly.

He didn't move. His smirk deepened.

Jeanette turned, fumbled with the lock, and yanked the door open. Her heels echoed down the stairwell as she rushed out of the theater and into the street, gulping cool night air.

The city lights blurred as tears welled in her eyes — not from fear, but from the heartbreak of a dream soured.

No, she wouldn't be a singer on Broadway.

Maybe that had always been a wishful dream — one meant to fade. As she stood beneath the buzzing glow of the marquee, she thought she heard her mother's voice again, soft and steady:

*"You don't need the stage to shine. You have your own light."*

***** 

Giuseppe walked up 18th Avenue toward the park where he used to play pinochle on the old concrete tables beneath the shade trees. But today, the familiar rhythm of the neighborhood was gone. Construction workers swarmed the park, tearing up pavement to fix a broken water line. The bone-rattling chatter of pneumatic drills echoed through the streets, drowning out the laughter of children.

He paused, watching them work, his heart heavy.

Since the death of his beloved Anna, nothing felt the same. The house, once filled with her gentle humming and the clatter of pots, had fallen silent. Her absence stole the joy from their home, leaving only shadows and stillness.

Giuseppe felt as if he had aged overnight. His steps had grown slower. His back, more stooped. He sat alone on a bench, surrounded by the noise of the city, yet feeling utterly disconnected from it. For the first time in years, he longed for Sicily — not just in the fond way of memories, but with a yearning deep in his bones.

When he returned home, Jeanette was in the kitchen, drying dishes.

"I miss my Sciacca," he said quietly, lowering himself into a chair. "The sea, the hills... and the way life used to be. I miss my sister, Maria. Her children must be grown by now. I should have gone back sooner."

Jeanette set the dish towel down and looked at him, unsure how to answer. She'd never seen her father so lost, so far away in thought.

That night, as she drifted to sleep, she heard her mother's voice—clear, calm, and close.

*"Go to Sciacca."*

***** 

Jeanette loved her job. She didn't mind leaving the house early each morning. The train ride into the city gave her a pocket of peace—a time to reflect, to dream. Over the next few months, her responsibilities expanded, and with them came a pay raise. Every extra dollar went straight into the *Sciacca can*—the old tin she and Giuseppe had labeled years ago with a strip of masking tape and a dream.

Four months later, the can was full—just enough for two round-trip tickets to Sicily.

In the evenings, Jeanette studied the island's map, tracing her fingers along the jagged coastline, imagining cobblestoned streets and the scent of sea salt in the air. For years, she had envisioned it. Now, the dream was coming to life.

She requested her vacation, two weeks in the spring, before the office scramble for summer holidays began. Easter felt right. The season of resurrection. It seemed like the perfect time to return to the land her family came from.

That afternoon, she finished her work and dashed out of the office, her heels clicking on the pavement as she hurried to the travel agency before it closed. The airline tickets were waiting for her, neatly tucked in a paper envelope. Everything was set—except the passports, which they were finalizing that week.

It would be the first time on a plane for both of them. Giuseppe had crossed the ocean by ship, a long, grueling voyage that took two weeks. Now they'd reach Sicily in just nine hours on United Airlines. Jeanette could hardly believe it.

Two months earlier, she had written to her great-aunt in Sciacca, hoping someone in the old country still remembered them. But the silence that followed made her wonder if the letter had been lost—or worse, if her aunt had passed away.

Then one day, the doorbell rang. It was the mailman.

"This letter's from Sicily," he said, holding it carefully. "Thought you'd want it hand-delivered."

"Oh—thank you," Jeanette said, heart racing. She took it to her room, sat on the edge of her bed, and held the envelope like it were made of gold. The paper was soft and worn from its long journey. Her fingers trembled as she broke the seal and began to read.

Dear Jeanette,
I received your letter two weeks ago, but I had to wait for my son to help me write back

since my English isn't very good. It has been many years since I've seen my brother. I have cried many tears, missing him. Your letter brought me such joy—I never thought I would hear from him again. The thought of him coming home feels like a dream.

My house is small, but you and my brother are welcome to take my room. Please write and let me know when you are planning to come.

I look forward to seeing you both very soon.

With love,

*Tua Zia Maria*


Included in the envelope was a photograph of Maria with her husband and their nine children—eight boys and one girl.

"Pop, look what I have," Jeanette called out as the aroma of frying fish drifted from the kitchen.

Giuseppe turned from the stove, slipping off his apron and wiping his hands on a dish towel. "What is it, Jeanette?"

She held out the photograph. He took it with care, staring intently. The longer he looked, the more his expression changed—until the light of recognition sparkled in his eyes.

"Where did you get this?"

"Your sister Maria sent it. I wrote her a letter, and she wrote back. We're going to see her—just you and me."

He blinked, still processing. "To Sicily?"

Jeanette laughed. "Yes, Pop. We're going to Sciacca to see Maria."

He shook his head in disbelief. "That's not exactly around the corner, you know."

"I have our tickets right here." She pulled the envelope from her purse.

"Tickets? Where did you get the money for them?"

"Don't you remember the Sciacca fund we started when I was a little girl?"

He looked up slowly. "Yes... but..."

"I've been adding to it all these years. There's enough now for both of us. We're going home."

He seemed at a loss for words. "What about your job?"

"I took a two-week vacation."

"How will we get to La Guardia?"

"Antonio's going to drive us. Everything is taken care of. Pop, this trip is everything we talked about."

Giuseppe looked down at the photo again. His voice softened to a whisper. "Sciacca..." Then louder, with joy in his tone, "Sciacca!"

# Sciacca Roots

Antonio honked the horn, and Jeanette opened the front                                           door.
"We'll only be a minute. I have to help Pop with his bag," she called out.

Mariella's daughters could hardly contain their excitement. They had never been to an airport before. Jeanette climbed into the back seat, squeezing in next to her father, Giuseppe.

"I wish I were going with you two," Mariella said wistfully.
"We'll take plenty of pictures," Jeanette promised, clutching her Brownie camera.

At the airport, they checked their suitcases and received their boarding passes. Janine watched wide-eyed as the luggage vanished on the conveyor belt into the plane. A large truck pulled up beside the aircraft and extended a ramp to load meal trays for the flight.

As boarding time neared, two men in blue uniforms approached the gate — one the pilot, the other the co-pilot. Noticing the young girl's awestruck stare, the pilot smiled and reached into his pocket. He pulled out a wing pin and gently fastened it to her shirt.

"What does it say, Daddy?" she asked. "United Airlines."

"Wow!" She beamed and touched it with her finger. "Look, Grandpa — I have wings!"

"You sure do, Angel," Giuseppe said with a proud smile.

Jeanette and Giuseppe embraced the family one last time before heading through the gate. At the top of the stairs leading to the plane, they turned and waved goodbye.

Onboard, a stewardess welcomed them and showed them to their seats.

"Is this your first time flying?" she asked.

"Yes," Jeanette replied, casting a glance at her father. He looked pale and tense.

The stewardess handed them each a small paper bag. "Just in case," she said with a kind smile.

"Everything's going to be fine, Pop," Jeanette said, patting his hand.

"This is a newer model — much sleeker and quieter than the old planes."

"I would've preferred taking the ship," he grumbled.

"The ship would've taken too long."

"Yeah, I suppose you're right… But I'll never forget the day I arrived in America. Aunt Caterina and Uncle Aldo were with me on the deck. It was a cloudy day, but the Statue of Liberty was just visible through the haze. I'd never seen anything so beautiful, shrouded in soft, gray rain."

The propellers began to spin, rattling the plane as it taxied into position. When the runway cleared, the aircraft surged forward, lifting off with a jolt that pushed them back into their seats.

Jeanette gazed out the window, watching the tall buildings of New York fall away beneath drifting clouds until they disappeared completely. She reclined her seat and smiled.

After a stopover in Rome, they finally touched down in Palermo.

"There! You see? That wasn't so bad," Jeanette said, turning to her father. "We'll be in your hometown in just a couple of hours."

They took a shuttle to the central station and had an hour to spare before the bus to Sciacca departed.

"Let's eat at that little café on the corner," Giuseppe said. "I ate there once as a boy."

Jeanette took his arm, and they walked slowly, soaking in the sights and sounds of Sicily. The people moved at a relaxed pace, so different from the bustling urgency of Brooklyn, where tempers ran hot, and everyone seemed in a rush.

As the bus wound through the hills, Giuseppe pointed out farms and vineyards he remembered from his youth. The ride took about two hours.

A cab was waiting at the terminal. The driver, a reed-thin man in his late fifties, wore a Capo cap pulled low over his eyes and barely acknowledged them — until Giuseppe greeted him in Sicilian. The driver's expression changed instantly, and they launched into an animated conversation.

Jeanette caught only fragments, but she understood enough. The driver asked, *"Chi è la tua famiglia?"—Who is your family?* When Giuseppe mentioned his sister's name, the man smiled warmly. *"Sì, sì. La conosco."* — *Yes, I know her.* He offered to drive them to her home.

"I never thought I'd stand on Sicilian soil again," Giuseppe said softly. "It feels like a dream."

He was eager to go straight to his sister's house, but Jeanette noticed how weary he looked. His beard was coarse, and travel had taken a toll. "No, Pop. Let's go to the hotel first. I'll give you a shave, and you can rest for a while." "That sounds good. I'd like to freshen up before I see Maria."

The cab pulled up to a cozy bed-and-breakfast a few blocks from the piazza. The driver nodded and shut off the engine. Together, they retrieved their luggage from the trunk.

Their apartment was on the fourth floor, but thankfully, there was a lift. As Jeanette opened the door, a musty scent greeted them. She quickly pulled back the curtains and opened the windows, letting the fresh sea breeze sweep in and scrub away the stale air.

The kitchen was small, but the dining area overlooked the marina. A warm Mediterranean wind flowed through the open balcony doors.

"This is heaven, Pop."

After a shower and a shave, Giuseppe looked like a new man, refreshed and ten years younger. Jeanette thought he had never looked more handsome. Proudly, she took his arm.

Maria's house was just four blocks away, in the same neighborhood where she and Giuseppe had grown up. He led the way up a long incline, turned left, and climbed a steep set of stairs. At the top, breathless, he paused to rest. Jeanette helped him sit on a low stone wall.

They continued into a courtyard, where children played, and mothers leaned over balconies.

"*Chi stai cercando?*" a woman called down. "*Sto cercando mia sorella, Maria Aruffo,*" Giuseppe answered in dialect.

"*Ahh… sorella!*" she said, pointing toward a gated patio.

"Grazie," Giuseppe replied, pressing the small button above the mailbox.

Moments later, a young man stepped out. "*Posso aiutarla?*"

"*Sto cercando mia sorella,*" Giuseppe said. "*Io sono Giuseppe.*"

Suddenly, a woman rushed out onto the patio. Her face went pale.

"Giuseppe!" she gasped. "Giuseppe! Mio fratello dall'America!"

The gate opened, and years of separation melted away in an instant.

"This is my son, Vincenzo," Maria said, hugging Giuseppe tightly.

"Buongiorno. I'm just here for lunch, but I need to return to the hospital soon," he said politely.

"He's a nurse. So is my other son, Giuseppe."

"Giuseppe?"

"Yes, I named him after you, dear *fratello*."

"I'm honored."

"And my oldest, Paolo, is named after our father."

*****

As word spread about the American brothers' return to Sicily, Maria's small kitchen quickly filled with voices and laughter. Her children gathered one by one, eager to meet the uncle they'd heard about since childhood. Giuseppe beamed as he listened to their stories, surrounded by a sea of smiling faces.

All the boys were fishermen — except for Giuseppe and Vincenzo, named after Jeanette's father and uncle. They were nurses, working long shifts at the local hospital.

Maria's husband, Salvatore, had passed away the year before. Giuseppe bowed his head. "I'm sorry I never got the chance to meet him."

At the stove, Brigida helped her mother prepare dinner, reminding Jeanette of scenes from her own childhood — her Nonna and Mariella standing shoulder to shoulder, stirring pots, their arms brushing as they worked in sync.

The last to arrive was Maria's youngest, Accursio, accompanied by a friend.

"Accursio, come greet your Uncle Giuseppe," Maria said. "The one I've told you so much about."

They embraced warmly. "It's good to meet you," Accursio said. "My mother has shared so many stories about when you were kids. She's missed you and your sister, Caterina. Is she with you?"

Giuseppe's voice softened. "*Mi dispiace*. Caterina passed away a few years ago."

Tears welled in Maria's eyes. "*La mia sorella*. I miss her so much."

"Did she have children?" Accursio asked gently.

"One son—Joseph. That's the American version of Giuseppe. He and his wife started a Christmas tree business. I think it's going to do well."

Maria placed a hand on Jeanette's shoulder. "This is your cousin, Jeanette."

"*Ciao, cugina!*" Accursio exclaimed, sweeping Jeanette into a bear hug.

His friend nudged him.

"Oh! I'm sorry," Accursio said. "This is my friend Francesco. He's an exporter of fine olive oil in Milan."

"Nice to meet you," Jeanette said politely. Francesco was striking—his dark hair threaded with silver, giving him a distinguished look. His tailored suit hinted at a taste for the finer things.

"The pleasure is mine," he said, lifting Jeanette's hand to his lips. She blushed, her eyes drawn to his bright blue gaze, his strong jawline, and Roman nose. Something about him stirred her—a quiet thrill at the possibility of something more.

Aunt Maria stood at the stove, tending to sizzling sausages and a pot of boiling pasta. Brigida set the table with practiced grace. On one end sat a dish of lemons and crusty bread, on the other, bowls of fresh basil and parsley. In the center: a mound of golden breadcrumbs.

"You make your own breadcrumbs?" Jeanette asked, impressed.

"Yes, of course. And we grow all our spices. The lemons are from our own tree. My son will pick oranges from the orchard for dessert."

Jeanette looked around the kitchen. It was modest, even a little worn, but the rich smells from the stove transformed it into something more. It felt like home.

Brigida placed a large bowl of olives on the table. "*Mangia!*"

Jeanette popped one into her mouth. "These are delicious! Don't tell me — you grow them too?"

Maria chuckled. "Naturally. My son Vincenzo runs a small farm. We're getting ready for harvest soon. That's actually why Francesco is here in Sciacca — he's helping us export our olive oil. Maybe we'll take you to see the orchard after Pasquale."

"I'd love that," Giuseppe said.

Francesco took the seat beside Jeanette, and as the meal unfolded, so did a conversation. He spoke English fluently, and by dessert, the two were deep in discussion. He offered to be her guide around the city.

Jeanette accepted.

Francesco assured Giuseppe that he'd return her safely to the hotel at a reasonable hour.

Their first stop was the marina. They watched local fishermen cast lines into the water, catching dinner in small silver buckets. Then he drove her to his favorite gelateria for a cold, creamy treat.

"You speak English so well," Jeanette said as they walked with their cones.

"I try. It's necessary in business. But there are still many words I don't understand."

"I'm learning Italian. I want to be fluent."

"Then we'll teach each other." He smiled.

They found a table outside and talked as the sky turned orange and gold. Culture, politics, literature, music — they touched on everything. Francesco asked about Brooklyn: its people, weather, and food.

Jeanette told him about the Chinese takeout, the clam bars, and, of course, the Italian food.

"We never went to Italian restaurants, though," she said. "We cooked our own. Everyone thinks their sauce is the best." She laughed. "But I do go out for pizza. Brooklyn has some of the best pies in New York."

"I imagine. Pizza isn't as common here as it is in Naples," he said. Naples is the pizza capital of the world. You might find your meatballs there, too. Here in Sicily, we eat a lot of fish."

Jeanette laughed. "Then this must be the squid capital of the world."

Francesco laughed with her, then paid the check. "May I see you again tomorrow?"

"Yes," she said softly. "I'd like that."

As they walked back to the car, he offered his arm. She took it.

They passed the piazza just as flocks of small brown birds swept into the treetops in rhythmic waves.

"Look at them," Jeanette said. "They're beautiful."

"It's a ritual," he explained. "Every night at dusk, they come to sleep. At sunrise, they fly to the marina in search of food."

Jeanette felt as if she were still in a dream. But it ended too soon when Francesco pulled up in front of her hotel. She looked up at the window. The lights weren't on. Her father was already asleep.

"I'll pick you up tomorrow. Around ten," Francesco said.

He kissed her hand again, and this time, she didn't blush. She smiled.

*****

The next morning, Jeanette rose early and stepped out onto the balcony. A soft breeze carried the scent of salt and seaweed as she watched the fishing boats chug out into the open water, their lights still flickering in the early dawn. Below, the town was just beginning to stir.

Giuseppe soon joined her, coffee in hand, his face peaceful, almost boyish in the morning light.

"You look younger, Pop," Jeanette said, smiling. "This town agrees with you."

He gave a soft chuckle and leaned on the railing beside her. "Maybe it's being home again."

He pointed toward the horizon. "My father's boat used to head out from that harbor. He'd be gone for weeks, sometimes a month."

Jeanette tried to picture it: a wooden vessel cutting through the Mediterranean, her grandfather at the helm, and her grandmother standing at the edge of the rocky shore, watching it disappear.

"How did Nonna manage while he was gone?"

Giuseppe's eyes grew distant. "The wives of fishermen wore black while their husbands were at sea. It was a tradition. A sign of respect... and a reminder that any voyage might end in widowhood."

"Do you remember those times, Pop?"

He nodded. "Sometimes, we thought he'd been lost. No word, no sign. And then — out of the clear blue sky — he'd walk through the door, smelling like salt and dead fish. We hugged him so tight, even though he was slimy from head to toe."

He fell silent, eyes fixed on the sea. Memories pulled him somewhere far away.

A sharp ring sounded from the street below. Francesco had arrived.

Jeanette kissed her father's cheek. "Will you be all right on your own?"

"Of course," Giuseppe said, waving her off. "I know this town like the back of my hand. I'll probably wander to the piazza and catch up with some old friends. Maybe even squeeze in a game of bocce."

She gave his hand a squeeze and hurried downstairs.

Francesco stood beside his little Fiat, smiling. "Buongiorno, bella. Ready for the best pizza in Sciacca?"

"Absolutely," she grinned. "Where are we going?"

"To a hidden gem up in the hills of San Calogero. It's called *Grande Valle Pizza*. Most tourists never find it — it's off the beaten path."

The Fiat groaned as it climbed the winding roads. At the top, nestled in the countryside, stood a large, plain building that looked more like a warehouse than a restaurant. Yet the parking lot was packed.

Inside, the air was warm and filled with the aroma of wood-fired dough. Flames danced in brick ovens lining one wall, and the hum of conversation filled the massive dining hall. Pizzas flew in and out of the ovens like clockwork.

"It's like a pizza factory," Jeanette said in amazement, watching the pizzaiolo expertly use the peel to slide pies in and out of the fire.

"They come from miles around," Francesco said proudly.

Jeanette's mouth watered as servers rushed past with pies bubbling with cheese and layered with eggplant, sausage, or anchovies. When they arrived, a plump green olive crowned the center.

She took a bite. The crust was smoky and crisp, the sauce bright with tomato and herbs. "This is the best pizza I've ever had," she said. "Better than Brooklyn. Don't tell anyone I said that."

Francesco laughed.

As they drove down the hillside, a soft spring rain fell — but the sun still shone brightly.

"It's a sun shower," Jeanette said. "We might see a rainbow."

They strolled through the piazza, the cobblestones slick and gleaming. Francesco reached for her hand. At first, it was casual, then natural. Jeanette felt her heart begin to race. She looked up at him, met his eyes, and everything else fell away.

He cupped her face in his hands and kissed her.

Children darted around them, laughing, caught in their own world of games. But for Jeanette, time had stopped.

Later, they watched the sun melt into the horizon from the marina. The boats bobbed gently in their slips, the sky streaked in hues of orange and rose.

It was another perfect day.

# Market

The next day, Francesco came to pick up Jeanette. Giuseppe peeked out the window just in time to see him open the passenger door with a gentleman's grace, then jog to the driver's side as the car behind him blared its horn. He smiled. Jeanette hadn't looked this happy since she lost her first love, Sonny.

"Where are you taking me today?" Jeanette asked with a playful smile as she buckled her seatbelt.

"Since it's Saturday," Francesco replied, brushing her cheek with his fingers, "I thought I'd take you to the market."

"The supermarket?"

He laughed. "No, *sciocchina*. The outdoor market. Every Saturday, local farmers set up tents to sell vegetables. But it's grown. Now you'll find cheese, olives, fish, meat from the butcher... even clothing and housewares. It's like a festival. You'll love it."

They drove across town, passing the cemetery and clusters of apartment buildings. Francesco parked near a narrow street and joined the crowd carrying empty sacks, while others passed them in the opposite direction with bags brimming with *cibo* and fresh goods. The scent of grilled meat and seafood wafted through the air. Fish sizzled on flat-top grills; whole chickens and legs of lamb rotated slowly on open spits.

The market stretched for blocks. Vegetable stands burst with blood-red tomatoes, glossy eggplants, and bundles of leafy greens. Vendors handed out samples: marinated artichokes, brined garlic, tender bites of grilled meat, and olives so rich they tasted like the earth. Sharing this with Francesco made it all the more magical.

They strolled arm in arm until they reached a cheese stall manned by a slender man and his young son. The older vendor greeted Francesco with a hug, exchanging lively words in Sicilian dialect. Jeanette was surprised by how many people knew him — and how warmly they greeted him.

The cheesemonger turned to her and smiled, as if discovering a secret. Before they left, he handed each of them a spoonful of fresh ricotta.

"Oh, my goodness," Jeanette said. "It's melting in my mouth."

"If you think that's good, you should've tasted my mother's. She and my aunt spent Saturdays making fresh ricotta and pasta. They hung it all over the house to dry. The best part was Sunday — everyone around the table, laughing, telling stories. I swear laughter makes food taste better."

Jeanette nodded. "I know what you mean. When my mom was alive, Sunday meant a big pot of sauce filled with meatballs. We'd sit at the table with our forks ready. But it wasn't just the food — it was being together. I used to sit next to my cousin Sonny. We were very close."

She paused, her gaze softening as she drifted into memory, wondering if Sonny had lived a happy life. She hoped so.

After a chilled fruit cup, they left the market and wandered toward the piazza. They passed the Basilica just as a wedding was beginning.

"Oh, I love weddings!" Jeanette said. "Can we take a peek?"

"Of course," Francesco replied. "I don't think the bride or groom would mind."

They stepped inside, blessing themselves with holy water, and slipped into the last pew. The organ swelled with Wagner's Bridal Chorus. The bride entered in a stunning gown with a train so long it stretched to the church doors. Ten attendants — five on each side — carefully guided the flowing fabric. Even the flower girls were dressed in white, scattering rose petals along the silk runner that led to the altar.

Jeanette reached for Francesco's hand and gazed into his eyes, intoxicated by the scent of flowers and the soft music of *Ave Maria* echoing from the organ. Her heart swelled with joy.

When Mendelssohn's Wedding March began, the newlyweds walked past their pew, the bride smiling at Jeanette as they stepped out into a shower of confetti. Jeanette noted the absence of rice — traditionally thrown for fertility — but the moment felt just as meaningful.

"Are you hungry for lunch?" Francesco asked.

"I had a small breakfast with Pop, but that was hours ago."

"Perfect. There's a seafood place near the marina. The owners are friends. They make the best *Zuppa di Pesce* in Sciacca."

At the restaurant, they sat by a window overlooking the boats and the flock of seagulls circling for scraps. Jeanette dipped crusty bread into golden olive oil, nibbling slowly. The fish soup was rich and fragrant, layered with saffron and fresh herbs.

"It's the best I've ever had," she whispered to herself—better even than her father's, though she'd never tell him that.

After two glasses of wine, Jeanette felt light and dreamy. They wandered back through the piazza toward the car and spotted the same bride and groom, now posing for photographs. Jeanette pulled out her Brownie camera and snapped a few candid shots.

"What should we do now?" she asked.

Francesco thought for a moment. "I know. Let's visit Luna Castle."

"A real castle?"

"Yes. It belonged to the Luna family—Guglielmo Peralta built it in 1380. There was a bloody feud with the Perollo family, a rival noble family. It all started when Guglielmo's daughter, Margherita, was jilted by Giovanni Perollo. Her cousin, Sigismondo Luna, launched an attack. Giacomo Perollo was killed, his body dragged through the city behind a horse. The feud lasted more than a hundred years."

When they arrived, they purchased two tickets and walked through the stone gates. The fortress bore the weight of its centuries. Worn walls enclosed the grounds, and narrow slits once used for archers lined the perimeter.

"Are these windows?" Jeanette asked, peeking through one.

"No. They were for weapons — to fire on ships as they approached."

She studied the sea beyond, trying to picture the ships coming into view, the guards preparing for battle.

Inside, they explored a small museum filled with preserved weapons, suits of armor, and faded portraits of kings, queens, and noble children. On the stone floor, deep pits were covered with iron grates.

"What are these?" she asked.

"Prison cells," Francesco said softly.

Jeanette shivered, then turned to study the painted faces on the walls — their elegant clothes and proud expressions the only remnants of lives once lived behind these cold, echoing walls.

"Thank you for bringing me here," she said. "It's been a beautiful day. But I should get back and check on my father."

"Of course," he said, offering his arm.

As they drove back through the glowing streets of early evening, Francesco glanced at her. "I'd love to see you again."

"Tomorrow is Easter," Jeanette said. "I'll be with my family. But maybe Monday?"

"Perfect. Monday is *Pasquetta*—the day after Easter. It's a holiday here. Most people have a barbecue or go for a picnic. Maybe we can go to the beach."

"That sounds lovely," Jeanette said. She kissed him on the cheek before stepping out of the car.

Upstairs, Giuseppe noticed something in his daughter's expression.

"What's wrong, Jeanette?"

She sat beside him. "I'm afraid, Pop. What if I fall in love with Francesco?"

Giuseppe reached for her hand. "If you do, and he makes you happy... then let yourself be happy. It's okay to move on."

That night, Jeanette lay awake, listening to the waves crash against the shore. She thought of Frank—how she'd once mistaken control for love. She thought of Sonny and how his face had grown blurry in her memory.

But when she closed her eyes, she saw Francesco—his voice, his kindness, his smile.

Was she ready to open her heart again?

Maybe.

Just maybe.

# Pasquale

Since their house was large enough to accommodate everyone, Calogero and his wife, Giuseppina, hosted Easter dinner. A long table stretched from one side of the room to the other, set with care for the joyful gathering.

Their children, Santo and Antonia, took to Jeanette immediately, peppering her with questions about life in America. One by one, Maria's children arrived, each accompanied by spouses and little ones. If Jeanette thought she had a big family in Brooklyn, it was nothing compared to the sprawling web of relatives in Sciacca. She could hardly keep up with all the names — Accursio, Paolo, Lorenzo, Antonino, Calogero, Vincenzo, Giuseppe, Salvatore, Giovanni — and those were just the boys.

Many of their children shared the same names, making it even harder to keep track. The girls' names, too, were often variations: Giuseppina, Antonina, Accursia, Vincenza, Giovanna — plus plenty of Marias and Annas. Brigida was easy to remember; she was Maria's only daughter. Her own daughter, Angela, played with the younger cousins.

The kitchen buzzed with activity as the women tied aprons around their waists and worked side by side, their hands dancing across pots and pans. Maria, for once, didn't cook—she chose instead to enjoy her brother's company. She insisted Giuseppe sit at the head of the table, her usual seat, while she sat to his right and Jeanette to his left.

"Do you remember when we were children?" Giuseppe asked, grinning. "We had to go to school every day. I hated it."

Maria laughed. "Oh, I remember. You found every excuse to skip. I was jealous that you got to go work with Papa on the boat while I had to sit in class."

"I thought you *liked* school." He turned to her sons. "Your mother was the smart one. Never once got hit with the ruler."

"No," Maria said, chuckling, "but Caterina sure did. Our sister was wild. The nuns didn't know what to do with her. Sister Agnes used to pace the classroom with her hands folded into her sleeves. She had a ruler hidden in there. If she caught someone daydreaming, she'd creep up in silence."

"And Caterina would just stare her down," Giuseppe added. "Until the nun whipped out that ruler and snapped, 'Hold out your hand, young lady.'"

"She obeyed," Maria said, laughing, "but always pulled her hand back just in time—until one day, she didn't. *Whack, whack, whack.* She never cried."

Everyone roared with laughter. The room felt as loud and lively as any family gathering back home in Brooklyn. Sicilian dialect flew through the air. Jeanette was glad she had paid attention to her father when he spoke to his friends at the park, especially when her mother, Anna, had frowned at it. Now, words she'd heard all her life returned to her like old friends.

The adults sipped Moscato wine from Calogero's vineyard, a rare red blend of Schiava and Muscat of Alexandria. Children ran in and out of the room, teasing, laughing, chasing one another. The older boys tried to impress their teenage cousins, while the girls huddled together, whispering and giggling about who was the cutest.

Even before the artichokes reached the table, the kids were tugging at the sautéed leaves, sliding the tender hearts into their mouths. Unlike the American tradition of a separate kids' table, everyone here dined together.

Most of the dishes were unfamiliar to Jeanette, but her adventurous palate welcomed each one. She thought back to sitting on her father's lap as a little girl, eating clams in garlic sauce and salty sardines, eyes and all. Her mother had been a good cook, but she leaned more American in her style of cuisine. Fish was Giuseppe's domain, and even then, it was usually squid, whole snapper, or fish heads for chowder. Shrimp was a rarity.

She tasted the shrimp in a creamy artichoke sauce and felt as if she were in heaven.

A massive pan of *Pasta con le Sarde* — a classic Sicilian dish with Arabic origins — came out next. For those who didn't care for sardines, a rich cheese pasta was served as well. A bowl of fried breadcrumbs made its way around the table. Jeanette sprinkled some onto her pasta, remembering her father's explanation that it symbolized the sawdust of St. Joseph, the carpenter. Still, she always thought it made the dish a little too dry.

Though fish was the mainstay of most meals in Sciacca, Easter called for lamb — *agnello*. Frank's family, being from Naples, had also eaten lamb, though they considered the head a delicacy. He once told her that, as a child, he avoided the eyes, afraid of leaving the lamb "blind." She sighed. If Frank hadn't buried his gentle heart in alcohol, he might've been a good husband. It was time to leave that in the past.

Roasted lamb with rosemary and potatoes was placed on the table, along with side dishes featuring eggs — symbols of rebirth. Even the bread had dyed eggs braided into it, something Jeanette had always thought was a Brooklyn bakery tradition. It amazed her to see how deeply her Sicilian roots had shaped her life, even when she hadn't realized it.

Instead of Easter baskets, the children were handed oversized chocolate eggs wrapped in gleaming foil. Each egg held a surprise toy inside.

Just when Jeanette thought she couldn't eat another bite, the aroma of espresso drifted from the kitchen, and the desserts appeared, one by one.

A stunning *cassata*, a glossy ricotta pie topped with glazed strawberries and kiwi, crumbly coffee cake, powdered pastries, and a plain yellow sponge cake for dunking in espresso. But Jeanette had her eye on the showstopper: a rich chocolate ganache cake filled with pistachio mousse. She and her father had picked it up at the bakery earlier that week. It was an indulgence, but today was a rare blessing — Easter, surrounded by family.

Accursio sat beside her, eager to practice his English. He had studied it in school and was happy to have someone to speak with. Of all her cousins, he was closest to her age and the most handsome. His dark brown hair curled slightly in front of his eyes. He looked so much like Sonny, it made her heart ache. They could've been brothers.

She sighed, wondering if Sonny would've enjoyed meeting their family here. She was sure he would have.

She looked over at her father, who was showing a group of children how to peel an orange using only a spoon. The fruit was so fresh that it still had its leaves. The kids crowded around him, enchanted.

As the evening wore on, Jeanette noticed the weariness in her father's eyes. She suggested it was time to head back to the hotel. They had planned to walk, but Salvatore and his wife — another Angela — were also leaving and insisted on giving them a ride. With six children between them, they packed up like a caravan.

Giuseppe and Jeanette kissed everyone goodbye. Maria invited them to the country house for *Pasquetta*, but Jeanette had already made plans with Francesco. She promised to visit again for lunch later in the week.

*****

Bright and early Monday morning, a knock came at the door.

Jeanette, flushed with happiness, sprang up to answer it. Francesco stood there smiling, holding a picnic basket and two rolled towels under his arm.

"Where are you two off to today?" Giuseppe asked from his chair by the window.

"I'm taking your daughter to the beach for a picnic," Francesco said with a grin.

"Oh yes — it's *Pasquetta*," Jeanette said. "Why don't you come with us?"

"You lovebirds don't need an old man tagging along," Giuseppe replied, waving a hand. "Besides, I promised Maria I'd spend the day at the country house with the family."

"Would you like a ride to her place?" Francesco offered.

"No, thank you. I think I'll walk — stretch these old legs."

"Take your cane, Pop," Jeanette reminded him.

"I will. Funny thing is, I don't seem to need it as much here. It's like my body remembers this place."

Jeanette hugged him tightly. "I'll see you back at the hotel later."

The drive took about an hour, winding through golden hills and clusters of olive trees until they reached a hidden cove. It felt like a secret — secluded, serene, with crystal-blue water, soft white sand, and a single palm tree casting shade just for them.

Francesco laid out a blanket, opened the basket, and poured wine into real glasses. He had packed aged cheeses, cured meats, crusty bread, and sun-dried tomatoes. Jeanette couldn't stop smiling. Everything about the day felt perfect—like something out of a dream.

They talked for hours, sharing stories, memories, and little pieces of their pasts they hadn't yet revealed. They swam in the clear sea, then dried off under the tree, letting the sun warm their skin.

Jeanette wasn't sure what made her so giddy—the wine or the joy of being with Francesco. She felt free, light, almost young again.

As the sun began to set, a cool breeze swept over the cove. Jeanette shivered. Francesco slipped off his jacket and placed it gently over her shoulders before pulling her close. She leaned into him, unwilling to let the moment end.

"I can't believe how fast the days have gone by," she said softly. "It feels like I just got here. I only have two more left... and I don't want to leave."

"Then we'll make the most of them," he said. "Have you ever heard of the enchanted garden—*Il Giardino Incantato*?"

"No. Is it a botanical garden?"

Francesco laughed. "Not quite. It's a garden of heads."

"Heads?" she repeated, confused.

"Yes. It was created by Filippo Bentivegna, a very eccentric man. He made his fortune in America and came back to Sciacca to live in solitude. He bought land, carved caves into the hillside, and sculpted hundreds of heads, their faces etched into stone, into trees. The locals called him *Il Signore delle Grotte* — the Lord of the Caves."

"Did he ever marry?"

"No. He lived alone until the end."

Jeanette shivered again, but not from the cold this time. "How bizarre."

They pulled up in front of the hotel. Jeanette glanced up and saw the light on in their room — Giuseppe was home, safe and warm.

Just as she reached for the door handle, Francesco gently pulled her back. He kissed her, soft and lingering.

"I'm falling in love with you, Jeanette," he whispered.

Her heart swelled. She smiled, eyes shining, and kissed him again. "I'll see you tomorrow."

Upstairs, Giuseppe was reading in bed. When Jeanette entered, he looked up and studied her face.

"You look like a woman in love," he said with a knowing smile. "So… I take it you and Francesco had a nice day at the beach."

"Oh, yes," Jeanette said dreamily, kicking off her shoes. "He's the most wonderful man. And tomorrow, he's taking me to a garden — a garden of heads."

Giuseppe chuckled softly. "Yes. I know it well."

# Enchantment

Jeanette inhaled the comforting scent of cigars as she slipped into Francesco's car. It mingled with the subtle aroma of espresso on his breath as he leaned in and greeted her with a warm kiss.

"Are you ready to experience something special today?" he asked.

Jeanette nodded, thinking every day with Francesco felt special, whether they were walking through a market or sitting quietly at a café.

The Enchanted Garden, or *Il Giardino Incantato*, was just outside town. Within minutes, they arrived, parked, and purchased tickets at a modest entrance booth.

"This garden used to be free," Francesco said. "But after thieves stole more than a thousand sculpted heads, they had to regulate it for tourism."

He placed a gentle hand on the small of her back as they followed a narrow path. Jeanette felt a jolt of electricity at his touch and turned to look at him — his dark eyes, his handsome face.

"Take my hand," he said. "The path is uneven."

She did, and her heart gave a flutter.

They wandered through the garden slowly, stopping often to study the strange stone faces — rows of them carved into walls, trees, and caves. Some were expressive, others blank, all weathered by time.

"Why do you suppose Filippo never married?" Jeanette asked.

Francesco shrugged. "Legend says he fell in love in America but got into a brutal fight over the woman. He was beaten badly... and returned here to live in solitude."

"Italians do seem to fight for love," she said, remembering the century-long feud between the Lunas and the Perollos.

Francesco smiled. "Love is worth fighting for."

They continued along the path, flanked by a short cement wall topped with more heads. Just beyond it, the sea glistened under a sun that was beginning to sink into the horizon. The sky grew heavy with clouds.

Soon, a drizzle began to fall. As it turned to rain, they took shelter in one of the caves. The downpour created a curtain of privacy. Francesco drew her into his arms, and Jeanette felt the heat of his body melt into hers.

His breath tickled her cheek as he whispered, "I've wanted to do this since the first moment I saw you."

Then he kissed her deeply, fully. She responded in kind, her doubts dissolving as his mouth and hands moved across her skin. It had been so long since she felt this kind of intimacy, not since Sonny.

"I want to take you to my country home," Francesco said, brushing a lock of hair from her face.

Jeanette hesitated. "What about my father? If I'm not back soon, he'll worry."

"I'll call my cousin Accursio. He'll tell your father you're with me—and safe."

Francesco held both her hands and looked into her eyes. "You *are* safe with me, Jeanette. I hope you know that."

"I do," she whispered.

When the rain slowed to a drizzle, they ran to the car. As Francesco drove up the hillside, the town disappeared behind them.

"You're going to love the view from up here," he said. "This is where I grew up. I want to move back one day—but for now, my business in Milan keeps me away."

The car followed a long dirt road lined with fencing to keep goats off the path. When they arrived, Jeanette marveled at the house before her.

"This is spectacular."

"My father was an architect. He designed it. I've modernized a few things since."

Francesco opened her door, and they walked up the stone steps to the porch. Inside, a crystal chandelier cast rainbows across the walls. A spiral staircase curled upward, disappearing from view. He gave her a tour of the kitchen and led her into the living room. The decor was minimalist yet warm—white walls, rich red accents, and a bookcase stretching the length of the room beneath five large windows overlooking the valley.

"Have a seat," he said, gesturing to a plush beige couch. "I'll open a bottle of wine."

While he stepped away, Jeanette wandered toward the bookcase. She'd always believed a person's soul lived in their books. Francesco's collection ranged from poetry to ancient history — proof of the depth she had sensed in him from the beginning.

He returned and handed her a glass.

"I'm lucky to have found you," he said, sitting beside her. "You're the most extraordinary woman I've ever met."

She blushed. "Have you ever been married?"

"Yes... briefly. About ten years ago. Her name was Angelina. We had a daughter — Antoinette. One day, Angelina was driving to visit her sister when a truck ran a stop sign. There was a terrible crash. Angelina survived... our daughter didn't."

Jeanette's heart ached. "I'm so sorry."

"She was a beauty," he said softly, his eyes distant. "You would have loved her."

"I'm sure I would've — if she looked anything like her father."

He gave her a faint smile. "I like to think she did."

"What about you?" he asked gently. "Were you ever married? Children?"

"Yes. I was married... briefly, like you. We had no children."

"What happened?"

She took a breath. "Frank was handsome, charming — but jealous, possessive. When he drank, he became someone else. We moved to Michigan for his Army assignment, but after his discharge, he wanted to stay. I didn't. I couldn't be that far from my family."

Francesco wrapped his arm around her. "That doesn't sound like love. You were right to leave."

Jeanette hesitated. "I... blamed him for my mother's death. I think that guilt hardened me. My father wanted me to forgive Frank, but I couldn't. I filed for divorce. The church denied my request for an annulment."

"I'm a man of faith," Francesco said, "but I don't believe you're tainted. You're brave for choosing peace."

She blinked back tears. "It sounds strange, but I hear my mother's voice sometimes. In dreams. She guides me."

"That's not strange at all. I dream of my mother, too. She died when I was young. I've forgotten her face... but I still remember her voice."

He held her in his arms, and together they found comfort in shared loss.

Francesco walked over to the record player and placed a vinyl record on the turntable. As soft orchestral music filled the room, he extended his hand.

"Dance with me?"

She nodded, rising. He pulled her close, his arms around her waist, her head resting against his shoulder. They swayed across the room. Jeanette closed her eyes and let herself fall deeper into his world.

When the music faded, she looked up, lost in his gaze. Her body tingled. Their lips met again, and without a word, he led her down the hallway into his bedroom. She let him unbutton her dress. It slid from her shoulders to the floor.

They tumbled onto the bed, their bodies tangled beneath the moonlight.

They made love until the stars blinked into the sky and the town below was hushed in sleep. For the first time since Sonny, her heart felt whole.

Later, as Jeanette freshened up in the bathroom, opera played in the background. She sang softly along.

"You sing beautifully," Francesco said as she returned.

"I used to sing. It was my dream to be famous. I even made a record once—it was on the radio. A Broadway producer gave me his card, but all he wanted was…" She trailed off.

"He wanted *you*, not your voice," Francesco said knowingly.

She nodded. "So, I walked away."

"I have friends in Milan—musicians, agents. Maybe someone at Teatro alla Scala would love to hear your record."

Jeanette laughed lightly. "It's too late for all that."

"Is it?"

She hesitated. "Wouldn't I have to move to Italy?"

Francesco's eyes gleamed. "Would that be so bad?"

# Previous Engagement

Their bond deepened swiftly, almost recklessly. Each day drew them closer. They strolled hand in hand through the narrow streets of Sciacca, dined in charming seaside restaurants, and visited her extended family, who welcomed Francesco as if he had always belonged. His ease with them, his warm smile, and the way he looked at Jeanette made it clear — he was already part of her life. Everyone noticed. Smiles widened when they entered a room. The air around them seemed charged with something electric, undeniable.

Though Jeanette never spent the night away from her father, her afternoons were Francesco's. They made love behind drawn curtains, wrapped in sheets, and whispered promises. In the soft light, their conversations grew more intimate. She told him things she hadn't told anyone since Sonny. With Francesco, she felt seen, safe, and desired in equal measure.

But time was running out.

"I'm going to miss you," she said one afternoon, her voice barely above a whisper. Her eyes shimmered with unshed tears. "When will I ever see you again?"

"We'll work it out," Francesco said, but his gaze drifted toward the window, unfocused.

A silence hung in the room. Heavy. Still.

Jeanette felt it immediately—something was wrong. He wasn't reaching for her, wasn't reassuring her in the way he always had. She waited, willing him to speak, to say something—anything.

Finally, she asked, "Francesco, is everything all right?"

He turned to her slowly. His eyes were dark with emotion.

"You're scaring me. What's wrong?"

"Come," he said gently, guiding her to the couch. "There's something I should have told you."

Her stomach tightened. She sat beside him, bracing herself.

"What is it?" she asked, already feeling the floor shift beneath her.

Francesco rubbed his hands over his face, tugging at his hair in distress. "I'm engaged," he said, barely above a whisper. "To a woman in Milan."

Jeanette blinked. "Engaged?" The word echoed through her like a slap. "But... how? Why didn't you tell me?"

"It was arranged," he said quickly. "An agreement between my father and hers. Her family is wealthy— old blood, very prestigious. My father believed it would strengthen our business ties. I was expected to take her out. Appearances had to be maintained. Everyone assumed she was my girl, and I didn't know how to correct them without seeming dishonorable."

Jeanette felt a cold, hollow ache blooming in her chest. "And you went along with it?"

His voice broke. "After Antoinette died, my life unraveled. The engagement felt like... background noise. It didn't matter. I thought it never would."

She looked away, fighting to breathe. "You lied to me."

"I didn't mean to." He reached for her hand. "Please, listen. I never expected to meet someone like you. You are the queen of my heart, Jeanette. I love you. Not her. I'll tell her—when I return to Milan, I'll end it."

Jeanette stared at him, stunned. The ground beneath her emotional foundation cracked open. What had felt like the beginning of forever now teetered on betrayal.

"You should have told me sooner," she said, her voice trembling.

"I know. I was afraid. Afraid of losing you before I had the chance to truly love you."

"But you *were never mine*," she whispered.

His eyes filled with regret. "Jeanette, I *want* to be yours. I'll do whatever it takes. Just give me the chance."

# Dear Francesco

Giuseppe sat quietly on the flight home, unusually subdued. Jeanette assumed he was simply sad to leave Sicily, but as the plane began its descent into New York, she noticed something was wrong. His speech became slurred, and his eyes grew vacant. His hands trembled.

"Pop? What's wrong?" she asked, alarmed.

He didn't respond—just looked at her with a hollow, distant stare.

Panic tightened in her chest as she flagged down a stewardess.

"Is there a doctor on board?" the announcement echoed over the cabin speakers.

No one responded—until a nurse rose from her seat and rushed over. After a quick exam, she looked at Jeanette gravely.

"He's had a stroke," she said. "I can't assess the full damage, but if we don't get him to a hospital immediately, he may not make it."

Jeanette's blood ran cold. "Pop. You can't die on me. Please, hang on."

An ambulance waited on the tarmac. As soon as the plane landed, Giuseppe was rushed to Kings County Hospital. Jeanette followed in a daze, barely aware of anything around her. She sat in the waiting room, rocking back and forth in a hard plastic chair, her hands twisted together.

*Dear God… don't let my father die.*

Her sisters were on their way. That thought gave her some comfort, but not enough. Closing her eyes, she whispered a desperate prayer.

"Please, Mama. Don't take Papa yet. I know you miss him, but I need him."

When she opened her eyes, Mariella was standing there. They embraced tightly, holding each other in silence. Thirty minutes later, Phyllis rushed into the waiting room.

"Sorry it took so long," she panted. "I had to wait for David to get home to watch the boys. How's Pop?"

"I don't know yet," Jeanette said, her voice thin. "We're still waiting for the doctor."

The three sisters huddled together, their tears falling freely.

Finally, the doctor stepped into the room. Jeanette leapt to her feet. "How is he?"

"Your father is stable," the doctor said kindly. "He did have a mild stroke. It's too early to know the extent of the damage, but he's conscious and responsive. He can nod when spoken to. His right arm is affected, but with therapy and rest, I expect a full recovery."

The relief was overwhelming. Jeanette collapsed into her chair, a clean tissue pressed to her damp eyes. She looked upward.

"Thank you, Mama," she whispered.

Giuseppe was released a few days later with strict instructions for rest and a small rubber ball to help rebuild strength in his hand. But he was never quite the same. A full medical workup revealed that he had diabetes — the same disease that had slowly robbed Anna's parents of their sight.

Sadness swept into Jeanette's life like a high tide.

She couldn't juggle work and caring for her father full-time. Phyllis suggested moving him to a nursing home on Long Island, but Giuseppe adamantly refused. He wouldn't leave Brooklyn. He wouldn't leave home.

Mariella, though busy with the bakery, agreed to check on him daily. Jeanette managed what she could between shifts and sleepless nights.

Letters from Francesco came at first, sweet, handwritten promises that warmed her aching heart. But gradually, they grew infrequent. She replied to each one, pouring her soul onto the page. Three letters went unanswered. Still, she told herself to be patient. International mail could take weeks.

But then a month passed. Nothing.

With each day, the silence became heavier. Her heart, once filled with hope, began to twist in uncertainty. *Where is he? Why hasn't he written?* Had it all been a dream?

Maybe he never truly loved her. Maybe he had gone back to the woman in Milan. Or worse — maybe something had happened to him.

Her thoughts spiraled into dread.

Desperate, she tried calling. She pressed the phone to her ear and waited, only to be met with a recorded voice.

"All circuits are busy. Please try again later."

She sat on the edge of her bed, clutching the receiver, listening to the mechanical voice repeat itself. And for the first time since Sicily, tears fell freely down her cheeks.

*****

Mariella arrived with her daughters, the scent of fresh bread trailing behind her.

"I brought some warm rolls from the bakery," she said cheerfully, heading straight for the kitchen. "I'll make some coffee."

She called over her shoulder, "Don't worry about Pop today, Jeanette. Antonio hired a new girl to work the front counter, so I don't need to be back at the bakery until late this afternoon."

Jeanette didn't respond.

Mariella turned and studied her sister's face. "What's wrong?"

"I don't know if I can go to work," Jeanette murmured. "I'm not feeling well."

Mariella walked over and placed the back of her hand on Jeanette's forehead. "You're a little pale, but no fever. Maybe you just need to eat something."

She broke off a piece of the roll and spread a thick layer of butter on it. Jeanette took a few bites, then suddenly pushed the plate away.

"Oh God. I feel sick."

She bolted to the bathroom and vomited into the toilet. After rinsing her mouth and splashing cold water on her face, she looked in the mirror, startled by the worn, pale woman staring back at her.

"I don't know what's wrong with me," she said, stepping back into the kitchen. "I've been dizzy. I can't hold anything down."

Mariella didn't hesitate. "Come on. I'm taking you to my doctor."

The wait at the clinic felt endless. Jeanette finally emerged from the exam room looking dazed.

Mariella stood up quickly. "What is it? Are you sick?"

"No," Jeanette said, her voice trembling. "It's not that."

"What, then?"

Jeanette drew in a breath. "I'm pregnant."

Mariella froze for a second, then wrapped her arms tightly around her sister. "Oh, Jeanette."

"It's Francesco's," she whispered.

Mariella pulled back slightly to look her in the eyes. "Have you told him?"

"I tried. I wrote to him, but I haven't heard back."

"Try again. Maybe if you tell him about the baby, he'll respond. Maybe he'll even come to America."

"I don't want him to feel obligated," Jeanette said quietly. "I want him to come because he loves me, not out of duty."

"He has to know, Jeanette. He deserves that."

Jeanette nodded. "You're right. I'll try again."

She sat at the kitchen table with a stack of fresh stationery and an airmail envelope. She picked up her pen and began:

*Dear Francesco,*
*I'm writing to tell you that you will be a father.*

Jeanette stared at the page, then crumpled it and started again. But no matter how she phrased it, the words sounded either too desperate or too angry. She wanted to scream. She wanted to cry.

Surrounded by balled-up drafts on the floor, she closed her eyes and forced herself to breathe. Then, slowly, she began again:

*Dear Francesco,*
*I've been so worried about you. I know you must have a good reason for not contacting me, but I have something important to tell you. Although the time we shared was brief, I am with child — your child.*
*I realize the distance between us is great, and I don't expect you to change your life because of this. Still, I thought you would want to know.*

*With affection,*
*Jeanette*

She folded the letter carefully and sealed it inside the envelope, then walked to the post office and dropped it into the slot with trembling fingers.

Two weeks later, she spotted Tony, their mailman, pushing his cart down the block. She hovered by the window, heart pounding. When he stopped at her gate and flipped through a handful of envelopes, she rushed outside.

"Hi, Tony," she said breathlessly. "Do you have anything for me?"

He handed her an envelope. "I'm sorry, Miss Jeanette. This one came back."

Her stomach sank.

"It was undeliverable. No forwarding address," he said gently.

Jeanette felt like the wind had been knocked out of her. "Oh," she said, trying to keep her voice steady. "Thank you, Tony."

She took the returned letter and walked slowly back into the house. She stared at the envelope, her name written in her own hopeful handwriting, now marked *Return to Sender*.

Now what?

She pressed a hand to her belly. *Our baby…*

"There's only one thing you can do," Mariella said firmly. "Raise the baby yourself. Everything's going to be all right. I'll help. I'll watch your baby. What's one more? Antonio won't mind."

Jeanette's throat tightened. A baby would change everything—her work, her home, her future. She felt lost. She longed for her mother's steady voice, her warm embrace.

"Mama would've known what to do," she whispered.

She turned into her sister's arms and sobbed. "I wish Mama was here."

Mariella held her, rocking her gently like a child. "I know, honey. I know."

# Ribbons and Bows

When Jeanette went into labor, she was alone in the house with her father.

Giuseppe panicked. He had no idea what to do. Desperate, he picked up the phone and called their neighbor, Tessie — the midwife.

Giuseppe had never liked her. She was a nosy old crony with yellowed teeth from smoking Guinea cigars and crooked fingers that looked like they'd been broken and reset wrong. Back when Anna was alive, Tessie had always inserted herself into their business, offering unsolicited advice. But now, with no one else to turn to, Giuseppe welcomed her wisdom.

"The first baby takes time," Tessie said after examining Jeanette. "It's going to take hours. I'll sit with her if you like."

Feeling helpless, Giuseppe stepped outside and sat on the stoop, clutching his rosary beads, worn smooth by time and memory. They were a gift from his grandmother on his first Holy Communion, a keepsake he had brought from Sciacca. He hadn't prayed with them in years, but now he clutched them tightly, his lips moving in silent, fervent prayer.

Inside, Jeanette's cries tore through the walls.

Hours passed.

Eventually, he returned to the bedroom, anxious. Tessie stood over Jeanette, frowning.

"The baby isn't dropping," she said.

She pressed hard on Jeanette's swollen belly, trying to shift the baby downward. Nothing. In a final act of desperation, she straddled Jeanette and attempted to apply weight.

Jeanette screamed, her face contorted with agony.

"Stop!" Mariella shouted from the doorway.

She had arrived in a panic after rushing over, leaving the kids with her mother-in-law. She stormed into the room and shoved Tessie aside.

"Are you trying to kill my sister?" she yelled. "Get away from her!"

Tessie, startled and shamed, muttered nothing in her defense. She slipped out of the room and was gone before anyone even noticed.

"Pop!" Mariella turned, furious. "Why didn't you call me sooner?"

Giuseppe's eyes filled with remorse. "*Mi dispiace*," he said softly, slipping into Italian.

"I've got this," Mariella said, pushing him gently toward the door. "You go rest. I don't need you having another stroke."

Giuseppe lingered in the hallway, still pale, listening to the sounds of his daughters on the other side of the door.

Mariella soaked a cloth in cold water and dabbed Jeanette's face.

"Mama… Mama…" Jeanette whimpered, half-conscious.

"I'm not Mama," Mariella whispered, "but I'm here. I'm here."

She sat on the bed and held her sister's hand, rubbing her arm in circles, comforting her through the waves of pain. She remembered her own births clearly — the fire, the exhaustion. "Men get all the fun," she said gently. "And we get all the pain."

Jeanette gave the faintest smile before it was swept away by another contraction. Mariella wiped the sweat from her forehead, studying her sister's gray-tinged complexion.

Something wasn't right.

"I think she needs to go to the hospital," Mariella said.

"I'll call Antonio," Giuseppe said, hurrying out of the room.

Another guttural scream echoed through the house just as he left. By the time Giuseppe returned with Antonio, Jeanette's skin had gone ashen.

"Should we call an ambulance?" Mariella asked, panicked.

"No time," Antonio said. "We'll take her ourselves."

Giuseppe looked frightened. "Are you taking her to Bellevue?"

Antonio shook his head. "No. They'll kill her there for sure. We're going to the hospital in Chelsea. It's run by the Sisters of the Holy Cross. I just hope we get there in time."

Mariella wrapped Jeanette in a blanket as Antonio gently scooped her up and carried her to the car.

"Stay here, Pop," Mariella said as she kissed her father's cheek. "We'll call you as soon as we get to the hospital."

Giuseppe nodded, pale and shaken, watching them drive off. He stood in the doorway long after the car disappeared down the block.

*****

Four hours after a difficult labor, Jeanette gave birth to a baby girl. Mother and child were safe.

Still weak, Jeanette carefully made her way up the steps of their Brooklyn brownstone, her baby swaddled snugly in a pink blanket. Antonio supported her arm in case she faltered.

Giuseppe waited in the doorway, his face etched with worry and wonder. Mariella stood beside him, cradling six-month-old Lynn, with Janine tugging at her skirt. Even Phyllis had driven in from Long Island, her toddlers, Alfred and Johnny, already dashing in circles around the living room, giggling and teasing each other with pent-up energy.

Giuseppe's eyes softened as Jeanette stepped inside. He took a cautious step forward, then stared down at the bundle in her arms.

"You sure had us all worried, little one," he said, his voice choked with emotion.

"I'm sorry if we scared you, Pop," Jeanette whispered.

"You're home now. That's what matters. And we've got another beautiful baby in the house to brighten our days."

"Have you picked a name?" Mariella asked.

Jeanette nodded, her voice tender. "Yes. Her name is Francesca."

Giuseppe's gaze flickered with recognition, but he didn't ask. "Ah… after her father."

They'd never spoken directly about her time with Francesco. The name said everything.

"Yes, Pop," she said softly. "I named her after him."

"Can I see her?" Janine asked, hopping on her toes.

"Of course, honey," Jeanette said, pulling back the pink blanket.

"She's beautiful!" Janine gasped.

"Would you like to hold her?"

Janine nodded, shy now.

"Okay, sit on the couch," Jeanette said, gently placing Francesca into her arms.

Giuseppe hovered beside them. "*Bella… bella,*" he murmured, fussing over his new granddaughter.

At the sound of his voice, Francesca stirred and opened her eyes.

"I wish your mom were here to see her," he said, his voice catching.

Jeanette's heart clenched. "I do too, Pop."

"I'm sorry. I shouldn't have brought that up."

"No, that's all right. She's been on my mind too."

She turned and offered the baby to him. "Here. Want to hold her?"

Giuseppe hesitated, then took the infant into his arms. He kissed her tiny forehead and looked upward. "I'm kissing your granddaughter, Anna," he said.

"We should get Jeanette and the baby into bed," Mariella said gently.

"That's a cute name," Phyllis added. "But maybe we should call her Francie. It's more American."

"Just like your mother," Giuseppe teased, shaking his head. "What's wrong with Francesca?"

The baby let out a soft fuss. Jeanette smiled. "I think she's ready for her nap."

"We set up a nursery in your room," Giuseppe said.

"Close your eyes!" Mariella said, leading Jeanette down the hall.

Phyllis opened the door with a flourish.

Jeanette stepped inside, stunned. The walls were painted a soft pink. A small white crib sat beside the window, with a delicate mobile turning gently above it.

"I placed the crib near the garden window," Phyllis said. "So she'll have something pretty to look at."

Jeanette bit back tears. "You are all incredible. I'm so lucky to have such a beautiful family."

"It's getting late," Mariella said. "You and the baby need rest."

"The crib is beautiful, but I think I'll keep her with me tonight."

"If you need anything, just call," Giuseppe said from the doorway. "I'll be in the living room."

Jeanette slipped into bed, her newborn tucked safely in her arms. Humbled, overwhelmed, she lay awake, listening to the rise and fall of the baby's breath.

"Oh, Mama," she whispered to the quiet night. "I wish you could have lived to see this."

She would never stop wondering what became of Francesco. But she took comfort in one thing: her daughter had been made with love.

In the middle of the night, a storm rolled in. Thunder cracked, and the windows trembled. Jeanette stared out at the streaks of lightning cutting through the sky. She looked down at her baby, who squirmed lightly in her sleep.

"Don't be afraid," Jeanette whispered. "Mommy's here."

By morning, the skies had cleared. Golden light slipped through the curtains. Jeanette exhaled and smiled. "Everything will be all right," she said softly.

She spent her days with Francie — her little miracle. On nice afternoons, she tucked her into the carriage and strolled down to 18th Avenue to meet Dorothy for lunch. They'd sit outside and park their baby carriages face to face, laughing as the girls kicked their little feet at each other, already forging a friendship of their own.

# Fire and Ice

When Francie turned two, Jeanette knew it was time to return to work. She couldn't go back to her old job on Wall Street, but she needed an income. Eventually, she found a part-time position at the local IGA market—not glamorous, but steady and close to home.

Giuseppe offered to watch Francie during her shifts, but Jeanette hesitated. Since his stroke, he'd grown more forgetful. He loved his granddaughter dearly, but she couldn't expect him to keep up with a curious, energetic toddler.

"You can leave Francie with me at the bakery," Mariella offered one morning.

Jeanette shook her head. "You've got your hands full already. I don't want to be a burden."

"Nonsense," Mariella said. "What's one more? Besides, the girls love having her around."

Jeanette reluctantly agreed—especially after Mariella promised to check in on Pop during the quieter hours between the bakery's morning rush and afternoon lull.

It was in those small, consistent acts that Jeanette realized just how much Mariella meant to her. There had been times in their youth when distance stretched between them—years, even. But now, that space had vanished. They were closer than ever, bound by shared loss, shared laughter, and a quiet understanding only sisters could have.

Before leaving for work each morning, Jeanette rose early to cook breakfast for Giuseppe, then bundled Francie up and walked her over to the bakery. Watching her daughter skip ahead and reach for Mariella's outstretched arms brought Jeanette peace.

She was starting over—day by day—and somehow, that felt okay.

*****

Standing in front of the stoop, Mariella caught the acrid scent of smoke before she even opened the door. Her heart jumped. She bolted inside and found Giuseppe in the kitchen, frantically swatting at a fire blazing on the stove. The flames had already leapt to the window curtains, crackling with fury.

"Pop, move!" she yelled.

She shoved him out of the way and grabbed the nearest pot of water, hurling it at the flames. Smoke billowed as fabric hissed and shriveled. Coughing, she pulled her father by the arm and dragged him outside to safety.

By the time the fire department arrived, flames had scorched the ceiling and eaten through part of the roof. A dark plume of smoke curled from the rooftop, rising like a warning to the sky.

"I'm afraid the smoke's going to ruin most of your belongings," one of the firemen told Giuseppe.

Giuseppe looked devastated. "Please... can you save my chair?"

The firefighter smiled gently. "I think we can manage that." He nodded to a colleague, and the two disappeared inside. A few minutes later, they reemerged with Giuseppe's well-worn chair. They set it down carefully on the lawn, where it sagged under its own weight, old and tired, just like him.

"Thank you," Giuseppe whispered. He turned to Mariella. "Maybe you should call Jeanette. Tell her to come home."

"I will, Pop. I'll call from my apartment. My mother-in-law's with the kids, so I can come back soon."

She made the call.

"Hi, Jeanette. It's Mariella."

"Mariella? What's wrong? Is Francie okay? Did Pop have another stroke?"

"Everyone's all right. But there was a fire. Pop left something on the stove. It got out of hand."

"Oh God," Jeanette gasped. "I'll be right there."

She dropped everything, told her boss it was an emergency, and rushed out the door.

By the time she arrived, the fire was out—but the damage was unmistakable. The kitchen was a blackened wreck, and smoke had crept into every room. Jeanette stood frozen in the doorway, her breath caught in her throat. Their home—the place where so much love had lived—was uninhabitable.

Mariella offered to take them in, but her small apartment couldn't hold everyone. After a family discussion, they decided Giuseppe would stay with Phyllis in Long Island while repairs were made.

He didn't take the news well.

"I don't want to go," he muttered. "My friends are here. My club's here. Brooklyn's home."

Tears welled in his eyes. On moving day, he walked through the empty rooms one last time. Every step echoed with memories. The wind whistled through the window cracks—a sound that always made him feel uneasy. He could almost hear Anna's voice calling from the kitchen, the laughter of the children, the rhythm of life that had once filled this house.

"Long Island's not so bad, Pop," Jeanette tried to reassure him. "You'll be okay."

Phyllis and David built him a small apartment in their basement. It had everything he needed—except the comfort of the old neighborhood. In Brooklyn, he could walk to the park, the butcher, the corner store. On Long Island, he was cut off—dependent on rides, routines, and the kindness of others.

No neighbors came to say goodbye. Most had either passed on or moved in with their own children. The world Giuseppe once knew had disappeared.

Phyllis spoke of sweet country air and the soothing sound of crickets, but Giuseppe missed the city's pulse—its trains, its music, its shouting vendors, and honking horns. Now he sat quietly under the oak tree in Phyllis's backyard, the same distant look in his eyes each day.

No one realized he was beginning to fade.

# Long Island

On a gorgeous Sunday morning in June, the whole family gathered on Long Island for Sunday dinner. Even Uncle Joseph and Aunt Genovese made the trip, along with Cousins Kathy and Robert. Phyllis was in her element, stirring a giant pot of sauce that filled the house with the smell of garlic and basil. She'd made enough meatballs to feed an army — and added a lamb shank, their father's favorite.

"Want to hear something funny?" Jeanette asked as she helped set the table.

"Please," Phyllis said, brushing a stray hair off her forehead. "I could use a laugh."

"Well, when Pop and I were in Sciacca, we didn't see a single meatball."

"You're kidding!"

"Not one. All we ate was fish. Pop says meatballs were invented in Brooklyn."

Phyllis burst out laughing. "That actually makes sense."

"It does," Uncle Joseph chimed in. "Most of the Italians who came to America didn't have money. Ground meat stretched farther — easier to feed big families."

"Maybe," Cousin Kathy added, "but even if we won the lottery, I'd still want meatballs on Sunday."

At the head of the table, Giuseppe smiled quietly as the voices of his family swirled around him. He watched the younger girls sitting neatly with folded hands while Phyllis's two sons darted between the chairs, drawing sharp glares and a frustrated outburst from their mother.

"These boys are driving me crazy!" Phyllis shouted. "Sometimes I wish I had girls."

"There's always next time," Aunt Genovese said with a grin.

Phyllis's face softened. "Maybe there will be. We're expecting another baby. I just found out."

Cheers erupted around the table.

"That's wonderful!" Mariella said. "Our babies will be close in age. I hope I have a boy this time. If I do, I'm naming him Giuseppe — after Pop."

Giuseppe smiled, touched. "You should call him Joseph. It's more American."

Mariella rolled her eyes. "Now you sound like Mama."

"If it's a boy," David added, "we may keep going until we have a full baseball team."

"Bite your tongue," Phyllis said, and everyone burst out laughing again.

Jeanette looked over at her father, whose hands trembled slightly as he lifted his coffee. "Isn't it wonderful, Pop? The family's growing."

Giuseppe nodded. "Yes. I just hope I'm around a little longer to see it."

Phyllis placed a generous slice of ricotta cheesecake in front of him. He took one bite and gently pushed the plate away.

"What's wrong, Pop?" she asked. "Did I forget the sugar again?"

Laughter bubbled up once more. Phyllis had a long-standing reputation for forgetting baking powder, salt, or sugar in her desserts.

But Giuseppe didn't laugh. He closed his eyes for a moment, looking as if he were trying to remember something, or maybe summon the energy to speak. The room quieted.

"You're not having another stroke, are you?" Jeanette asked, alarm rising in her voice.

"No, no. I'm just tired." He opened his eyes and gave her a weak smile. "Think I'll turn in early."

After dinner, as everyone helped clear the table, Mariella pulled Phyllis aside near the kitchen sink.

"Keep an eye on him," she whispered. "I don't want to upset Jeanette, but... he doesn't look good."

Phyllis nodded, her face serious. "He's been depressed. I thought he was adjusting, but maybe he's not."

They both glanced toward the hallway where Giuseppe had disappeared. The laughter from the dinner table still lingered in the air, but a quiet unease settled between them.

*****

Phyllis went to check on her father early that morning. As soon as she stepped into his room, she knew something was wrong. Giuseppe was burning with fever, his skin flushed, his breath shallow. She pressed her hand to his forehead, scalding.

"Daddy?" she whispered, but he didn't respond.

She called the ambulance, then her sisters.

Jeanette drove back to Long Island with Mariella, hearts pounding with dread. Antonio gripped the steering wheel, weaving through traffic on the Belt Parkway, then flying down the Southern State. No one spoke. The silence in the car was suffocating.

By the time they reached Mid-Island Hospital, it was too late.

"I'm sorry," the doctor said gently. "Your father passed. His kidneys had failed. We did everything we could."

Jeanette staggered back, her hand over her mouth, the tears coming hard. Mariella caught her in her arms.

He was gone.

As she sat in the hospital waiting room, numb, Jeanette's mind wandered back to the day they left Brooklyn. Her father's face had been etched with grief—his hands trailing the walls of the old brownstone one last time, as if trying to absorb its memories. He never said much about it, but she knew what it cost him.

Brooklyn was his second homeland. Just as Sciacca had shaped his boyhood, Brooklyn had shaped his manhood. It was in his stride, his voice, his stubbornness, his laughter. He had belonged to its streets as much as to his family.

Jeanette wiped her eyes and looked toward the hallway, half-expecting to see him shuffle out, cane in hand, offering some old-school advice or asking for a cup of espresso. But there was only silence.

*****

David made all the arrangements and asked his sister to watch the children. Jeanette was relieved—she didn't want Francesca to see her grandfather in a coffin.

In Sciacca, it was common practice to lay out the dead at home. Jeanette remembered her father telling stories of how, as a child, he and his siblings played near the casket when their grandmother died, as if it were just another piece of furniture. He had even insisted that Anna be viewed in their living room when she passed. Jeanette and her sisters hadn't liked the idea. They knew their mother wouldn't have wanted to be on display, but they'd respected their father's wishes. He had needed to grieve in his own way.

Now it was up to them to decide how Giuseppe would be sent into the next world. This time, Phyllis put her foot down. She refused to have him laid out at home and paid for a wake at the funeral home instead.

Giuseppe's nieces and nephews all came to say goodbye to the man they affectionately called Poppy.

The moment Jeanette stepped into the funeral home, the scent of carnations overwhelmed her. It sent a shiver down her spine. Ever since her mother's death, she'd hated the smell. Roses, too. Their sweetness felt too close to sorrow.

Across the room, she saw Sonny standing with his parents. There was no sign of his wife.

Jeanette hesitated. Her heart stirred at the sight of him, and for a moment, she wanted to run to him — to tell him that despite everything, he still meant something. But Aunt Evelyn stood near him like a sentry, and that was enough to ground her. A tear escaped and rolled down her cheek. If her aunt noticed, she didn't let on. Tears were expected at a funeral.

Sonny caught her eye and smiled — his same old sunny smile that once warmed her through the coldest winters.

"Did your wife come with you?" Jeanette asked quietly.

"No. Jiao's home with our son."

Jeanette wanted to ask if he was happy, but Sonny quickly changed the subject.

"I heard you have a daughter."

"Yes," she said, softening. "Her name is Francesca. We call her Francie."

"My sister Rosetta showed me her picture. She's beautiful — like her mother."

"Thank you," Jeanette replied, then excused herself to rejoin her sisters.

Standing beside the casket, shoulder to shoulder with Mariella and Phyllis, Jeanette kept her gaze low.

She was afraid to look directly at her father. But after a moment, she found the courage to lift her eyes.

Antonio had done a good job picking the clothes. Giuseppe wore a crisp new blue suit, his hands folded gently over a silver crucifix. He looked peaceful. The worry lines that had creased his brow for years had faded. Seeing him that way — serene — was unexpectedly comforting.

At the funeral mass, Jeanette sat in the pew closest to the flower-draped coffin. Her mind wandered through memories. She smiled as she recalled his stories, his stubbornness, and the joy he had taken in their trip to Sicily. She was proud to have given that to him — one final journey home.

After the service, four pallbearers — Uncle Joseph, Uncle Carlino, Uncle Paul, and Antonio — carried Giuseppe to his final resting place beside his beloved Anna.

Later, the family gathered at a local restaurant to celebrate his life. Giuseppe had saved a small sum and left instructions for Jeanette to use it to take the family out for a meal. It was his final gesture — to keep them together, even in death.

As they sat at the long table, Jeanette's heart felt heavy with one more concern.

Luciana.

Still in Africa, she hadn't made it home. They had managed to get word to her, but she hadn't called or written. That silence gnawed at Jeanette. It wasn't like

Luciana to go dark. She'd always found a way to stay connected.

Something was wrong. Jeanette could feel it.

# The Letter

That night, Jeanette lay awake long after Francie had fallen asleep beside her. The letter felt like it radiated heat through the mattress beneath her, as if it had a heartbeat of its own.

Francesco's words played over and over in her mind.

*I never stopped thinking about you. I failed you.*

She had imagined this moment so many times — receiving a letter, hearing his voice again, being swept back into the tide of what they'd shared. But now that it was real, her heart wasn't as sure.

Francie stirred beside her. Jeanette brushed a curl from her daughter's forehead and whispered, "Your father wrote to me." The little girl didn't stir. "You're the best thing that ever happened to me," Jeanette whispered. "I don't regret a single thing."

The next morning, she busied herself in the bakery, hoping work would dull the ache in her chest. She kneaded dough with extra force, scrubbed the display cases twice, and kept the radio low to drown out her thoughts. Still, Francesco's letter haunted her — every word, every unspoken apology.

That afternoon, when the bakery quieted, and Mariella poured two cups of coffee, Jeanette finally spoke.

"I don't know what I'm supposed to feel," she admitted.

Mariella looked up from her pastry, patient. "Do you still love him?"

Jeanette didn't answer right away. "I loved who he was. Who I thought he could be. But he left... and life went on."

Mariella nodded. "That doesn't mean your heart turned to stone."

Jeanette laughed softly. "No. But I can't go back to who I was. I have a daughter now. I have responsibilities."

"Maybe he should know he has a daughter," Mariella said gently.

Jeanette's eyes welled up. "I'm afraid. What if he doesn't want to know? What if it doesn't change anything?"

"Then nothing changes," Mariella said. "But at least *you'll* know you gave him the chance."

Jeanette sipped her coffee, staring into the swirl of cream. "I need more time."

Mariella reached across the table and gave her hand a squeeze. "Take it."

*****

The next day, after the mid-afternoon rush, Mariella and Jeanette grabbed two Crullers and put up a pot of coffee.

The children were still at the park with Cousin Ronnie and his family. Ronnie grew up to be one of the kindest people Jeanette ever knew. Nothing like the bully he had been when they were growing up. He and his sisters lived on Staten Island. They returned to Brooklyn often to visit Uncle Alberto and his wife, Josephine. Like Giuseppe, they were getting up in their years and having some health issues.

Jeanette took a sip of her coffee. "I received a letter from Francesco yesterday."

"After all these years?" Mariella looked amazed. "What did it say?"

Jeanette took the envelope from her apron pocket and stared at the return address before removing the letter.

"He's living in Milan."

"Well, go on, read it to me."

Jeanette sighed.

*Cara Jeanette,*

*There isn't a day that passes that I don't think of you. I should have written sooner, but shame and confusion held me back. I don't expect forgiveness. I only want you to know the truth.*

*When I returned to Milan, I ended my engagement. It was difficult, but I couldn't live a lie. I thought I would return to you, but then your letters stopped coming. I feared I had lost you forever.*

*Only recently did I find the last letter you sent — tucked away in a drawer at my cousin's house. He had forgotten to forward it. My heart broke when I read your words. Jeanette, I never knew about the baby. I can only imagine how alone you must have felt. Please, if there is any space left in your heart, write me back. Let me know if you're well… and if you would ever consider letting me meet my daughter.*

*Con affetto eterno,*
*Francesco*

Mariella was silent for a moment. The only sound was the bubbling of the percolator and the low hum of a delivery truck idling outside.

"What are you going to do?" she asked gently.

Jeanette folded the letter again, pressing it back into the envelope like it might break. "I don't know," she whispered. "Part of me wants to scream at him — for not trying harder, for disappearing. But another part… wants him to meet Francie. I think she deserves that."

Mariella reached across the table and wrapped her hand around Jeanette's. "Whatever you decide, I'm here. And so is your family."

Jeanette nodded, her eyes misty. "I just hope it's not too late."

Jeanette sat at the small desk by the bedroom window, staring down at the blank page in front of her. The first draft came quickly, almost impulsively:

*Dear Francesco,*

*I was unprepared for your letter after so many years. You have a daughter.*

She froze. The words looked harsh, stripped of the warmth she still carried for him. She crumpled the page and tossed it into the wastebasket. It wasn't something she could write so bluntly — not like that. She wanted to tell him in person. To look into his eyes and let him see the truth for himself.

She took a breath and tried again:

*Dear Francesco,*

*I was quite unprepared for your letter. For a long time, I feared something terrible had happened — an accident, or worse. But then I reminded myself that if anything had happened to you, your cousins in Sciacca would have reached out.*

*Still, silence has a way of becoming its own answer. I thought you had forgotten me. And yet, your letter brought back memories I'd carefully tucked away — of the garden, the sea, your home on the hill. I'm glad to hear you're well. And I'm happy for you, returning to Sciacca. It's where you belong. My father passed shortly after our trip to Sicily. Life hasn't been easy, but I've been surrounded by family, and I am grateful for that. It's just my daughter and me now.*

*If you're open to it, I would love to come for a visit. Let me know if that would be all right with you.*

*Affectionately yours,*

*Jeanette*

Jeanette folded the letter neatly and slipped it into an envelope.

In the days that followed, Jeanette often wrote to Francesco. She told him about Francie's laugh, the way she scrunched her nose when she was being stubborn, and how she liked to sing while helping sweep the bakery floor. But she left out the part about the night Francie was born, about how close they had come to losing her. She couldn't find the words. Not yet.

Some truths were better spoken face-to-face.

# Parasite

Assisting Dr. Trent Arnold in the ER, Luciana was on the verge of collapse. The heat clung to her like a second skin. Sweat trickled down her spine beneath her scrubs, which were stiff with dust and streaked with blood. The doctor looked just as spent, in wrinkled green scrubs, drooping eyelids behind black-rimmed glasses.

"Luciana, can you bring me a clean bandage?"

"Yes, doctor." She rubbed her temple as a dull ache pulsed behind her eyes, then turned to the supply cabinet.

Dr. Arnold glanced up again. "Are you okay? You look overheated."

"I'm fine. Just a headache."

"Have you taken anything?"

"Aspirin. It helps… for a little while."

As she began gathering instruments to sterilize, Dr. Arnold gently took her wrist. "I'll take care of this. Go drink some water. Cool off."

Grateful, Luciana stepped outside and bent over the old metal waterspout. She cupped her hands under the flow, letting the water pool before drinking. The moisture was a small mercy against the scorching sun and the exhaustion creeping deeper into her bones.

A moment later, Dr. Arnold joined her.

"How long have you had the headache?" he asked.

"Three days."

His eyes softened with concern. "You should lie down. Mary can cover for you."

"Thank you, doctor. I'll rest a bit. If you need me…"

"I'll find you," he assured her.

Luciana reached her tent and peeled off her sweat-soaked scarf. By the time she lay down, her clothes clung to her like a fevered second skin. Her body trembled, her head spun. She pulled the thin sheet over her and closed her eyes.

"Luciana," Dr. Arnold's voice pierced the fog. He was shaking her awake.

She opened her eyes slowly, the room spinning. Her stomach lurched. She reached for the tin bucket beside her cot but couldn't lift her head. He rushed to her side and held it for her as she vomited violently.

For two days, Luciana burned with fever. Through waves of delirium, images flickered — her sisters, her father's warm hands, the familiar scent of home. Somewhere in the haze, she thought she heard someone say he was gone. *Was it a dream?*

Dr. Arnold diagnosed malaria. They gave her quinine, strong doses that eased the fever but left her weak and trembling.

"Luciana," he said one evening, sitting by her cot. "Your work here is done. We're sending you home."

"No," she whispered hoarsely. "I can't leave. What about Nadia?" The little girl she had bonded with, orphaned by machete-wielding rebels.

"She's safe, but we can't locate her in time. You have to go."

"I can't—" Her voice cracked. "They need me."

"You can't help anyone like this. If you stay, you'll die."

She looked at him, tears welling in her fever-glossed eyes. "I'll die there too."

"Perhaps," he said quietly. "But at least you'll be with your family."

He made the arrangements. She packed her meager belongings in silence. There was no chance to say goodbye to Nadia.

When Luciana heard the helicopter approaching, its distant thump-thump echoing across the arid plain, her chest tightened. This wasn't how she had imagined leaving. She had planned to stay until the war ended. To stay until they no longer needed her.

But they still did.

And she was going anyway.

\*\*\*\*\*

The front door opened with a jingle of the bell.

Luciana stepped inside the bakery, the late afternoon sun glinting off the glass display. Even though Francie had never met her, something about the woman's face felt familiar.

"You must be Francesca," Luciana said gently.

The little girl nodded.

"Where's your mother?"

"In the kitchen." Francie turned and darted to the back. "Mommy, there's a lady out front."

Jeanette looked up from arranging a tray of warm Italian bread. "A lady?" she asked, wiping her hands on a dish towel.

She stepped into the shop and froze. The tray nearly slipped from her hands.

"Luci..." Her voice cracked. "You're home."

Jeanette rushed forward and wrapped her arms around her sister. When she pulled back, she turned to her daughter. "Francie, this is your Aunt Luciana. The one I always tell you about."

Luciana knelt. "Hi, Francie. I've heard so much about you."

"You live in Africa, right?" Francie asked, recalling the stories her mother read about the children in Sudan.

"I did. But I've come home now."

Luciana brushed a dark lock of hair from her niece's forehead, then looked up at Jeanette.

"Where's Mariella?"

"She took little William for his three-month checkup. Wait till you see him—he's the most beautiful boy in the neighborhood. Big brown eyes, curly hair. And the girls? They've grown so much."

"They finally got their boy," Luciana said softly. "Their family's complete."

Jeanette caught the faraway look in her sister's eyes—the shadow of something unspoken.

"Francie, sweetheart," she said gently, "why don't you set your dolls up for a tea party?"

"It's no fun without Janine."

"She'll be home soon. Go on now — Mommy and Aunt Luciana need to talk."

"Okay." Francie ran off.

"I'm glad you're home," Jeanette said, her voice quiet. "I've missed you. Where are your bags?"

"Just this one."

Jeanette frowned. "I'm sorry, we don't have a proper house. It burned down. The contractors are still fixing it. Francie and I have been living here, above the bakery."

She hesitated. "You can take my bed. I'll sleep on the couch."

"I can't put you out — "

"You're not. After living in the desert for years, you deserve a soft bed. Don't argue."

Luciana smiled faintly. "You've always taken care of me."

"Remember what I told you when we were little? I'll always be here for you. I meant it."

Luciana reached for her sister, and they embraced again. But when she pulled back, her eyes were shimmering with unshed tears.

"Luciana?" Jeanette's heart started to pound. "What is it? What's wrong?"

"I'm sick, Jeanette."

"No… what do you mean? What kind of sick?"

"I contracted malaria. They treated it, but…" Her voice faltered. "There may be lasting damage. To my organs."

Jeanette clutched her sister's hand. "You're here now. We'll find the best doctors. There's always hope."

Luciana's eyes brimmed. "I wish I believed that."

"You have to. Promise me you'll try."

Luciana gave a small nod. "I promise."

"Do you want to sit outside? Get some air?"

"I need a cigarette."

Jeanette blinked. "You smoke?"

"I picked it up… out there." She laughed quietly, almost ashamed.

They stepped outside. Luciana lit a cigarette and took a long drag. A coughing fit overtook her.

Jeanette raised an eyebrow. "You sure that's helping?"

"No," Luciana rasped. "But it doesn't matter anymore."

Jeanette stared at her. "Why not?"

Luciana didn't answer.

"Come on," Jeanette said softly. "Let's go upstairs. We can close early."

She flipped the sign to *Closed* and locked the door. Upstairs, Luciana noticed Giuseppe's empty chair in the living room.

"We couldn't get rid of it," Jeanette said. "It's all we had left of him."

Luciana ran her hand along the worn armrest.

"I tried to come back for the funeral," she said. "But it was impossible. You know I would've…"

"I know." Jeanette's voice broke. "It's okay."

"I didn't want to leave Sudan. Not while the war still raged, but—"

A noise broke the moment. Janine came rushing up the stairs, followed by Lynn, and behind them was Mariella, cradling baby William in her arms.

"Luci?" Mariella gasped.

She handed the baby off quickly to Lynn and flew into her sister's arms. "Oh my God. You're really here."

# Caregiver

Jeanette stirred at the sound of voices in the kitchen. Groggy, she pulled the blanket over her head, trying to find a more comfortable spot on the lumpy sofa — until a familiar voice made her sit up.

Was that… Phyllis?

She threw off the covers and padded into the kitchen. Her sisters were seated around the table, sipping coffee, already mid-conversation.

"You girls sound like a bunch of chickens," she said, smiling despite the early hour.

"Then come cluck along with us," Mariella said, scooting over to make room.

Jeanette rubbed her eyes. "Aren't we supposed to be getting ready for the bakery?"

"Antonio's covering today — with the girls' help," Phyllis said. "We've got more important things to do."

Mariella leaned in. "We're taking our sister to the doctor. But first, we're having breakfast together. It's been ages since all four of us were at the same table."

Jeanette looked at Luciana, who offered a faint smile.

After breakfast, the sisters bundled into Phyllis's car — Luciana in the front, the baby nestled in

Mariella's arms in the back—and drove to Dr. Zuckerman's office.

The doctor took Luciana's vitals, drew blood, and asked an endless stream of questions. He scribbled notes as he spoke, his brow furrowed in concentration.

"You most likely contracted malaria from a mosquito," he said finally. "There are a few strains, but if it's *Plasmodium ovale*, there's a risk of relapse."

Jeanette blinked. "Relapse?"

Dr. Zuckerman nodded. "With *P. ovale*, the parasite can stay dormant in the liver for months—even years—and reactivate later. That might explain your recurring symptoms."

Luciana sat quietly, her face unreadable.

"I'd like to admit your sister to the hospital," the doctor continued. "We need to run more tests—to make sure there's no lasting damage to the kidneys, heart, or brain."

Phyllis reached over and took Luciana's hand.

"We'll do whatever it takes," Mariella said firmly.

Jeanette looked at her sister, remembering the little girl who once clung to her in thunderstorms and followed her everywhere.

"We're not losing you," she said quietly. "Not without a fight."

*****

Two weeks passed. The hospital called with news Jeanette had been dreading: there was nothing more they could do for Luciana. She would be transferred to a long-term care facility.

Jeanette's heart sank. The thought of her vibrant, compassionate sister living out her final days in a sterile institution was unbearable.

"We're not sending our sister to a home," she said, her voice trembling. "I'll take care of her."

Mariella, exhausted from her long hours at the bakery, nodded in agreement. "We'll make it work."

Jeanette rearranged the small bedroom, moving Giuseppe's worn recliner beside the window. Every morning, she helped Luciana from the bed to the chair with slow, careful movements, trying not to show how heavy her heart had grown.

"What would you like for breakfast?" she asked one morning, drawing back the dark curtains to let in a stream of golden light.

Luciana blinked against the brightness and smiled weakly. "I'm not very hungry, Jeanette… but I'd love a cup of tea."

"I'll be right back with it," Jeanette said gently.

Outside the room, Francie and Janine hovered in the hallway.

"You girls need to stay out for now," Jeanette said, holding a finger to her lips. "Your aunt needs her rest."

"Can we sit in the doorway?" Janine asked.

Jeanette paused, then softened. "All right. But no loud voices."

Francie tiptoed to the edge of the doorframe. "Can she tell us a story?"

Jeanette smiled faintly. "Only if she's feeling up to it."

A few minutes later, she returned with the tea and placed it carefully on the table beside Luciana. Her sister reached for the cup, her frail fingers curling around it for warmth.

The smell of the tea filled the room—chamomile and lemon—and Luciana inhaled deeply before taking a small sip.

Francie peeked around the door again, eyes wide with anticipation. "Can you tell us about Nadia?"

Luciana glanced over, a tired but tender sparkle in her eyes. "Of course," she whispered. "Nadia was a little older than you, Francie. She had the kindest heart—and she was brave, too. Even when the world around her was full of danger…"

The girls sat quietly, listening, as Luciana's voice wove through memories of dusty villages, wild mango trees, and children who played with pebbles and string instead of toys.

In those moments, the sickness faded into the background. What remained was her strength—and her stories.

*****

Jeanette had never been particularly religious. Growing up, she often found excuses to skip Sunday services, and even when she'd gone with Sonny, they were known to slip out early or not show up at all. But now, something in her spirit felt unsettled. She needed more than comfort—she needed a conversation with God.

The church was quiet, the kind of hush that made you tiptoe even when no one else was there. She slipped into the front pew, its surface smoothed by generations of prayerful hands and kneeling souls. With a deep breath, she closed her eyes, trying to shut out the world, and began to pray.

When she opened them, she saw Father Hubert standing nearby, his expression gentle and curious.

"Well, hello, Jeanette," he said, his voice warm. "What brings you into the house of God? Is it the end of the world?"

Jeanette gave a nervous laugh. "I suppose it feels like it. I should've come sooner, but…"

He held up a hand to stop her. "There's no need for explanations. I'm just glad you're here. Would you like to talk?"

She hesitated, then nodded. "It's Luciana. She's very sick. The doctors can't do anything more. I think… I think we're losing her."

Father Hubert's smile faded into something more solemn. "I'm so sorry to hear that. You've already lost your mother and father. This must feel unbearable."

"It does," Jeanette whispered. "Mariella and I are doing everything we can, but I see Luciana getting weaker every day. And I feel so helpless. I promised I'd always take care of her, and now I can't fix this."

"You're not helpless," Father Hubert said gently. "You're giving her comfort, dignity, and love in her final days. That's more powerful than any cure."

Jeanette blinked away tears. "Mariella won't even talk about it. She insists Luciana will recover."

"Maybe that's her way of coping," he said. "We all face grief in different ways. But you're doing the right thing—facing it with honesty, even if it hurts. And remember, you're not alone. My door is always open."

"Thank you, Father."

She stood, crossed herself slowly in front of the altar, and stepped out into the light.

*****

Luciana fought to hold on for another month, but in the end, the fluid that built up in her lungs became too much. Pulmonary edema took her last breath.

"Don't grieve for me when I die," she had said. "Know that I'll be in a better place. I'll be with Mama and Pop."

"You'll be with the saints and angels you've loved all your life," Jeanette whispered back.

"Yes," Luciana murmured, her voice frail. "But before it's too late… will you call Father Hubert? I want him to hear my confession."

"Of course." Jeanette hid her tears and left to find the priest.

Father Hubert arrived shortly after. He entered Luciana's room with calm assurance, clothed in a white satin chasuble embroidered with golden crosses on the front and back. There was no fear in his step — only grace.

Luciana could barely lift her head, but she opened her mouth to receive the host. The priest placed the wafer gently on her tongue.

"Glory be to the Father, and to the Son, and to the Holy Ghost," he chanted. "As it was in the beginning, is now, and ever shall be, world without end. Amen."

Luciana moved her lips. *Amen.* No sound came out, but her face glowed with peace. Her eyelids fluttered closed. "Mama," she whispered.

Jeanette knew in that moment that Luciana was seeing their mother. She couldn't see what Luciana saw, but she felt its beauty through her sister's expression. It made the pain of letting go just a little more bearable.

At the funeral home, people filled every corner. There were barely enough paths between the floral sprays to reach the coffin.

Our Lady of Guadalupe Church had sent a large cross of red roses in her honor. To them, Luciana had always been one of their own. Her head rested on a soft pillow of white carnations. Everyone who came whispered the same thing: she looked like an angel.

After the mass, the family followed a procession to the cemetery. Mariella and Phyllis clung to each other. Antonio and David wrangled the children, keeping them from wandering too close to the open grave.

Jeanette stood alone near the edge, the cold earth heavy in her hand. A sharp wind cut through the warmth of the day, and her tears streaked her powdered face.

She released the small clump of soil. It fell with a soft *thud* onto the coffin lid, sending a shiver up her spine.

Giuseppe used to say she was made of Sicilian steel.

But standing there, Jeanette didn't feel strong at all.

# Big Girl Pants

Francesca was now five. She had the look of a Roman beauty — fair-skinned, with waves of chestnut hair that glowed red in the sunlight. Her high cheekbones and delicate features echoed Luciana's, but it was her sky-blue eyes that drew the most attention — a gift from her father.

She also had a gift for song. Jeanette was thrilled. They sang together every Sunday morning to the melodies of *The Italian Hour*, the same radio show Anna had once adored.

When Jeanette was young, she had idolized American singers and ignored the Italian classics. Now, those old songs were all she wanted to sing — and Francie picked up the language as if she'd been born to it.

One morning, another letter arrived from Francesco.

*"I'd love for you to come to Sciacca during Carnevale next month. It's a grand celebration. I'm sure your daughter would love it. Just say the word, and I'll send tickets for you both."*

Jeanette reread the letter, her thoughts adrift. She barely noticed Francie tugging at her sleeve.

"Mommy! Can we?"

"Can we what, sweetheart?"

"Go to the park!"

Jeanette smiled. "Of course — but finish your lunch first. We'll have to bundle up. Winter's almost here."

The air was crisp, but the sun was bright. They held hands as they walked, and the sunshine did them both                                          good.

Jeanette settled on the same bench where Giuseppe had sat every day, watching the world go by. Being there made her feel closer to him. She remembered his stories about Sicily and how he always said, *"When you lose your way, go back to where you started."* *Oh, Pop,* she thought. *I wish you were here to guide me.*

At Francie's fifth birthday party, the little girl had asked a question that stuck with her.

"Why don't I have a daddy like my cousins?"

Jeanette had hugged her tightly and kissed her forehead.

"I love you, baby."

"I love you more, Mommy."

Now, sitting beside her on the bench, Jeanette turned to her daughter.

"Honey, come sit with me. There's something I want to tell you."

Francie climbed up eagerly. "What is it?"

"Well, remember I told you your father lives far away?"

"Yes. That's why we don't see him, right?"

Jeanette nodded.

"Maybe we can go visit him?"

"Maybe," Jeanette whispered.

The next morning, Jeanette awoke from a deep, peaceful sleep, her mother's voice echoing in her dreams. She threw back the covers and padded barefoot into the kitchen, where Mariella was pouring coffee.

"You look happy," Mariella said. "What's going on?"

"I meant to tell you yesterday, but… I heard from Francesco again."

Mariella raised an eyebrow. "You mean he didn't get struck by lightning or fall off a cliff?"

Jeanette laughed. "I've decided to go to Sciacca. I'm going to see him. I need to tell him about Francie — and I can't do it in a letter."

"You're leaving Brooklyn?"

"I'm not sure yet. There's not much left for me here anymore."

Just then, Francie wandered into the kitchen, rubbing the sleep from her eyes.

"We're going to see my daddy in Sicily?" she asked.

"Yes, honey."

"Oh boy!" Francie squealed. "I'll go pack my stuff!" And she dashed off to her room.

"I'm happy for you," Mariella said. "But…"

"But what?"

"Call me selfish, but I'm going to miss you. I don't want you to leave."

"I haven't said I'm going forever. I just... need to see what's there. Maybe Francesco will be angry. Maybe he won't want us."

"He'd be a damn fool if he didn't."

Jeanette's eyes widened. "Mariella! I've never heard you curse before."

"Well," Mariella smirked, "times are changing."

"If it doesn't feel right, I'll come back. Maybe I'll move to Long Island. Phyllis keeps saying I should move in with her and David, but I'd rather have my own place. Something small. Something cozy. I'll find work and take care of my daughter."

Mariella smiled. "You'll be fine."

*****

On Sunday, Mariella had the whole family over for dinner. The children took the seats once held by Anna, Giuseppe, and Luciana — a quiet gesture that somehow softened their absence. Mariella's two girls, Phyllis's boys, and little Francie sat at their own small table, laughing and playing between bites. The sound of their voices filled the room like music.

Jeanette watched them, her heart full. *La famiglia* was everything. It reminded her of childhood dinners, of crowded tables and the comforting chaos of family.

"I have a going-away present for you," Phyllis said, handing Jeanette a neatly wrapped box.

"You didn't have to get me anything," Jeanette said.

"It's from Mariella, too," Phyllis added.

"Yeah," Mariella said with a smirk. "But I would never be caught dead in it."

Jeanette peeled off the white and silver foil. "Bonwit Teller?" she gasped. "Whatever's in here, you spent too much."

"You're worth it," Phyllis said. "Go on, open it."

Jeanette lifted the lid and stared. Nestled in layers of tissue paper was a black lace brassiere adorned with satin ribbons.

"Oh!" She quickly lifted it out of the box and held it out of the children's view. "This is... risqué."

"Can I see it?" Lynn asked, trying to peek.

"Never mind that," Jeanette said, laughing. "You're too young to be concerned with such things."

"I think any damage to her innocence has already been done," Phyllis joked. "Look—there's a matching pair of panties."

Jeanette held them up, laughing harder now. "What would Mama say?"

"She'd say, 'Make sure it fits properly, or you'll ruin your back!'" Mariella chimed in, and the whole table erupted with laughter.

For a moment, the sisters weren't grieving or worrying. They were just girls again—laughing, teasing, and wrapped in the comfort of each other.

# Leaving Brooklyn

Jeanette peeked out the window and saw the postman's mail cart parked in front of the house. He never rang the bell unless there was a special delivery.

The doorbell buzzed.

"Hello, Miss Jeanette," Tony said, tipping his cap. "I was hoping I hadn't missed you before you left for Sicily."

"I'm waiting for the taxi. It should be here any minute."

"I won't keep you then. But—eh—I came across this letter, forwarded from Boston. Handwritten, addressed to you."

Jeanette took the plain white envelope from his hand. The handwriting sent a jolt through her. She traced the letters of the return address. *Sonny?*

"Thank you, Tony."

"Safe travels to you and your little girl."

Jeanette closed the door and leaned against it, trying to breathe. She stared at the envelope, fingers trembling. Why would he write now, after all these years?

She loosened the flap and unfolded the letter. Her eyes dropped to the bottom of the page.

*"I'm still in love with you."*

The words blurred as her heart pounded in her ears. She pressed the letter to her chest, overwhelmed.

A horn blared outside.

"Mommy, it's time!" Francie stood in the doorway, clutching her teddy bear.

Jeanette tucked the letter into her purse, grabbed their suitcases, and stepped outside. The cab driver loaded their bags into the trunk. As the car pulled away from the curb, Jeanette turned back, watching the roof where she and Sonny had once fallen in love. They passed the apartment building where she grew up, the corner pizzeria, and the park bench her father loved.

Brooklyn faded behind her, but her memories clung tight.

In the back seat of the taxi, Jeanette sat quietly. The letter from Sonny was a weight in her purse — a whisper from the past. Why now? What did he want her to know?

She didn't have all the answers, but the words gave her strength. She had always known it. Even time couldn't break their bond.

*****

Francie gripped her mother's hand as they walked through the airport, wide-eyed with a mix of excitement and fear. She clutched her favorite bear tightly to her chest — it was her first time on an airplane.

Jeanette was anxious, too, but not because of the flight. She kept second-guessing herself. *Am I doing the right thing?*

At the gate, Francie pressed her nose to the window, watching in awe as the giant jet waited for them.

"Don't be scared, honey," Jeanette said, brushing a curl from Francie's face. "You're going to love flying. It's like one of those rides at Coney Island — only better. You'll see."

Francie nodded, but her eyes followed another little girl about her age who was boarding the plane with her father. The girl seemed calm and confident, chatting away and tugging her suitcase behind her.

The stewardess announced the start of boarding. Jeanette handed over their tickets, and they stepped onto the jet bridge toward their new life.

Their seats were directly across the aisle from the girl and her father. She immediately called dibs on the window.

"Would you like to sit by the window?" Jeanette asked.

Francie hesitated. "Maybe… okay."

When the plane lifted off, Francie squeezed the armrests so tightly her knuckles turned white. She shut her eyes and leaned back.

Jeanette gave her a reassuring smile, remembering her own first flight to Sicily six years earlier. Since then, airplanes have improved — less noise, less turbulence — but the nerves stayed the same.

Once they were cruising, the cabin settled, and Francie relaxed. The stewardesses wheeled out dinner carts. Jeanette pulled down their tray tables as the first stewardess handed out plates, utensils, glasses, and cups. A second followed with salad, pasta, and sliced ham.

Francie picked at her food. "My tummy hurts."

"Just eat a little, sweetie," Jeanette coaxed.

After a few small bites, she perked up. When the scent of fresh cookies floated through the cabin, Francie sat up straighter.

The girl across the aisle beamed. "I hope they're chocolate chip. Those are my favorites. What about you?"

Francie nodded. "Mine, too."

"I'm Emily. What's your name?"

"I'm Francie."

"My doll's name is Molly."

Francie smiled. "She's pretty. This is Teddy."

Emily giggled. "Teddy... bear."

Soon, the two girls were inseparable. Their parents traded seats so the girls could sit together by the aisle.

"We're going to see my *Nona*," Emily explained.

"I'm going to meet my *Papa*. He lives in Sicily. I've never seen him before."

"I'd be scared too," Francie admitted.

"There's no reason to be scared," Emily's father said gently. "I'm sure your Papa loves you very much."

With Francie happily chatting, Jeanette finally relaxed. The cabin lights dimmed. Passengers settled in, and a soft hush fell over the plane.

Francie drifted off mid-sentence, her head resting against Teddy.

Jeanette leaned back and exhaled deeply. But the letter from Sonny burned in her mind like a fever. She reached into her purse and felt for the smooth envelope.

Taking a deep breath, she opened it again.

Dear Jeanette,

I don't know if the news has reached you, but Jiao and I are divorced. I loved her, but I never stopped loving you. You were always there — just beneath the surface — like a ghost haunting my dreams. I think she sensed it. I may have mentioned you in passing, but she was intuitive. After our son was born, the distance between us only grew wider.

You may have wondered why I married her. The truth is, I thought I had no choice. We were young, and I let everyone else decide what was best. I didn't want to disgrace our families. I should've fought harder. I should've cared less about what they thought and more about what I knew to be true. But I was a coward. I couldn't stand up to my mother, and so I left Brooklyn — because I knew that if I stayed, I'd never be able to stay away from you.

College filled my days, but nothing filled the space you left behind. I convinced myself I had done the right thing, but every time I closed my eyes, I saw you. I've carried the weight of that mistake every day since.

Jeanette, I know I hurt you. You were the one person I never wanted to hurt. You were right — life was simpler then. All we had to do was dodge my little sister. We belonged together, even back in elementary school. I used to scan the cafeteria just to find you. Seeing you smile was the best part of my day.

I'm still in love with you. I don't care who knows it. Maybe it's too late — but maybe it's not. If there's still a place for me in your heart, I hope you'll tell me.

Always,
Your Sonny


Tears welled in Jeanette's eyes as she reread Sonny's words. She had spent years trying to forget him — tucking his memory into the far corners of her heart — but now, here he was again, reminding her just how deeply she had loved him. Still loved him. And yet, she was crossing the Atlantic to be with another man.

She turned to the window, staring out at the white, cottony clouds that floated beside the plane. With a sigh, she closed her eyes, letting the steady hum of the engines lull her into a twilight slumber.

In her dream, she was walking down a white satin aisle. At the end stood Sonny, waiting with open arms. Her family and friends lined the pews, their faces glowing with joy—even Aunt Evelyn smiled. As Jeanette passed them, she felt their love lifting her, step by step, until she reached him. Sonny took her hand and led her gently up the altar steps. Just as the priest was about to pronounce them husband and wife, the dream shattered.

The plane jolted violently as it touched down, skidding roughly along the runway. Jeanette woke with a start, heart pounding, the image of Sonny still lingering in her mind like the final note of a forgotten song.

# Carnivale

Jeanette and Francie stepped off the plane at Punta Raisi Airport and followed the crowd toward the baggage area. Francesco had promised to meet them, but an emergency meeting at work kept him away.

Once they collected their luggage, they exited the terminal. As the sliding doors parted, a soft breeze swirled around them, ruffling the hem of Francie's pretty pink dress.

Jeanette raised her hand, and a taxi pulled to the curb. The driver stepped out, hoisted their bags into the trunk, and opened the rear door with a polite nod.

"Dove vuoi andare?" he asked.

Jeanette rummaged through her purse and pulled out the slip of paper. "I need to go here," she said, pointing to the address.

"Ah, sì!" the driver said with a smile, then pulled away from the terminal.

Francie pressed her face to the window, eyes wide with wonder. Rolling farmland and hills stretched along the right side of the road, while the shimmering Tyrrhenian Sea sparkled to the left. Within an hour, the landscape changed—the roads narrowed, houses and apartment buildings rose along the streets, and scooters zipped by in the light mist beginning to coat the windshield.

The taxi came to a stop in front of a tall, modern building on the outskirts of town.

Francesco's house was under renovation after sitting vacant for years, so he had arranged a temporary apartment for them—secure, furnished, and close to everything. Jeanette appreciated his thoughtfulness.

Inside the marble-floored lobby, they approached the front desk. Francie turned in slow circles, captivated by the shimmering Venetian mirrors on the walls and the crystal chandeliers overhead.

"Buongiorno," the clerk greeted.

"Buongiorno. Inglese?"

"Yes, I speak English."

Jeanette gave her name, and the clerk handed over a key. "You're in apartment 406. If you'd like, I can help with your bags."

"Thank you," Jeanette said, "but I think we can manage. Do you have an elevator?"

"Elevator?" he looked puzzled for a moment. "Ah—you mean a lift. Yes, just around the corner."

Francie giggled with delight as the small lift jolted upward, then sailed smoothly to their floor.

"Look for number four-zero-six," Jeanette told her.

Francie darted down the hall, reading each number aloud. "Here it is, Mommy!"

"Very good, Francie. You're my smart little girl."

"Can I open the door? Please?"

"Of course." Jeanette handed her the key.

Inside, the sitting room glowed with warmth and elegance. A plush gold carpet made the sleek white sofa look even whiter, its cushions plump with gold satin pillows. French doors led to a small terrace overlooking the city skyline, soft lights beginning to twinkle in the distance.

"Oh, how beautiful," Francie breathed. "Look, Mommy—flowers and wine!"

Jeanette crossed the room to read the note tucked into the arrangement.

*Welcome, Jeanette. I thought you might need a little rest to shake off your jet lag. Everything has been taken care of. The refrigerator is fully stocked, but please call the front desk if you need anything. I will come for you tomorrow morning at eight.*

Jeanette held the note to her chest, unsure what tomorrow would bring—but for now, she felt safe. And home, wherever that would turn out to be, suddenly didn't feel so far away.

*****

There was a loud knock on the door.

Startled, Jeanette shoved Sonny's letter back into the envelope and tucked it beneath the clothes in her suitcase. She smoothed her blouse, took a deep breath, and peered through the peephole.

Francesco.

He was even more handsome than she remembered. His hair, now more salt than pepper, made him look distinguished, and the scarf around his neck added to his effortless Italian charm. For a moment, they hesitated — unsure how to greet each other after all this time. Then he smiled and opened his arms.

She stepped into his embrace, and for a fleeting second, she thought she might melt into the gold carpet beneath her feet if he hadn't been there to catch her.

Behind her, Francie lingered, watching him warily. Jeanette had told her everything she could about her father, but seeing him in real life was something else entirely.

"And this must be your lovely daughter," Francesco said, stepping closer. He paused suddenly. A flicker of recognition swept over his face. Then shock. Then something deeper.

He turned to Jeanette, questioning.

She gave a slow, quiet nod and lowered her gaze. "This is Francesca," she said softly.

Francie blinked up at him. "Are you my daddy?"

Francesco's face turned pale. He looked from the child to Jeanette.

"I wanted to tell you," she said quickly. "I tried. I couldn't reach you."

"I... I'm so sorry, Jeanette," he murmured. "I didn't know."

"I sent a letter. You never answered. I didn't know what to think."

"I should have been there — for both of you. Can you forgive me?"

"Forgive you?" Her voice trembled. "Francesco, of course, I forgive you. I was hurt. I was angry. I couldn't understand why you would sacrifice what we had for a woman you didn't even love. But maybe—if you'd known about Francie—you would have chosen differently."

Before he could answer, Francie tugged at Jeanette's sleeve.

"Can we go to the castle now?" she asked, eyes wide with expectation. "Mommy told me about it."

Francesco knelt down to her level. "Yes, Francesca. But today, I'm taking you and your mother somewhere very special."

"Everyone calls me Francie."

"Francie, it is," he said, smiling. "Tell me, Francie—do you like parades?"

"I love parades!"

"Then you're in luck. Today is Carnivale. There are floats made from papier-mâché and people in costumes—pirates, queens, angels, even clowns."

"But I don't have a costume."

"That's all right. Maybe we'll find you some angel wings or a princess crown from one of the vendors."

Francie clapped. "Let's go, Mommy!"

"Okay, sweetheart. But grab your sweater—just in case it gets cool."

As she darted off, Francesco looked to Jeanette. "She's wonderful. I think she likes me already. Does she know... I'm her father?"

Jeanette nodded. "Yes. She was nervous at first. It's always been just the two of us. But she's brave."

Francie reappeared wearing her pink sweater and holding her teddy bear. Together, they stepped into the Sicilian sunlight.

"There's going to be a lot of traffic," Francesco said. "Instead of driving, we should walk. It's not far."

He offered his arm, and Jeanette took it. Their daughter led the way, drawn by the scent of roasting sausage and the distant sound of drums.

"I think the festival has already started," Francie said, skipping ahead. "I hear music!"

"Oh, I can smell the food," Jeanette added. "In all the excitement, we forgot to eat."

Francesco chuckled. "We'll stop at one of the vendors. Carnivale sausages are famous around here. And orange soda too — it's tradition."

\*\*\*\*\*

Many people lined the streets to watch the parade, and Francie struggled to find a clear view.

"I can't see," she said, straining on tiptoe.

"Get on my shoulders," Francesco offered.

Francie hesitated, glancing at her mother. But the music was getting louder, and the first float was drawing near. She reached up, and with a smile, Francesco lifted her onto his shoulders.

"Can you see the floats now?" he asked.

"Oh, yes! There's a big head coming this way."

"That's Peppe Nappa," he explained. "He's always the first float. He's the mascot of Sciacca."

"Why him?"

"Legend says he symbolizes the Sicilian soul — joyful, full of laughter, and a lover of life's simple pleasures."

Eight elaborate floats rolled past, one more colorful and outrageous than the next. Dancers twirled in vibrant costumes, and musicians filled the air with Sicilian folk tunes. Some of the giant figures moved their heads, and Francie found a few of them scary. She turned her gaze instead to the children tossing handfuls of confetti high into the air like magic.

"Would you like to throw some?" Francesco asked.

Her face lit up. "Oh, yes!"

He set her gently on the ground and bought a large bag of confetti and a lioness mask from a nearby vendor.

"Here you go," he said, adjusting the band around her head. "Now you're part of Carnevale."

Francie beamed and ran to join the other children along the curb. Jeanette watched as her daughter disappeared into a whirl of music and color, dancing confetti and wide-eyed laughter.

The parade continued to the Piazza, where the main stage stood surrounded by lights and draped flags. Francie insisted on seeing all the floats again and eventually declared Peppe Nappa her favorite. Music and performances went on as the sun dipped low, casting the square in a warm golden haze. Even as night fell, the city pulsed with celebration.

Jeanette rubbed her temples, feeling the weight of the day. "Would it be all right if we skipped the gelato?" she asked. "I didn't get much sleep last night."

"Oh, my dear, of course," Francesco said gently. "You've traveled halfway around the world. I should have let you rest more. I'll take you both home."

"Thank you," Jeanette said, her voice soft.

But travel wasn't the reason for her weariness. From the moment she had opened Sonny's letter, she'd felt like the floor had shifted beneath her feet. She had thought she knew where her life was headed, but now, everything felt uncertain.

"I'm not tired," Francie murmured, mid-yawn. Her eyelids drooped, and her apple-shaped cheeks were rosy from the cold air.

"Tomorrow's another day," Francesco said. "And I have a surprise."

"What is it?" she asked, barely keeping her eyes open.

"Do you like puppets?"

Francie tilted her head. "I think so."

"Then you're going to love the puppet show. It's very Italian. We're going tomorrow."

"Oh, boy," she whispered, yawning again.

Later that night, once Francie was fast asleep, Jeanette stood by the window with Sonny's letter in her hand. The sounds of the parade still drifted faintly through the open shutters. She ran her fingers across the page, rereading every line.

For years, she had built Sonny up in her mind, turning memories into myth. But now, the fantasy could become real. What she had always wanted — what had once been impossible — was suddenly within reach.

# Breathe

Francie ran to the door at the sound of the knock. Francesco scooped her up in his arms, and she kissed his                                                                                                      cheek.

"Who wants to go to a puppet show?" he asked.

"I do! I do!" she shouted, bouncing with excitement.

On their way to Palermo, they stopped in the small village of San Biagio. The townspeople were busy crafting intricate sculptures out of bread for the upcoming spring festival. The creations adorned tall bamboo poles—some religious, others celebrating the rebirth of spring—flowers, fruits, vegetables, and mosaics of grain and pasta. Grand arches spanned the narrow street, forming a cathedral made of wheat.

"Oh my," Jeanette said, gazing around. "They could feed an army with all this bread."

"In feudal times, the church required part of the harvest to be used for the arches. After the festival, the bread was given to the poor," Francesco explained.

"I wish we could eat some," Francie said, rubbing her tummy. "I'm hungry."

"They mix a resin into the dough to protect it from the rain, so it's not edible," Francesco replied. "But I know a lovely pasticceria where we can have lunch. They have plenty of real bread."

They stopped for pasta with clam sauce and shared the largest ricotta-filled pastry Jeanette had ever seen.

"When do we see the puppets?" Francie asked between bites.

"As soon as you finish your lunch," Francesco said.

Jeanette gently wiped powdered sugar from Francie's cheeks, and they headed to the theater.

The drive to Palermo took two hours, winding through farmland dotted with cows and sheep. At times, the sheep blocked the road, forcing Francesco to stop the car, much to Francie's delight.

When they arrived at the Opera dei Pupi, long lines already trailed down the block. "Don't worry," Francesco said, reaching into his jacket. "I bought our tickets ahead of time." He handed them over with a wink.

Inside, the lobby buzzed with chatter. Francie clutched her parents' hands tightly—hers the only small figure among a sea of grown-ups. Overhead, a crystal chandelier sparkled with candlelight. They followed the crowd down the aisle, and Francesco led them to their seats.

The theater dimmed. The curtain lifted. Onstage, a beautiful puppet princess in a pearl-trimmed pink gown turned to a puppet prince. "Oh, my love," she said, raising one dainty hand to her head. "Our families are at war. We must keep our love a secret."

Francie giggled, craning her neck to see above the stage. "She's not really climbing down—I can see the strings!"

The prince bowed. "We'll speak to your father. He must understand."

The curtain closed briefly. When it reopened, the puppet king sat on a throne in a purple robe, his gold crown glittering with red stones.

"Halt!" he commanded as his daughter's lover appeared. "Leave my kingdom!"

"Please, Father. Hear our pleas."

Suddenly, a masked figure with horns swooped down between them.

"Oh, great king," he said darkly. "If you concede now, you'll appear weak. Your power will wither on the vine."

The king rose tall. "Guards!" he bellowed.

Six soldiers marched onstage, swords drawn. "Arrest him! To the dungeon!"

Francie's smile vanished. She closed her eyes and squeezed Jeanette's hand. "I'm scared. Can we go?"

"It's only make-believe," Francesco assured her, but Jeanette was already rising, guiding Francie up the aisle.

In the lobby, Francesco joined them.

"I'm sorry," Jeanette said. "We're not used to puppets like that."

"I understand." He scooped Francie into his arms.

"I'm sorry it scared you. Do you forgive me?"

She nodded, wiping her eyes.

As they walked toward the exit, Francesco paused.

"Jeanette, I don't want today to end on a sad note. I have an idea."

"What is it?" she asked.

He turned to Francie. "Let's visit the gift shop. We'll find a puppet you like — one that's not scary."

Inside, they avoided the wall of soldier puppets. On the opposite side, a row of princesses in pastel gowns stood waiting. Francie chose a yellow one with blonde hair and a rhinestone tiara. She clutched it tightly as Francesco paid.

In the backseat on the ride home, Francie made the puppet dance across the seat.

"Who's hungry?" Francesco called. "I know a quaint little place in San Michele — it's at the highest point in town."

"That sounds lovely," Jeanette said. "What do you think, Francie?"

"Yes, we are!" Francie chirped, raising her puppet's strings.

The restaurant's walls were lined with large fish tanks. Colorful fish swam inside, waiting to become someone's dinner.

"Do you like to fish?" Francesco asked. "We could go to the marina tomorrow."

Francie wrinkled her nose. "Do I have to touch worms?"

Francesco laughed. "No, I'll handle the bait."

When their table was ready, the hostess seated them. The waiter noticed the little girl watching the fish with fascination, and her parents, locked in each other's gaze.

As he cleared their plates, he leaned toward Francie. "Would you like to feed some of our big fish by hand?"

"Can I, Mommy?"

"Of course," Jeanette said. "But come back for dessert."

Francie skipped away with the waiter.

Francesco reached across the table and took Jeanette's hands.

"I've missed so much. If only I had written... I would've known about our daughter."

"You're a good man," Jeanette said. "You were there for Angelina when she needed you."

"But you needed me, too. I failed you."

"No," she said softly. "Don't say that. We're together now. There's so much more life to live."

Later, they returned to the hotel. Francie had fallen asleep in the car, the puppet resting beside her. "She must be worn out from all the excitement," Francesco said, carrying her to bed. He tucked her in gently and kissed her forehead.

Jeanette watched from the doorway, tempted to stay, but she let him have the moment.

In the sitting room, Francesco opened the bottle of wine he had once sent her with flowers. They sat together on the couch. He hesitated, then reached for her. She leaned in, resting her face against his chest. She could hear his heartbeat as he lifted her chin and kissed her. His lips tasted of sweet red wine, just as she remembered.

*What about Sonny?* she wondered. *Is it possible to love two men at once?*

Sonny, with his bold, American ambition. Francesco, with his gentle Italian charm. Both are good men. Both pulling at her heart.

"I love you, Jeanette," Francesco whispered, leading her to the bedroom.

Her breath caught as he undressed her. Swept up in the moment, she surrendered to his touch. Every nerve awakened beneath his hands.

Afterward, wrapped in his arms, she listened to his even breathing.

But Sonny's letter still burned in her heart.

*Oh, Mamma. What should I do? I love them both.*

# Donna di Sciacca

Jeanette opened her eyes and reached across the bed, but Francesco wasn't there.

Hearing laughter from the kitchen, she slipped out of bed and padded barefoot across the cool tile floor. Pausing in the doorway, she smiled at the sight before her.

Francesco and Francie were at the stove, completely engrossed in their task. Francie stood on a chair, stirring a bowl of pancake batter. Most of it had ended up on her arms, face, and the floor, but she was beaming.

"Hey," Francesco said, chuckling, "save some for the pancakes, or we'll go hungry."

That only made Francie stir faster, reveling in the mess and her father's attention.

"Can I pour, Daddy?"

Jeanette's breath caught. *Daddy*. Hearing her daughter call Francesco filled her with emotion. Her heart swelled.

"Okay," Francesco said gently, "but let me help." He guided her small hand as she scooped the batter onto the pan.

"Now, stand back, little lady. I don't want you to get burned."

Jeanette stepped into the room. "Do I smell pancakes?"

Francie spun around, holding up a spatula proudly. "Look, Mommy! I'm a cook, just like you!"

"Oh, good. I'm starving." Jeanette bent down and kissed her flour-dusted daughter on the head.

"Sit down, Mommy," Francie said with exaggerated authority. "We've got this."

Jeanette laughed and backed away from the stove. She took a seat at the table, watching them work side by side. A wave of peace came over her. *This* — the smells, the sounds, the joy — felt like home.

"This is our first breakfast as a family," she said softly.

Francesco turned to her with a smile. "Yes, but I hope it's only the first of many. Jeanette, you and Francie should move to Sciacca. Come live with me at my country house. Just think about it."

"Please, Mommy, pleeeease," Francie begged, clasping her batter-covered hands.

Jeanette chuckled. "I know you're having a wonderful time, sweetheart. But not every day is Carnevale."

"But I *love* it here!"

"We'll see," Jeanette said, her tone teasing, though her mind was racing.

*Sonny's letter.* Should she tell Francesco? *No — not yet.* She needed time to sort out her heart.

Francesco turned to Francie. "Are you ready to go to the garden?"

"Yes!" she squealed, hopping off the chair and clapping her hands.

Then he looked at Jeanette. "Pack an overnight bag. I have a surprise for you girls later."

Francie's eyes sparkled. "Another surprise? What is it, Daddy?"

"You'll see," he said, winking.

*****

Il Castello Incantato was just as beautiful as Jeanette remembered. It was a place filled with magic, where she had once fallen in love with Francesco. Now, sharing it with Francie made it even more special.

Francie moved from sculpture to sculpture, tracing each stone face with her fingers. She darted in and out of the softly lit caves, her laughter echoing through the enchanted space.

Afterward, instead of heading back toward the apartment, Francesco turned the car in the opposite direction. They drove past the edge of town, down a winding dirt road. Finally, he pulled into a long driveway and brought the car to a stop.

Jeanette looked out the window, her eyes widening.

"Your house," she said softly. "It looks brand-new."

"It is. The builders finished just yesterday. Everything inside is modern."

Francesco opened the front door, and Francie burst inside ahead of them.

"Is this our house?" she asked, spinning around in the entryway.

Francesco glanced at Jeanette. "It is — if you want it to be."

Jeanette looked away, unsure how to respond. She exhaled slowly, caught between the warmth of the moment and the weight of her thoughts.

"Mommy, Mommy! Come look!" Francie's voice called from somewhere down the hall.

Jeanette smiled, shaking her head. "What did you do now?" she asked Francesco playfully. "You're going to spoil her."

They followed the sound of Francie's excitement to a small room and stepped into a world of pink.

It was every little girl's dream. A white canopy bed draped with tulle, shelves filled with dolls and stuffed animals, and a closet packed with colorful dresses and shoes to match. Francie's eyes sparkled with delight as she twirled in the center of it all.

Jeanette had never seen her daughter so happy.

"Let's go into the kitchen," Francesco said. "I want to cook a delicious dinner for my girls. But I'll need help."

Francie leapt off the bed, eager to assist. This time, it was a true family affair. Francesco prepared the sauce and set a pot of water to boil. Jeanette and Francie made a salad together while Francie also set the table, humming to herself.

"I didn't know you were such an expert cook," Jeanette said.

Francesco shrugged modestly. "I studied at a culinary school in Paris when I was young. Cooking was always my first love. But my father didn't approve—he thought it was a hobby. He pushed me into the family export business instead."

"I want to go to Paris," Francie said suddenly, looking up from the salad bowl.

Francesco smiled. "If your mom says yes, maybe we can go there for our honeymoon."

Francie gasped. "Really?"

"Yes. I even know a beautiful castle we could stay in."

Even Jeanette was taken aback. "A castle?" she said, laughing. "You make it hard to say no."

"Can I have a day to think about it?"

"Of course," Francesco said gently.

He opened a bottle of wine and poured a glass for Jeanette, then poured sparkling water into a smaller glass for Francie.

"A toast," he said, raising his glass. "Alla famiglia."

They clinked glasses—three cups meeting in the golden glow of the kitchen, the sound of laughter, promise, and possibility floating in the air.

*****

Jeanette tossed and turned, careful not to wake Francesco, who lay sleeping peacefully beside her. The room was still, the only sound the rhythmic whisper of waves beyond the window. She closed her eyes, trying to silence her racing thoughts.

And then—like a breeze stirring the soul—she heard her mother's voice one final time.

*Listen to your heart, my daughter. It will lead you to your destiny.*

Tears welled in Jeanette's eyes as she slipped out of bed and tiptoed into the sitting room. Moonlight streamed through the curtains as she reached for the letter — Sonny's letter — worn at the edges from being read so many times.

She unfolded it gently, as if touching a memory.

But something had shifted.

Jeanette realized, with aching clarity, that she didn't truly know Sonny anymore. And he didn't know her. Not the woman she had become. The girl who once fell for him under a Brooklyn sky no longer existed — not fully. She had lived through heartbreak, buried her mother, her father, and her sister. She had been reshaped by life, by love, by loss.

And in the rubble of it all, she had found something new: Francie. And Francesco.

Her mother's words echoed again, softer now, but surer.

*Listen to your heart...*

Jeanette picked up a pen and turned over the letter. Her hand trembled as she began to write.

Dear Sonny,

I received your letter the same day I left for Sicily. I must have read it a hundred times. Part of me wanted to board the next plane, run straight into your arms, and pretend no time had passed. I can't begin to tell you how many nights I've imagined that moment—replayed it in my mind, again and again.

You finally said the words I've waited my whole life to hear: that you love me. That you always have. I wish you'd told me when we were still young and free—before time got in the way, before we both became different versions of ourselves.

You will always have a special place in my heart, Sonny. But the truth is, I don't think we can turn back the clock. Too much has happened. Too many seasons have passed.

I've fallen in love with someone else. And for the first time in a long while, I'm truly happy.

I won't be coming back to Brooklyn.

I am now a *Donna di Sciacca*.

With love,
Jeanette

*Thank you for reading Brooklyn Love Story by Janet Sierzant. Please take a minute to post a review on Amazon.com.*

Please send feedback to jsierzant@gmail.com

*Dedicated to my Mother*

Jeanette Corrao – 1949-2018

Other novels by Janet Sierzant

Asunder
Sauce on Sunday
Gemini Joe
The Green Room
Justice Rules
A Made Man